Good
Little Wives

By Abby Drake

GOOD LITTLE WIVES

Good Little Wives

Abby Drake

AVON

An Imprint of HarperCollins*Publishers*

GOOD LITTLE WIVES. Copyright © 2007 by Abby Drake. All rights reserved. Printed in the United States of America. No part of this book may be used or reproduced in any manner whatsoever without written permission except in the case of brief quotations embodied in critical articles and reviews. For information address HarperCollins Publishers, 10 East 53rd Street, New York, NY 10022.

HarperCollins books may be purchased for educational, business, or sales promotional use. For information please write: Special Markets Department, HarperCollins Publishers, 10 East 53rd Street, New York, NY 10022.

FIRST EDITION

Interior text designed by Diahann Sturge

Library of Congress Cataloging-in-Publication Data

Drake, Abby.
   Good little wives/Abby Drake.—1st ed.
      p. cm.
ISBN: 978-0-06-123221-3
ISBN-10: 0-06-123221-1
1. Wives—Fiction.   2. Marital conflict—Fiction.   3. Middle age—Fiction.
I. Title.

PS3604.R345G66   2007
813'.6—dc22   2007012608

07 08 09 10 11   ❖/RRD   10 9 8 7 6 5 4 3 2 1

To the Wives . . .

🍃 One

It started because of a facelift. A second face-lift, actually. Caroline Meacham, after all, was now fifty-two, and her first cosmetic surgery had been twelve years ago, a fortieth birthday present from her husband, Jack. Or *for* him, Dana's husband had chuckled back then at the thought that one of the trophy wives was beginning to tarnish in visible places.

Dana gripped the stem of the champagne flute. She stood with several ladies, semicircle, arced around Caroline, extolling the delicate work of Dr. Gregg (his first name, not his last, for none of the wives called him Dr. Rathberger).

"A teeny tuck here . . . another one here . . . ," Caroline explained to the women she'd invited for cracked crab and conversation at Caroline and Jack's palatial home in New Falls, New York. She'd dubbed the meeting her rite-of-spring luncheon for her fifty closest friends, though there was no doubt the real reason they'd gathered was to view the new lift.

"And my lips," Caroline continued. "Remember how thin they'd become?" The women—Dana, Bridget, Lauren, and three others Dana knew Caroline deemed unimportant— nodded as if they truly remembered Caroline's pencil mouth. "Well, Dr. Gregg—the man is sheer genius—took a touch of fatty tissue from the cheek of my butt, and see how he plumped up my lips?" She outlined the edge of her upper lip with the tip of a lightly frosted, manicured fingernail. She smiled.

"Amazing," Lauren said, her Mikimoto triple strand of pearls clasped tightly to her neck, masking a hint of early wattle that Dr. Gregg surely would excavate as soon as Lauren got up the nerve.

"*Magnifique*," Bridget added. They counted on Bridget to toss around French words and bring a flair of the EU to any party she attended. Despite that she'd been in America more than two decades, it was something her husband encouraged.

Dana would have liked to ask how much the surgery cost, but in New Falls, no one discussed money. She tuned out the chatter, looked around at the tall crystal vases of artfully drooping yellow tulips, at the Matisse by the long window and the Renoir over the mantel, at the cluster of petite-ribboned hostess gifts that spilled from the Louis XV table that had cabriole legs *avec pied de sabots* ("with hoof foots"—a favorite style of Bridget's). The gifts careened from the foyer into the music room where the ladies now stood, bundled in small groups of tennis partners, country club foursomes, and spa buddies.

There was Rhonda, who seemed over the top today, but apparently her doctor had just changed her meds.

There was Georgette, who'd recently learned that, for twenty-five years, her husband had been an undercover informant for the IRS, when all along she thought he merely had a mistress.

There was Chloe, Caroline's clonelike daughter, whose engagement ring was the size of Japan.

And there was Yolanda, who once had been their hairstylist, but now was one of them, sporting pink diamonds, a gift from her new husband, Vincent DeLano, who'd been married to Kitty—whatever happened to her, anyway?

There were pastel cashmere twin sets and massive solitaire diamonds (more carats than at Whole Foods) and peachy complexions and white, orthodontically correct smiles.

Dana sipped from her glass and wondered how soon they could leave. It wasn't the first time in recent weeks that she was simply bored.

As if reading her mind, Lauren spoke. "I hate to break up the party, but Bob's coming home on the early train and he's bringing Mr. Chang."

Yi Chang was the new head of Xiamen Electronics (ticker symbol, XmnE), which most of the women there understood, because they were wed to the men who ran Wall Street or at least perceived that they did.

"Well," Dana said, "the three of us rode over together, so I guess we're off." They kiss-kissed Caroline, waved to the others, and escaped without incident onto the front walk. They hiked around a string of European cars, clipped past a row of arborvitae and a lily-padded water garden, and climbed into Lauren's big Mercedes before Dana dared to say, "It has occurred to me that we just kissed Caroline's ass."

They drove off in silence until they reached the main road, at which time Bridget said, "*Mon dieu*, what have we become?"

Three streets from Caroline and Jack Meacham's, Kitty DeLano stood in the hollow living room of the ten-thousand-square-foot mausoleum that once had been hers, or rather, had been theirs, before Vincent had decided he liked a hairdresser better than he liked her.

She chewed the tip of a fingernail she could no longer afford to have manicured, realizing there really was a fine line between love and hate, sanity and insanity; a flimsy curtain that hung between man and wife like the veil of a bride, which, once lifted, revealed irreversible truth.

Vincent, of course, had given her everything, according to him: the boy and the girl from her womb, the furs and the jewels, the villa in Naples (Italy, not Florida), the too-large house in New Falls that was now empty of furnishings.

Most of all, he had given her status.

And while Kitty could do well enough without all the stuff (except for her kids, who had sided with him, because though they were grown up and successful, Daddy still subsidized their Manhattan apartments, their BMWs, their Visa cards), it was the status that could not be replaced.

She was no longer Mrs. Vincent DeLano.

She was no longer welcome in New Falls, not at the deli,

not at the dry cleaner, not at Caroline Meacham's rite-of-spring luncheon.

And now Vincent lay at her feet, dead on the floor, a trickle of blood oozing from his left ear, a gun slack, still smoking, in Kitty's right hand.

🍃 Two

That was how the <u>New Falls Journal</u> *described* the crime scene in the paper the next day: that the former wife of futures trader Vincent DeLano was found standing over the corpse, *a trickle of blood oozing from his left ear, a gun slack, still smoking, in Kitty's right hand.*

Dana sat at the breakfast table and stared at the newspaper. She supposed they'd referred to Kitty as "Kitty" because it was a small town and it wasn't really socially appropriate to call her "Mrs. DeLano" since she was no longer wed to Vincent but Yolanda was.

But a murderer?

Kitty?

Of all the women in New Falls, Kitty was one of the least

likely. She kept a nice house, raised two acceptable kids (an unattractive yet quite talented physician and a startlingly gorgeous redheaded supermodel), and never made a public fuss, not even when Vincent walked out on her in the middle of dinner at Rosa's with half the town looking on.

They had been friends once, Kitty and Dana. They had served together on the town arts council and on the elementary school PTO. Kitty had been with Dana the day Dana decided to go blond (a big mistake; she since had reverted to her natural, premature silver, a look her husband said made her green eyes even more radiant). More importantly, it had been Kitty who'd been at Dana's the day the huge oak tree was struck by lightning and fell through the roof and into the sunroom and knocked Dana out. Kitty did CPR and called the fire department and kept Dana calm until the ambulance got there.

But that had been a half dozen or more years ago now. Before life had changed, Kitty's especially.

Dana looked at the clock: seven-fifteen. She wondered whom she should call first. Steven was in San Francisco today, or was it L.A.? No matter. He wouldn't appreciate being awakened at four-fifteen even for the news of Kitty and Vincent. She could call her sons (any or all three), but Michael was probably dashing from his Dobbs Ferry apartment to catch the commuter (like his father, he was a tireless worker), and the twins, Sam and Ben, might have their phones turned off because wasn't that what college students did when they were trying to sleep? Surely it was too early for them to be at classes, even at Dartmouth, where studies seemed to matter.

God, she hated her empty nest and how it fostered such a restless malaise.

With thin resignation, Dana realized that because her family was inaccessible, that left Lauren. Bridget. Maybe even Caroline, who must have already seen the story. Caroline, after all, rose most days at dawn, then ran two miles before the commuters began clogging their shady, stone wall–lined back roads. The fact that it was the day after the luncheon would not alter Caroline's schedule. Plenty of people had no doubt been hired to deal with the aftermath.

Dana eyed the cordless phone. She'd never cared much for gossip, a carryover from when she'd been a senior in high school and her father's name had kept popping up in the newspaper of their small Midwestern town:

POLICE UNION BOOKS FAULTY

UNION HEAD QUESTIONED

GEORGE KIMBALL ARRESTED FOR EMBEZZLEMENT

He pleaded guilty and was sentenced, ten years in prison, two years' probation. In the meantime, Dana's middle-class life disintegrated. She missed her senior prom (who on earth would go with her?), lost all her friends, and had been shipped off to an elderly aunt's on Long Island, where she finished high school by corresponding with her teachers.

After the shame-dust had settled, it seemed easier to stay where she'd been transplanted. She was accepted as a continuing ed student at Columbia. She studied hard and made it into the school of journalism the same month her aunt died, leaving her a little money and a lot alone. She had a brief stint as an investigative reporter for the *New York Post*, but after what her family had been through, courtrooms and crime made Dana uneasy. So she took a job as an assistant-to-an-assistant editor at *Fortune* magazine, where she met Steven

Fulton, Harvard BS in economics '70, Wharton MBA '72, while interviewing him for a story on "Investments for the New Generation."

Within months they were married, and Dana no longer had to worry about writing headlines—or about having her father make them. By that time it had been years since she'd spoken to her father; by now it was decades.

She took another sip of coffee, reread the article, and realized that if it hadn't been for gossip, however, she would not have met or married Steven, but might have remained rooted in Indiana and married Mr. Nobody.

Gossip, she decided, had ended up serving her well, if "well" meant unlimited credit at Neiman Marcus and modest, but adequate, trust funds for her kids. If "well" meant a decent, if not perfect, marriage, a healthy family, a place as Mrs. Steven Fulton at the respectable New Falls table.

Yes, gossip had served Dana well.

As for Kitty DeLano . . . well, Dana wondered, Kitty had once been a good friend, so would it really be gossip? And wouldn't it be better than sitting around her too-empty house waiting for someone to come home?

"Caroline," Dana said into the phone with feigned nonchalance. "I wanted to say thanks for the delightful luncheon yesterday."

"It's too early in the day for thank-yous," Caroline replied. "You must have seen the paper, too."

One thing Dana had instantly recognized about Caroline when they met at a "Newcomers" meeting twenty-five years ago, was that Caroline was always in the know, the puppeteer for the New Falls social life. Dana sighed. "Do you think she really killed him?"

Caroline laughed a short, sharp laugh. "Who would blame her? Did you see Yolanda yesterday? It's not as if Vincent left Kitty for a Radcliffe alum."

Like the rest of them, Caroline was a snob. Unlike Dana, she had the right to be a snob, having been born and raised in another Westchester County town that was level with New Falls on the highbrow barometer. Unlike Dana, Caroline hadn't come there by way of Indiana.

With a twinge of guilt for having stepped onto a rung of the social ladder under spurious pretenses (not that any of them knew Dana's humiliating past), she said, "But do you think Kitty's okay? I mean, good Lord, she's in *jail.*"

"I doubt if she's okay. She's probably cold and scared as hell."

Dana's father had said he'd been cold. He never said if he'd been scared. "Should we do something?"

"Like what? I don't expect they'll let us bring her blankets. Besides, if we show up, she'd only be embarrassed."

"I think she's already been embarrassed, Caroline. By the divorce and everything." Of course, Caroline hadn't helped by inviting Vincent's new, *underage* missus (Yolanda was barely out of her twenties) to the rite-of-spring luncheon, thereby perpetuating the notion that, in New Falls, men ruled.

But Dana had lived there long enough to know that was simply the way things had worked for generations, as if women's lib had never happened, as if this were not the twenty-first century and women had never been granted the right to vote, let alone to abort. The reasons were simple: The

men did business with one another, played golf, commiser-
ated. Their wits and their egos—and who knew what else—
were measured daily by themselves and by each other, and
their prizes were dollars and cents. At their sides were their
prerequisite wives—their Stepford Middle-Aged Mamas—
fine-tuned and well-oiled in diamonds and pearls, in cracked
crab and champagne.

When divorce came calling, the men retained all the status;
the women were paid off and cast out. Shunned. Brushed off
like lint on navy cashmere, the way Kitty had been brushed
off by Caroline.

It was sad, true, inevitable.

"Does she have family?" Dana asked, suddenly more interested in Kitty's survival than in the gossip.

"Her children, of course, though from what I understand
they've clung to Daddy and might not be sympathetic to her
cause. She has a mother in a nursing home upstate. Other than
that, I think Kitty's alone." She said the word "alone" with a
hint of sorrow and compassion that surprised Dana.

Does she feel it, too? Dana wondered. Does Caroline feel the
same dread—no matter how seemingly remote—that she,
that any one of them, was just one Yolanda away from being
cast aside, too?

"Caroline," Dana said as epiphany struck, "we have to help
her."

There was a pause of time and space and social class. Then
the woman said, "My husband would be furious."

Dana didn't think Steven would be as furious as Caroline
thought Jack might be. Unlike most of the husbands, Steven
saw the world the way it was. He often, in fact, laughed out

loud at their own behavior as much as at the behavior of their friends.

"Well," Dana said carefully, "I understand. But I can't sit here knowing that Kitty is in trouble and that I might be able to help." It was hard to admit that, like the rest of them, she hadn't once called Kitty since the marriage broke up.

Caroline paused again as if she were smoking a cigarette with her new plumped-up lips. "Give her my best" was all she said.

It was spring, too warm a morning to wear the Polarfleece Dana had on. She could not, however, rid her mind's eye of the image Caroline had planted there: that Kitty was cold and scared as hell. Besides, Dana didn't suppose she'd run into the fashion police at the county jail where the newspaper article said Kitty was being held pending arraignment.

She wondered if the guards would let her give Kitty the jacket. Then again, she thought, as she wheeled her Volvo past the tall chain-link fence that was topped with barbed wire corkscrewed like a big, unfriendly Slinky, maybe one of Kitty's kids had bailed her out by now.

She parked, she turned off the ignition, she got out of the car and locked it as if she were simply going into the market, or into the nail salon for a manicure. Unlike the other New Falls ladies, Dana did not find jail a foreign land.

She remembered the drill:

"Name."

"Driver's license."

"Inmate number."

Crossing the parking lot, Dana zipped the Polarfleece, glad

she'd remembered to wear a jacket that did not have a hood. As she recalled, a hood was deemed a suspicious hiding place for a packet of cocaine or a loaded gun.

Pulling open the heavy glass door, Dana wondered where on earth Kitty had gotten a gun and when she'd learned how to shoot.

The waiting room was harsh from too many fluorescent lights. A large, uniformed young man sat behind a desk next to a wall of computer screens. There had been no computers thirty-plus years ago.

What was familiar, however, was the air. It was stale and still, scented by bodies that had not been washed often or well enough. Dana knew if she closed her eyes, she might think she was back home, that it was Monday evening visiting hours, and she'd come to see Daddy.

"May I help you?" the uniformed young man asked.

Dana blinked. "Yes," she said, her voice just a whisper, as if not to disturb her long-ago ghosts. "Can you tell me if Kitty DeLano is being held here or if someone has posted her bail?"

The young man smiled. Well, that was certainly something else that was different from the stern, bullying looks of the Indiana guards. Maybe the prison system had decided to soften its approach.

"She's here," he said. "Are you her attorney?"

It should have occurred to Dana that she might not get in to see Kitty without some credentials. At home, after all, she'd been "family."

She considered leaving, then realized that because Kitty was still there, her children apparently hadn't yet appeared.

Not her children, not even an attorney. Perhaps Kitty was so cold and so scared that she hadn't known what to do or whom to call. Perhaps she truly was all alone.

Dana cleared her throat. "We haven't decided whether or not Ms. DeLano will retain me." Her journalism voice had returned, the voice that implied she was a professional and she was in charge. As long as the guard didn't ask for a card that stipulated she was a member of the bar.

He looked at his watch. "Her arraignment isn't until one. The judge is real busy this morning."

"I know," Dana said, as if she did. She was glad the guard did not question why an attorney would wear Polarfleece.

Then he stood up and leaned across the desk. "May I see your driver's license?" he asked, and Dana's heart skipped a past-memory beat. She dug into her purse and extracted the document.

His eyes scanned it briefly, then he pointed to a tall, white archway that looked like the metal detectors in airports. She sucked in her breath and stepped toward the arch, thankful she hadn't put on an underwire bra when she'd dressed that morning.

🍃 Three

It was a small, square room—not a big, open one like the one George Kimball had been escorted into so he could receive Monday night visitors.

There was a lone table the same size as the cozy kitchen table in the split-level where Dana had grown up—not a configuration of bureaucratic, banquet-style tables shaped into a "U" with inmates parked on one side and visitors directed to the other.

It was almost friendly—not at all like in Indiana.

Dana waited in the room alone, looking out a window that had wire honeycombed inside the glass. She clicked her fingernails together and wished Kitty would get there before she spent too much time thinking about her father and wondering if he was still alive.

A heavy door creaked open.

Kitty stood in the doorway. Her jaw went slack; her eyebrows knitted into a waxed "W". "Dana," she said.

Dana wrung her hands. "Kitty. Are you all right?"

She didn't look all right. Her muddy brown hair was sticking up as if she'd had an electric shock; her skin was pale, in grave need of a good foundation and a little blush. The body that Kitty used to hate (no matter what diet or exercise regimen she followed, she could never quite flatten her tummy) had grown thin and frail since Dana had last seen her.

But Kitty said, "I'm fine," because that was what the women of New Falls had been trained to say. "The bed's not very comfortable, but I didn't feel like sleeping anyway."

Dana sat down because her legs were suddenly weak. "Are you cold?" she asked. "You can have my jacket."

"That would be nice. I'm freezing." She wore only linen pants and a short-sleeved sweater, which must have been the outfit she'd had on yesterday when they'd found her standing over Vincent, *a trickle of blood oozing from his left ear, a gun slack, still smoking, in Kitty's right hand.*

Short sleeves and linen, Dana thought. No wonder Kitty was freezing.

Dana unzipped the jacket and wondered how Caroline would have known that. Did she, too, have a father in another state that she didn't talk about? She handed the jacket over to Kitty, who slipped it on quickly and huddled against its warmth. A guard in the doorway didn't seem inclined to take it away. In fact, he didn't seem to be paying attention to them at all.

16

"Your arraignment's scheduled for one," Dana said as if Kitty didn't know. She lowered her voice. "Has your attorney been here?"

Kitty sat down across from her. "I don't have one."

Surely Dana misunderstood. "What do you mean? Of course you have an attorney."

"Only a court-appointed one. A young girl right out of law school. I'm her first murder case."

Dana leaned closer. "Kitty, that's ridiculous."

Kitty shrugged.

"What about the man who did your divorce?"

But Kitty shook her head. "Sean isn't a criminal lawyer. I don't know any of those, do you?"

Dana could hardly say the only one she knew was back in Indiana. "No. But if you need help. . ."

Kitty shrugged again.

"What about your children?"

"I guess they're too busy making funeral arrangements."

Dana wondered what her boys would have done if she'd been arrested for killing Steven. Would they rally to her side or his? She stared out the window again.

"It's nice of you to come," Kitty said. "Thank you for the jacket."

"It was Caroline's idea."

The eyebrows scrunched back into the "W".

"We're all concerned about you, Kitty." She said it as if all the women who'd been at the rite-of-spring luncheon were now lined up at the barbed wire with fleece jackets of their own.

Kitty didn't respond, perhaps because she knew better.

"I'll come to the arraignment," Dana said. She didn't say she'd post her bail because even tolerant Steven might draw the line at that. "In the meantime, is there anything I can do? Call your kids? Anything?"

"You can find Vincent's killer," Kitty said.

"Pardon me?"

"I said you can find Vincent's killer. You don't really think I murdered him, do you?"

"Mrs. DeLano killed her husband?" It was Sam, calling from Dartmouth. He sounded anxious, the most sensitive of Dana's boys, the one who cared too much about other people.

"Mom?" Michael was next. "What's going on?" He was between meetings, had heard the news on Wall Street.

Steven did not call. Apparently the Kitty/Vincent saga hadn't made *USA Today* yet.

She had just finished assuring Michael that Mrs. DeLano was fine when the doorbell rang. It was Bridget.

"You went there?" she accused as she pushed past Dana and moved into the living room without being invited. She wore a pink jogging suit that accented her round boobs—"all-natural, no implants, *merci beaucoup,*" Bridget was fond of saying. (Unlike Lauren, Dana, and Caroline, who wore sizes four, six, and eight respectively and had heights according to that, Bridget, at five-five, was a twelve on the top, six on the bottom; so much for French women being scrawny.) She also wore too much Chanel for this time of day, not even lunchtime. She went to the twin love seats by the fireplace and made herself at home.

"Coffee?" Dana asked.

Bridget shook her head. Her black curls danced and bounced. "Answers. I want answers. How is our dear Kitty?" She pronounced "is" like "ees" and "Kitty" like "Keety." Sometimes her accent was more than annoying.

Dana dropped onto the sofa across from her. "She didn't do it," she said.

The phone rang again. That time it was Lauren.

"Whatever has happened?" Lauren cried in tiny, childlike sounds.

"I'll tell you both at the same time," Dana said. With her eyes on Bridget and the phone to one ear, she drew in a long breath and said how she'd gone to see Kitty and how she'd given her the jacket and how Kitty said she didn't do it. She did not tell them how terrible Kitty had looked. That fact seemed too much like the gossip that Dana detested.

When she was finished, she handed the phone to Bridget. "Talk to Lauren if you want. I'm going upstairs to get ready for the arraignment."

Neither Bridget nor Lauren offered to go with her.

Caroline sat at her vanity table, pulling her short, sun-colored, painted hair under a terry headband. She studied her reflection, pleased at the absence of the finest lines around her amber eyes, her now-full, coral lips. She wondered if she'd need another facelift when she turned sixty-four. Would twelve years be too much time between her second and her third?

"Everyone is different," Dr. Gregg had said. "You have exceptional skin tone. You may be able to wait fifteen years."

It wasn't as if he needed to drum up more business. Though his waiting room was like a therapist's—with an entrance

and an exit positioned so patients did not see one another—
Caroline knew that, in addition to the women of New Falls,
Dr. Gregg had amassed a clientele of men who wanted to be
nipped and tucked, too, who were desperate to avert the on-
rushing train of that hideous thing called time.

One would think we lived in L.A., Caroline mused as she picked
up the silver pot of face powder and dabbed the sable brush.

"Do you think New Falls will make the evening news?" her
husband, Jack, said as he entered her dressing room, the *New
Falls Journal* in his hand.

"Doubtful," she said, curving the brush from nose to ear
with a swift, circular sweep. "It's not as if Vincent was an up-
and-coming player."

She knew, because Jack had told her in confidence, that
Vincent's client list had begun to shrivel a year or so ago, that
his edge had lost its sharpness, his drive had slowed its pace—
a lethal combination when money was at stake. It had happened around the time that he'd met Yolanda and, according
to Kitty, his brain was lobotomized by his dick.

Still, Vincent DeLano had found a way to survive until now.

Setting down the pot of powder, she picked up a light brown
eye pencil and started to enhance the half moons above her
eyes. In the mirror, she saw Jack sit on the velvet side chair
and cross his legs as if he were a girl.

"I don't think I have to suggest that it's best if you stay out
of this," he said.

He had on a light blue shirt, a gray-blue tie, and gray flan-
nel pants. He was dressed for the office today (an increasingly
rare occurrence), though he wouldn't leave for the city until noon, leaving rush hour to the "amateurs" and lunch to

the hungry. Jack Meacham, after all, no longer hungered for anything. He had started his own mutual fund a number of years ago, sold out when mutual funds were hot, made a great fortune, and only dabbled now and then for fun: a few million here, a few there. Mostly Jack played golf.

"I do not intend to get involved," Caroline replied. She noted that Jack looked older in his reflection, his face showing wear, his eyes downcast as if he were tired. "Are you all right?" she asked.

"Me?" He raised his head. He stood up. "I'm fine, Caroline. I just find this sort of thing extremely sad."

"That a friend of mine is in jail?"

"No," he said. "That a friend of mine is dead."

It was about the men, of course. It always was.

"Oh," she answered, and resumed the task of her makeup.

She was aware he still stood there, though she didn't expect he was looking at her, thinking about her. When they'd been young she'd often thought his pensive moments were spent in obsessive thoughts about her; how she was the most regal of all their friends; how she strode so elegantly into a room and paused to be admired; how only Jack knew that beneath her silk and satin, she wore nothing at all; how they'd had awesome sex the night or the week or the month before (he especially loved to watch while she masturbated, an act that always engorged his member and resulted in power-thrusts she did not understand).

It had taken a few years for Caroline to realize that in those pensive moments, her husband had not been thinking about her at all, but about his next mega-deal, the next client he would land, the next eagle/birdie/hole-in-one he would score.

"Well," he said, "I'm off to work then."

He left the room without kissing her good-bye, no doubt because he hadn't thought of that, either.

She set down the eye pencil, picked up the palette of blush, blended peach with rose, and applied it to her cheeks, wondering what Jack would say if he knew that, not so long ago, she had considered having him disposed of, not unlike the way Vincent was disposed, deposed, yesterday.

❧ *Four*

Kitty's son, Marvin, showed up at her arraignment and posted his mother's bail. Then he asked if Dana would mind taking her home. "I must get back to work," he said, pushing his round, black-framed glasses up onto the bridge of his sloping nose. Though not quite thirty, he was a top proctologist at Cedars-Sinai. It was a profession so fraught with innuendo that most people didn't say a word, they just tried to hide their smiles.

Kitty kissed her son and thanked him for the bail. As dispassionate as Dana's life had become, she was grateful that she was not Kitty.

"Shall we stop for lunch?" Dana asked, once they were seatbelted inside the Volvo.

Kitty sort of nodded. "If you'd like," she said, her head tipping curiously to one side, her arms wrapping themselves around her too-thin middle, her gaze fixating on the dashboard.

They went to The Chocolate Flan because it was on the way to the apartment where Kitty had been staying since the movers had absolved the marital house of its furnishings. Like the apartment, the restaurant was in Tarrytown, so it would not matter that Kitty looked like a zombie, or that she wore Dana's Polarfleece with linen pants.

They ordered salads. Kitty also ordered wine.

"You need a real attorney," Dana said.

Kitty flinched as if she only just then realized that they were in the restaurant and not still in the car. "It won't matter," she replied. "I was the one who was holding the gun. No one's going to believe I didn't do it."

Dana spread the mocha-colored napkin across her lap. "What happened, Kitty?"

Kitty zipped the fleece as if it were as cold in there as at the jail. Her eyes did not meet Dana's but attached themselves to the small sunflower in the center of the table. "I went to the house to meet him." The waiter brought her wine. She took a long, slow sip. "Vincent was already dead. Right there in the living room." She took another drink. Dana wished she'd ordered wine, too. "I got scared," Kitty added. "I took out my gun."

"Your gun? I didn't know you owned a gun."

"Vincent bought it for me. He was so worried about all the cash he always carried. He was afraid someone would think I carried a lot of money, too."

Dana didn't ask why a futures trader—or his wife—would carry a lot of cash. Steven rarely had more than a hundred dollars, relegating the space in his wallet to American Express. Dana wasn't much different.

"But..." Dana stumbled for the words. "The article said the gun was still smoking." Since the boys had grown and gone and Steven was traveling so much, Dana spent too much time home alone, watching too many *Law & Order* reruns. She supposed it was a throwback to her early years as a cop's daughter and her brief journalism dreams. But even before Lennie Briscoe and Jack McCoy, Dana would have known that when a gun was "still smoking," it had just been fired.

Kitty lifted her glass again. "Ah," she said, "a smoking gun. Right out of a Sue Grafton novel."

It was the first spark of life Dana had witnessed since seeing Kitty that morning.

Then, lowering both her eyes and her voice, Kitty said, "I heard a noise. I thought the murderer was still in the house. I took out my gun and pulled the trigger by mistake. I shot the Oriental rug."

"Excuse me?" Dana asked.

"The rug," Kitty said, lifting her head again, this time her blue eyes wet with tears. "I shot the bloody rug that we bought when we went to Istanbul for our twentieth wedding anniversary."

Dana frowned. "Isn't the house empty?"

"Yes. Except for the rugs. A dealer from Newbury Street in Boston was coming to give us a price. Vincent promised to split the cash with me. Keep it away from the lawyers, you

25

know. They already were charging the net worth of the house and the villa combined. Anyway, that's why I went there. To meet Vincent and the rug dealer. We have nine carpets, in all. Scattered all over the house." She waved her hand as if she were talking about dust mites and not valuable antique rugs.

"Did you tell the police?"

"Tell them what?"

"That you shot the rug?"

"Yes."

"What did they say?"

"They told me I had the right to remain silent."

The salads came, the waiter left.

"And did you?"

"I didn't think I had a choice. What with the way it looked and all."

The boys from *Law & Order* no doubt would have agreed.

Bridget had tried to be a good wife to Randall Haynes, a *joyeux fille* who would make his life a pleasant one. She did not care that some people thought she was a trophy: That was an American slang term; Americans could be so *grossier*, so *visqueux*.

Last year she had made certain her daughter was finally going to school in Provence—Ecole Ste. Anne—where Bridget would have gone if her parents could have afforded it. But Aimée was an only child, and Randall had finally agreed to send her, though he lamented that three times a year— Christmas break and spring and summer—would not be often enough to see his fourteen-year-old daughter.

Still, he'd allowed it because he knew his wife was from Provence. Luckily he did not know the rest.

But Bridget had tried to be a good wife. They'd had their ups and downs, like when he'd wanted more children and she'd said absolutely not, that she had not liked being pregnant, that she'd thrown up all the time. His good nature had vanished like a blip on a screen. He'd threatened to send her back to France without their daughter and without a dime. He said that in America the courts always sided with the parent with the money, especially if he could prove that prior to meeting him, she'd merely been a waitress and not a good one at that.

She hadn't known if his caveats were true; she hadn't known how to find out.

She hated Randall during that horrid time, hated him *très terriblement*. She thought of kidnapping Aimée and running away. But Bridget had nowhere to go, no longer anyone to go to.

She decided if she couldn't have a good life, at least her daughter could. So she pretended to change her mind, to agree with Randall that another child would be worth a few months of illness. His humor, his love, returned. For several years she pretended to be trying to get pregnant, but instead she took the pill. Lucky for her, Randall was Catholic. As time went by he began to think that God had intervened (Bridget paid off a wayward priest to delicately plant the suggestion). When she turned forty, Randall woefully gave up, and now they only had sex on occasion, like Christmas and birthdays and when the Dow broke twelve thousand.

Through it all, Bridget had not once thought of shooting him.

She stood in the middle of her daughter's enormous walk-in closet now, surveying the skirts and shirts and pants and cotton sweaters Aimée might want at school in the next couple of months. It had been a thin excuse for not accompanying Dana to Kitty's arraignment. But the truth was, she couldn't fit one more drama into her life.

"So sorry, darling," Bridget had whined when Dana emerged from upstairs, dressed for the courtroom, keys to her Volvo in her hand. "But I'll be leaving in days to get Aimée—I have so much to do!"

She could have lied and said she had a doctor's appointment, but she'd had enough of those lately and didn't want to jinx her diagnosis.

"Most women survive cervical cancer," her doctor had told her.

No one else, of course, knew. Not Dana or Caroline or Lauren. Not Aimée. Not Randall.

When Bridget had her hysterectomy, they'd thought she'd gone into the city to have some work done on her thighs (liposuction wasn't just for fat people anymore) and her tummy (tucking was so easy). It was amazing how the latest patient rights' legislation helped you burrow like a little mole in a medical backyard, helped you keep your private things truly private, God bless America.

Radiation treatments were even easier to pull off: She'd claimed to be a volunteer for a French program at the United Nations. Every day for seven weeks, she took the train into the city. No one questioned, not even Randall, why she was exhausted. Nor did anyone question why she was having god-awful hot flashes because no one knew her body had been hurled into menopause ahead of its natural time.

Still, the doctors wanted Bridget to have chemotherapy. But she wanted to put it off until she'd told Luc.

Luc, after all, had been her first husband, though her second didn't know it; he'd fathered her son, whom Randall didn't know about, either. Luc was the man Bridget had loved forever, the man who lived across the sea, not far from where Aimée now went to school, *quelle coincidence*. Bridget needed for Luc to know she still loved him, in case she was not like "most women" and did not survive.

Plucking a pretty pink sweater from a cubbyhole, Bridget smiled. She folded it, dropped it into the suitcase. She'd leave for Provence this coming weekend to spend a few days in the country before bringing her daughter home. While she was there, she'd tell Luc about the cancer. Maybe then he'd tell her that he still loved her, too.

With slow, deliberate motions, she packed the suitcase. If she finished early enough, she might go back to Dana's and ask how Kitty had made out.

It was after five o'clock when Dana finally arrived home. She went into the living room, poured a glass of wine, and sat down on the love seat, propping her feet on the low coffee table, the way she'd often admonished her sons for doing.

She'd hated leaving Kitty. The apartment Kitty was renting (two bedrooms, two baths, no ambience) was partially filled with the landlord's unimaginative furniture, poorly framed floral prints, and thin window blinds that at least blocked the view of Interstate 287. She said she'd be fine but Dana wasn't convinced.

Nor was she convinced Kitty hadn't shot Vincent.

It had been nearly a year since Kitty had been one of "them," nearly a year since Vincent had left her and snatched her credentials the way the Queen of England had once revoked Princess Di's "HRH" just because her husband couldn't get his priorities straight. It was abominable, Dana thought, the way men could be the screwups, yet emerge the victors.

Her cell phone and the house phone rang simultaneously. Dana closed her eyes and considered answering neither. But she'd spent too many years as a mother to be comfortable with that ("Michael"—or Ben or Sam—"fell on the playground and split his forehead open") and too long as a New Falls wife to expect such a luxury ("Honey, my driver can't get to La-Guardia. Do you feel like taking a ride?").

So she opened her eyes, checked caller ID (Caroline, not the school, and Bridget, not her husband), and answered them both anyway.

"We all need to do lunch tomorrow," Caroline said, and Dana agreed and passed the query over to Bridget.

Lunch, of course, was not about food, which none of them ate much of anyway. It was, instead, their justification to talk, their venue for resolving the persistent issues that had a way of creeping into their lives.

The issue, right now, being Kitty, though Dana was surprised Caroline was feigning interest.

"She called me," Caroline said.

"She called her," Dana relayed to Bridget, who was on the cell.

"She wants the name of an attorney."

"She asked Caroline for the name of an attorney."

"She doesn't understand that I can't get involved."

Dana wasn't sure how to translate that to Bridget, so she merely tucked the receiver between her neck and her chin and took a drink from her glass.

"What time?" Bridget was asking. "And where?"

"Where?" Dana asked Caroline. "What time?" She'd have to reschedule her pedicure, but this was more important. Steven wouldn't be home for another few days, and it wasn't as if anyone else saw her toes.

"Twelve-thirty. At Calabrese."

"That's in Tarrytown," Dana said.

"Yes. It's near where Kitty lives. She'll join us there."

Dana passed the information on to Bridget, who asked, "Shall I call Lauren?"

Dana turned from her cell back to her landline. "What about Lauren?"

"No," Caroline said. "I already called her. She said she can't make it."

Can't. *Won't* was more like it, Dana suspected. Lauren, after all, was afraid of her own silly shadow.

"Shall we meet at the restaurant?" Dana asked.

"Yes," Caroline replied. "I have an early appointment at the museum." She was on more boards of directors than seemed physically possible.

"We'll meet her there," Dana told Bridget.

"I'll pick you up," Bridget said to Dana, which would happily allow for pre- and post-lunch discussion.

They said good-bye all around, then Dana hung up both phones, stared at her wineglass, and wondered how it happened that life did these kinds of things, that as soon as you felt restless and bored, along came a distraction to keep you from losing your mind.

She thought she was going to go crazy.

Lauren sat on the window seat in the master suite, looking out at the rolling green lawn and the towering oak trees and the flower beds that had been tended by Jeffrey, the gardener, who once worked for Martha Stewart but now worked for her and for Caroline, too, doing twice the work for four times the price. He had, after all, married Lauren's stepdaughter Dory, and the women took care of their own.

Lauren sat on the window seat, toying with her triple strand of pearls, her eyes stinging with tears, her throat closing with fright.

She was alone in the "big house on the hill," as Bob called it because of the way it was perched, overlooking (over*seeing*) the town as Bob liked to do. Bob and Mr. Chang had gone into the city, after Mr. Chang said he'd very much enjoyed his visit to their home.

She'd smiled and bowed and said, "It was a pleasure to have you," all the while holding her secret close to her chest, so close that Mr. Chang could not suspect anything might be askew, so close that Bob wouldn't know, either.

Finally they'd left. She'd sat there and watched as Jeffrey packed up his rakes and his hoes and departed, too. And now she stared at the stillness of the earth and the quiet of the sky as the sun slid toward the horizon, its soft salmon color stretching its arms.

She sat there in the silence and wondered how soon it would be before everything erupted. How soon it would be before someone, somehow, would learn that, before Yolanda, Vincent DeLano had been sleeping with her.

🍃 Five

Lauren Halliday had been born Lauren Bryson of the Boston–Palm Beach–Nantucket Brysons. The silver spoon in her mouth had literally been a ladle, intricately carved by Paul Revere himself and owned by her industrialist and abolitionist great-great-great grandfather, who'd been gifted it for his "statesmanlike spirit" in helping desegregate Boston.

From the Beacon Street brownstone where she'd been raised, to the waterfront mansion where the family wintered, and the sprawling, gray-shingled "cottage" where they summered, Lauren had it all.

She was quiet and sweet, always eager to help. She went to the right schools, had the right friends, wore the right clothes, smiled the right smile. She never had acne, had perfect blond hair that to this day she wore demurely long, tied back with a pretty ribbon. As a young girl she'd been a natural at dancing and on horseback, and she loved her volunteer job giving out books at the hospital because it made her father so proud. At twelve, however, she was whacked in the head by the boom of a sail mast (did her cousin Gracie really not see her?) and soon after, she developed ulcers, which the doctors said she'd outgrow. When she didn't, they put her on Xanax, which she still enjoyed on occasion.

Bob had been a friend of her father's, a member of the Harvard Club, an investment manager for First New York National, where he'd gone from New Boston Bank & Trust, where her father had been senior vice president.

Lauren married Bob eighteen years ago when she was thirty-one and he, forty-nine. It was a second marriage for both. (Her first to the son of a lobsterman who was more enamored of her cash than of her—as her father, too late, had predicted; Bob's first to a woman who'd borne him seven children, then had the misfortune to be hit by a bus. "A *city* bus, of all things," Lauren's mother had wailed. "*Public transportation.*")

Unlike less privileged Gracie, who'd been raised with Lauren's leftover clothes and accessories once Lauren had tired of them or they'd gone out of style, this was the first time Lauren had been given a hand-me-down. Fortunately, by the time she and Bob married, two of his kids had their degrees and were living on their own, two were still in college, and only three were still "school age"—nine, twelve, and fifteen—still in need of some sort of mothering, which Lauren would have done if only she knew how.

But like her father, Bob was rich, so instead of patience and hugging, Lauren offered nannies (they were too old for that), then summer camps, then child psychologists. When the kids finally grew up she was hugely relieved, though she never said so.

The thing with Vincent had been a fluke.

Bob had turned sixty-five, and along with the milestone came impotence. With impotence came frustration, then confusion, then anger.

He was angry, she supposed, at the clock and the calendar and the fact that, though he played racquetball and golf and ran three miles a day, Mother Nature had pointed her finger and said, "Done."

So his penis was wilted like overcooked pasta and he refused the Viagra and the rest of the stuff, citing that this must be a "virus" or some other phenomenon, that surely his noodle would come back to life and spring forth once again from his pants.

He had, after all, fathered seven children. Clearly he had no problems in the bedroom.

She tried blowjobs and oils and getting on top. She tried whipped cream and pornography and negligees with the nipples cut out.

None of it worked.

After a year, Lauren was horny. Well, the truth was, after two weeks, Lauren was horny, but it took her a year to admit it. And that long to wonder if Bob's "virus" would define the rest of her life.

Then, on a simple, run-of-the-mill Tuesday, there was Vincent.

She'd been in the city buying china because Dory's wedding

was in a few weeks, and Lauren wanted to be certain the girl had the best. She'd taken the train because Bob was using their driver, and she hated the traffic and the hassle of parking.

There had been an accident of some sort on the tracks north of the city. The train to New Falls was delayed. She went into The Campbell Apartment—a chic bar in Grand Central Station—for wine and the wait. Within five minutes Vincent DeLano sat down beside her.

"If it isn't Lauren Halliday," he said with a grin.

They talked.

They drank.

The train was stalled another hour.

They discussed having dinner, but drank more instead. Then Vincent told her she was the prettiest of all of Kitty's friends. That she was the sweetest, the absolute sexiest. That whenever he saw her, his penis got hard. Very hard.

Did Bob know how lucky he was?

If he hadn't mentioned Bob, Lauren might have escaped. Instead her hand traveled to Vincent's crotch, right there in The Campbell Apartment in Grand Central. He was right: His package bulged.

Luckily the Helmsley was within walking distance.

By the time they were finished, Lauren was weak-kneed and raw. And God, she felt good. If she felt any guilt, it was over the fact that she didn't feel guilty. For once in her life she had been a bad girl, and God, yes, it had felt good.

A few months and dozens of lusty afternoons later, she found out that Vincent was also seeing Yolanda. The thought of him touching the woman whose hands touched her hair had been too repulsive for words.

Now that he was gone, she should feel relieved, the way she'd felt when Bob's kids finally left. But as she sat in her boudoir, staring out at the sunset, Lauren could think only one perilous thought: Had Vincent told anyone about their affair, and if so, would they tell the police?

🌿 Six

Tarrytown, New York, was where Washington Irving had penned *The Legend of Sleepy Hollow*, so it wasn't unheard of for odd things to happen there. It was also downriver from Ossining, the home of notorious Sing Sing prison that now boasted twice as many annual visitors as inmates. Kitty wouldn't go there if she were convicted because she wasn't a man.

Instead she'd no doubt end up in the quaint little hamlet of Bedford Hills, which housed the only maximum-security facility for women in the state, or at least that's what Dana figured would happen, though no one at the table seemed to want to address it.

They were at Calabrese the day after Kitty's arraignment.

They sat in a private spot in a corner as Caroline had requested.

"It's our fault, isn't it?" Bridget said before Kitty arrived.

"That Kitty killed her husband?" Caroline asked. A hint of disdain laced her voice, as if to ask how Bridget could entertain such a thought.

"That Kitty *allegedly* killed Vincent," Dana corrected.

"Why on earth is it our fault?" Caroline asked.

"Because we are *dégout* snobs," Bridget continued. "Kitty was our friend, and when Vincent dumped her, we all did, too."

Caroline made no comment.

Dana didn't, either. It had, after all, been only yesterday that she'd reminded herself that they were, indeed, snobs. Instead of commenting, she looked around the restaurant. It was decorated in red and green, Italian colors. The tables were dressed up with Chianti bottles whose necks wore long shawls of candle wax. The walls displayed harbor scenes that looked as if they'd been painted by number.

All in all, the place was tacky enough to minimize the number of patrons who might recognize them. Besides, they were in Tarrytown.

Bridget was right, Dana thought. They were *dégout* snobs.

Caroline selected wine and told the waiter they'd wait for the rest of their party to order their food.

"And now Kitty's late," Bridget added, eyes scanning the room. The women of New Falls *never* were late, no matter how small the event. They might be snobs, but they were not prima donnas, at least not about time.

"I asked her to be here at one," Caroline said. "I wanted to speak with both of you before she arrived."

You spoke with both of us—sort of—on the phone yesterday, Dana wanted to say. But she supposed the wine and the setting were part of Caroline's plan. She always, after all, had a plan. It was how she was able to successfully juggle so many boards of directors.

"I've located an attorney for Kitty," she said, hand sliding into her Gucci daytime bag and extracting a business card. "Paul Tobin," she said. "He's in White Plains. She has an appointment Monday at eleven."

There were two things that Dana found disturbing: first, that Caroline hadn't "located" a Manhattan lawyer; second, that she handed the card to her.

She tried handing it back. "I think you should give this to Kitty yourself," Dana said. Caroline had been a good friend over the years—well, as good a friend as a New Falls wife could be—but lately she'd begun to irritate Dana. The charities, the agendas, the quest for perfection . . . God, was Caroline ever not perfect? Then Dana's eyes moved to Caroline's lips. She couldn't hold back a tiny smile.

"I can't stay for lunch," Caroline said. "In fact, the truth is, I can't be any part of this. I've secured Mr. Tobin and paid his retainer. But that's all I can do on Kitty's behalf."

Dana's smile waned. She had paid a retainer?

"How generous of you," Bridget said before Dana could ask what on earth had motivated Caroline to pay thousands of dollars to help a friend that she'd written off.

The wine arrived; Caroline stood up. "Enjoy your lunch,"

she said, adjusting Gucci on her shoulder. "The waiter has been instructed to put it on my card. And by the way," she added with a cool grin through those lips, "Please tell Kitty not to call me again."

It was a great exit line, so that's what she did.

Dana's husband came home that night, two days ahead of schedule.

She was back on the love seat, feet propped on the coffee table, mulling over the lunch where no one had ended up eating or even drinking. She was thinking about Bridget and Kitty and odd Caroline, when Steven walked through the door.

"Is fifty-eight too young to retire?" He dropped his suitcase on the floor and flopped on the love seat across from her.

Of all her friends' husbands, Steven had retained his looks best of all. He'd never been a Hollywood type, never chiseled and schmiseled and drop-dead Redford or Pitt. But Steven was tall and straight-backed with startling cobalt eyes and good cheekbones and a slightly receding hairline that, along with his wire-framed glasses, made him look sincere. *Sincere* was a good thing for a man who specialized in mergers and acquisitions.

He was not the sort of man a woman might murder.

But did they have enough money for him to retire? After today, she was wincingly aware of the parallel between having money and being a *dégout* snob. She'd never minded being a lighthearted, regular snob, because she'd never really taken it seriously. But now Bridget had made them sound so, well, appalling.

"Was your trip that exhausting?" Dana asked, then added, "Would you like a drink?" It was, after all, a New Falls wifely duty to honor and serve, even if it only meant bourbon.

He waved his hand. "No drink. Not tonight."

She was grateful she didn't have to get up off the couch. "You're early. Does that mean things didn't go well?"

Rubbing his hand over his hairline (probably encouraging it to recede all the more), he said, "Actually the deal went fine. Quickly. We wrapped it up in record time."

"And now you're exhausted."

"Yeah. I really hate all this traveling lately."

"Then retire."

He laughed. "And do what?"

Dana shrugged. "Play golf. Take up sailing. I don't know. What do other men do?"

He laughed again, dismissing the notion. "Tell me what you've been up to while I was away. You looked rather thoughtful. Is anything wrong?"

With a giant sigh, Dana told him that Vincent DeLano was dead and Kitty had been arrested and Bridget thought all her friends were snobs and Caroline was acting peculiar.

"Caroline Meacham has always been peculiar," Steven said, "so that part's not news. And you probably are snobs, so what?"

Dana laughed and poked her foot at his, which was now parked on the coffee table, too. "You didn't say anything about Vincent and Kitty."

"I'm digesting that."

"It's murder, Steven. Not chicken soup."

"Speaking of which, what's for dinner?"

"Steven!"

Now it was his turn to sigh. "I could say I'm not surprised. I could say it's too bad that Kitty has been arrested, but who could blame her?"

"Blame her? Because of Yolanda?"

"Yolanda? The hairdresser?" Steven chuckled. "Christ, what about your friend Lauren?"

Dana blanched. "What? What about Lauren?"

He rubbed his hairline again. "Didn't I tell you I saw them?"

"Saw who?"

"*Them.* It was a while ago. Months. Maybe a year. I don't know. I thought I told you."

Dana sat up straight. "Steven," she said. "Spit it out."

"I was meeting Ed Cannon from the UK for drinks. When was that? Was it last summer? Well, whatever. We were going to Harry's but it was packed. No. It wasn't summer. It was in the spring. Right around . . . oh, I know. April fifteenth. Which was why the bar was packed." He smiled as if he were a genius.

Dana held herself back from lunging at him.

"I decided to wait for Ed in the lobby. At the Helmsley, you know?"

Of course she knew Harry's Bar was at the Helmsley.

"That's when I saw Lauren and Vincent get off the elevator. They were all over each other, like they'd just come from enjoying one of the Helmsley's fine rooms."

If he'd said the earth had cracked open and sucked in Manhattan, it might have made more sense.

Lauren and Vincent?

Their Lauren and *Kitty's* Vincent?

Steven pulled his long legs from the table and slowly stood up. "I think I'll get that drink after all. Do you want anything?"

But Dana sat mute, too stunned to drink or to move or to breathe.

If it weren't for Luc, Bridget would cancel her trip to Provence and let Aimée fly home alone. She would go with Kitty and Dana to the appointment with attorney Paul Tobin and help provide backup, the way singers did, her alto to Kitty's soprano. It was bad enough the women were snobs. At least they could stick together.

Bridget was so pissed that Caroline had so blatantly blown off Kitty that she would do just about anything to help the poor woman. Except, of course, cancel her trip.

Back in Aimée's closet, Bridget began counting and folding sweaters again, wondering why she'd let her daughter accumulate the trappings of the wealthy that she was beginning to hate.

Of all the women of New Falls, Bridget was the one who knew what it was like to be the outcast, society's rubbish, the one without money and material stuff.

Her father, after all, had been a French cowboy. Bridget had been raised on the Camargue in southwestern Provence amid the white horses and pink flamingos and the Gypsies who gathered in spring. She'd attended school in Ste. Marie de la Mer—where Mary Magdalene was thought to have landed after Jesus' crucifixion—where the Petit Rhône meets the Mediterranean Sea, where shellfish were abundant and olives and figs were trucked in from the hills. She'd worshipped in the ninth-century church, rebuilt by the monks into the town's fortifications.

It was a lively, safe, healthy place to be raised, even in the sixties and seventies, when the rest of the world seemed to be falling apart with protests and riots and wars.

When she was eleven, Bridget fell in love with Luc, a cowboy like her father, though he was just thirteen. At seventeen Luc was fighting the black Camargue bulls at the medieval arena in French style, so the bulls were not killed.

They were meant to be together, Bridget and Luc.

When he was twenty, they married. When he was twenty-one, and Bridget, nineteen, they had a son, Alain, who they named after her father. When Luc was twenty-four, and Bridget, twenty-two, Luc was gored by a bull. He lost the use of both legs but not of his penis, though his depression was so great, he hardly cared about sex.

Even a place as idyllic as Ste. Marie de la Mer could not renew Luc's spirits.

He wanted her to leave, to take Alain with her, to have a chance at the normal life she deserved.

But Bridget would not go.

They had little money; they moved in with her parents; when her mother died, they stayed with her father, and Bridget took care of them all. Alain was the glue that held them together, the charming little boy with his father's sensitive soul and his grandfather's name.

Then, one day after school, five-year-old Alain wandered off through the marshes, perhaps following the wild horses. He was found the next day, drowned in the swamp, his perfect little body already bloated with death.

The year that followed was a long bad dream, with time passing like the speed-train from Marseilles to Paris, the image out the window too blurred to allow for emotion. The next thing Bridget knew, she was waiting on tables near the Sorbonne, a woman who had lost her child, and whose husband had become bitter and loveless and so she'd divorced him.

"Life on the Camargue is no life for me now," she'd said to Luc when she said good-bye. He did not disagree.

Six years later, when Bridget had already been married to Randall for five, had been living in New Falls among the rich Americans, her father died.

She returned for the funeral. She seduced Luc; she wanted him back. He said no: He had another wife now, another child. Apparently his depression had lifted.

She had no pain after that, only a dull, aching loss that never left her, winter, spring, summer, fall. Her life was with Randall, but her heart was not there.

When Aimée was born, Bridget was determined her daughter would have all the things Bridget had not, that her life would be better than life on the Camargue with the white horses. But as time passed, Luc had not left Bridget's mind, and last fall she returned to Provence, under the ruse of enrolling her daughter in a French private school.

She'd seen him then, though not alone. Randall had been with her, after all. She'd introduced Luc as an old family friend, a protégé of her father's, a cowboy long ago.

At Christmastime she convinced Randall to let her cross the Atlantic to escort Aimée home. How could she have known Luc was on holiday in Paris?

Maybe this time, Bridget thought with a smile. *Maybe I will see him, and I will tell him I am sick, and then he will come back to me.*

Her daydream was interrupted by her husband's footsteps across the bedroom carpet. "I thought I'd find you in here," Randall said. He was shorter than most men and wore a toupee to which his stylist had recently begun adding gray. He had kind eyes and a kind heart and deserved someone better than her. "I heard about Vincent DeLano."

Bridget nodded. "*C'est terrible*," she said.

"And Kitty. Your friend."

"She did not kill him."

"Do you know that for sure?"

"*Non.*"

He gestured toward the suitcase. "I will go get her," he said. "You stay here in New Falls. I suspect Kitty will need you."

It took a moment for Bridget to understand what he had said. "What?"

"I said I will go to France to pick up our daughter. There's no need to thank me, it's what I want to do."

He turned and left Aimée's closet, with Bridget still standing, clutching a Ralph Lauren.

🍂 Seven

The funeral was orchestrated by Premiere Parties, which had done Caroline's daughter's engagement festivities and the holiday museum ball.

Lauren arrived at the cemetery in a Marc Jacobs silk sheath with embroidered shrug because the outfit was navy and therefore seemed appropriate. She was glad it was only a graveside service. Vincent, after all, hadn't been a churchgoer, so Yolanda had spared everyone the pomp and procession.

In the backseat of the limo Lauren shivered to think Yolanda was the one making such decisions. Yolanda, who, with her youth and her looks and the wiggle in her walk, had stolen Vincent's attention from her.

The driver opened the door for Bob, who stepped into the

sunlight, buttoned the center button of his gray Jon Green suit, and inhaled the spring air as if it were an outing and they had all day. Lauren held on to her wide-brimmed navy hat, took the driver's gloved hand, and emerged outside next to her husband.

"Everyone's already here," she whispered, and Bob nodded because it never bothered him to be late to the party, never made him nervous or shy to walk into a room—or in this case, a graveyard—surrounded by others, friends, strangers, everyone. She wondered if that was because he was usually the oldest one there.

He took Lauren's elbow and guided her toward the mourners, who, instead of looking at the minister, were now looking at them.

"Hello," Bob said quietly here and there. "Hello. How are you?"

She leaned into his shadow, wishing she'd invented a migraine and refused to come. Even without the bizarre circumstances, Lauren had simply never liked funerals. They were too reminiscent of her angst-driven childhood when the family all gathered for births and for deaths and for milestones in between, which mostly provided a soundstage on which to critique one another, especially her. "She's too thin," "She's too quiet," "She's not nearly as smart as Harold, Celia, or Marge," Aunt Clara would mutter to Aunt Bertie and Aunt Bertie would pass on to Aunt Jane.

It had been at Lauren's grandfather's funeral that Uncle Raymond had fondled her at the back of the hearse, when he'd lured her to peer past the dark velvet drapes that hung, slightly parted, at the rear window. When Lauren leaned down, he swooped in from behind her, clasped his hands around her, and caressed her twelve-year-old buds.

No wonder she didn't like funerals.

Bob led her over the uneven grass to a small opening between Dana and Steven and Caroline and Jack, who stood next to Bridget and Randall. It wasn't strange, Lauren thought, that they were all there. Most times the people who were gossiped about were the ones who didn't show up. Besides, she realized, it wasn't as if any of them was crying.

Across from the metallic blue coffin that held what was left of Vincent DeLano and the deep pit that was poised to swallow him up, dozens of potted lilies were positioned as if it were Easter and resurrection were near. Behind the plants stood Yolanda, draped in layers of frothy black. It would be too much of a farce, Lauren supposed, if Yolanda tripped over the lilies and fell headfirst into the grave.

Lauren straightened her back and tried to pay attention.

"Vincent was a devoted father," the minister began, and all eyes turned toward Kitty's homely proctologist son, who propped up Yolanda on her right side, and toward the supermodel daughter who flanked her right. Just because the kids were Kitty's blood, that was apparently no cause for allegiance.

"He was a wonderful provider," the reverend continued, though Kitty might have protested if she were in attendance.

"And he was also proud of his Italian heritage."

Italian heritage?

Lauren sucked in one corner of her lower lip and gently bit down with her teeth.

"The guys in the high school locker room called me the

'Italian Stallion,'" Vincent had said to her once. "What do you think? Does it fit?"

Though they'd both been naked and he had just climaxed, Lauren was embarrassed. Yes, his penis was big. Yes, it was hard, and yes, it had more staying power than Bob's ever had to her knowledge. But as much as she liked it—indeed, as much as she coveted the very *thought* of it when she was at home in her bed, eyes closed, feeling herself grow damp way down there—Lauren did not want to *talk* about it, at least not to Vincent. She would have *loved* to tell Dana or Bridget or even Caroline at one of their lunches after a glass of wine, but Lauren couldn't, wouldn't, do that because, after all, she was married to Bob, and Vincent had still been married to Kitty, and as delicious as her secret was, it just couldn't be shared.

Besides, what would she tell them? That Vincent had a dick the size of an Italian flagpole?

She felt Bob's eyes on her; she realized she had giggled. Well, at least the minister's words had helped take her mind off Aunt Clara and Aunt Bertie and Uncle Raymond with the traveling hands . . . and off the fact that a small part inside her felt sad that Vincent was dead, and angry at Yolanda because he'd no doubt still be alive if she hadn't come to New Falls and ruined the one great thing in Lauren's life.

They said the Lord's Prayer and then it was finished quite fast, unlike Vincent. The minister told them to go with God, but before they went a loud wail erupted from behind a tall granite tombstone, and everyone knew who had wailed it.

"Mom!" cried Marvin, the proctologist, as he raced toward the tombstone. "Mom! Don't!"

And there stood Kitty, maniacally waving something in her hand, something black, something shiny.

Everyone ducked, including the minister.

"No!" shouted Yolanda just as Kitty's daughter grabbed her by the arm and yanked her in the opposite direction.

"Mrs. DeLano!" the minister shrieked. "Please! Stop!" No one seemed sure if he was addressing Kitty or Yolanda.

"NO, NO, NO!" Yolanda's voice echoed as supermodel Elise dragged the woman away, her chiffon fluttering like an obscure apparition.

From the tombstone came another big wail.

Heads poked up to see Marvin restrain his mother, then pluck the black, shiny object from her hand. Kitty collapsed against him and sobbed. One by one, the mourners began to emerge from their crouch.

"God help her!" the minister shouted again.

"God help *us*!" someone, maybe Jack Meacham, muttered.

Life returned to the group. Steven stepped forward because he was always the one who was willing to help.

"Kitty," he said, "it's all right," and Dana nearly wept because she felt so proud.

The rest of the crowd remained half standing, half stooping, frozen in the moment. Then they backed up as Steven moved toward Kitty and Marvin, who slowly approached. Marvin cradled his mother with one arm. "It was her purse," he said to Steven, as if all the others were gone. He waved the black, shiny thing that Kitty had waved. "It wasn't a gun. It was her purse."

Dana recognized Kitty's patent leather, Bottega Veneta handbag that Kitty had bought at Bergdorf's last year. It was nice that she hadn't lost everything in the divorce.

"I just want to say good-bye to my Vincent," Kitty quietly said. "Please, let me say good-bye."

The crowd remained frozen, none speaking, as if they'd been paused on a big plasma screen.

Steven guided Kitty to the blue coffin, where she placed both her palms on the lid. She bent her head and simply said, "Vincent, you bastard. God help me, I loved you. God help me, I still do."

Then she shook off Steven's hand and ambled away from the people who had once been her friends before she'd lost Vincent and everything changed.

🌿 Eight

The post-funeral luncheon was served at Alio's because the house Vincent had bought for Yolanda hadn't been decorated yet. They had, after all, been married only five or six months.

Dana would have bet that most of those in attendance would have preferred to go home. But Yolanda had somehow composed herself and Kitty was nowhere in sight, and apparently the mourners had decided to continue this charade to the end.

At Yolanda's direction, Premiere Parties had arranged an eight-course degustation of Vincent's favorite dishes: antipasti, osso buco, pasta vongole, and other items Dana did not recognize and would not eat, certainly not at noon and definitely not while surrounded by the sickish scent of lilies that

Yolanda insisted be hauled from the grave and distributed around the banquet room.

As soon as Dana had seen Kitty's compelling display of sorrow at Vincent's casket, she knew she must talk to Lauren. It was too hard to believe that Kitty had pulled the trigger.

Between the fourth and fifth courses, Dana leaned across Steven and caught Lauren's eye and asked if she needed to use the ladies' room.

The men half stood as the women got up because they knew their wives peed with each other. They'd long ago given up stupid jokes about that.

Not surprisingly, the ladies' room was decorated in black, red, and gold. Dana knew Kitty would have been horrified, that she would have held the event at a place with a less boisterous color palette.

Then she remembered that Yolanda was not Kitty and this wasn't a party.

"Well, this has been positively awful," Lauren said once they were inside. "Who ever expected Kitty would show up?" She seemed more demure than usual.

"Vincent was her husband almost thirty years," Dana said. "He was Marvin and Elise's father."

Lauren offered no response.

Dana went to the vanity and set down her purse. She straightened her hair, which had been confined under her small hat. She adjusted the collar of her deep pewter weskit. It was easier to straighten and adjust, after all, than to address what needed addressing.

"Lauren," she said, eyes transfixed by the mirror. "I need to know about you and Vincent."

Lauren took a step back the way everyone had at the grave when they thought Kitty would shoot them all, too. Dana thought if she were closer she might see Lauren grow pale; she might witness the pinkness drain from Lauren's forehead the way the blood in an IV bottle empties during a transfusion.

She's going to deny it, Dana surmised.

But Lauren regained her footing and tightened the ribbon that held back her hair. "Oh, Dana," she said with a bewildered smile. "His dick was the size of an Italian flagpole."

❦ Nine

Bridget drove Caroline home because Jack had convinced Randall to go to the club and play golf.

"No sense wasting a beautiful day," Jack said when the funeral drudge was finally completed. "You girls go have a good time."

The men went in Jack's car because the Meachams had more money than the Hayneses.

When Bridget directed Caroline to Randall's silver Mercedes, she knew they would not have a "good time" because Caroline never laughed when she was in the passenger seat.

"I'll just go home," Caroline said once they were belted into the soft leather.

Bridget pulled out of the lot, then drove a few blocks,

past the Episcopal church and the Protestant church and the Catholic church Randall supported. "It was a nice turnout," Bridget said, because it would have been absurd to say the funeral itself had been nice.

Caroline's twice-lifted face was turned toward the churches and not toward Bridget. "I must change the seating for the hospital gala. Vincent and Yolanda were supposed to sit with us."

Us, of course, meant Caroline and Jack, Bridget and Randall, Lauren and Bob, Dana and Steven. The funeral now over, Caroline had clearly moved on.

"Can't we be eight at the table, not ten?" Bridget asked.

"Heavens, no. A successful fund-raiser should never appear to have more comforts than the paying guests."

It was amusing how Caroline danced the dance.

"Well, who then?"

"Chloe and Lee. Do you think the others would mind?"

Though Bridget often made fun of the New Falls hierarchy, it didn't seem right to have Caroline's daughter and her fiancé sit where Vincent and Yolanda should have been.

"Lauren's stepchildren might feel slighted."

"Well, there are seven of them and only two chairs." She snapped her head toward Bridget. "What else can I do? Cover Vincent's chair in black velvet? Besides, Lee is perfectly suitable."

It went without saying that Chloe's betrothed had more money than the rest of them put together. Bridget sighed. "Forget the gala," she said. "I'm worried about Kitty."

Caroline moved her eyes back to the tree belt. "Kitty will be fine."

"Fine? *Mon dieu*. Did you see her today?"

Caroline said nothing. Several minutes passed, as did two SUVs and a Subaru station wagon.

"Well," Bridget said finally, "I intend to be supportive. I plan to go with Dana and Kitty to see the lawyer on Monday." She'd told Dana that, when they'd been at the funeral, right after Kitty made her dramatic appearance. If Bridget couldn't be in France, she might as well be in Tarrytown.

"Do as you wish," Caroline remarked, tiny icicles forming at the corners of her newly done mouth. Then, as the car turned up the long Meacham driveway, she added, "And I will seat Chloe with us."

A few weeks ago, Bridget had planned—a declaration from Luc that he still, indeed, loved her and would leave his wife and remarry Bridget notwithstanding—to return from France in time to go to the gala. Randall would not want to miss it. Who would? They'd go with their checkbooks and buy their visibility in the form of black and white snapshots for the local newspapers and, if they were lucky, for the Sunday style section of the *Times*.

Randall and Bridget Haynes shown here with Steven and Dana Fulton.

Bob and Lauren Halliday share a cocktail with Jack Meacham and his wife, event chairperson Caroline Meacham.

The images would be clipped and pasted into thick scrapbooks that would serve as a standard for the next generation of *dégout* snobs.

It was, indeed, pathetic.

"It's only a damn gala, Caroline," Bridget said abruptly as she stopped the car at the front entry. "It's hardly as important as Kitty—who once was your friend, and who now has to fight for her life."

Caroline waited a moment, as if expecting a driver to open her door. "Bridget," she said, "you're right about one thing. I used to be one of Kitty's friends. Just as I am one of yours. But be careful, my dear. This is too small a town to take the wrong side." If her voice hadn't cracked in the middle of the last sentence, Bridget might have suggested that Caroline go to hell.

Instead she simply watched Caroline exit the car, clearly not having had the good time her husband had instructed.

Thank God that was over.

Caroline swept into her foyer and called out to Jennie, who hadn't been waiting at the entrance. One would think that after working five years for Caroline, the young woman would know better.

She moved into the music room as Jennie materialized in a simple black dress with a white, starched collar, and black, on-your-feet shoes. At the end of the month, her attire would change to warm-weather light gray. Caroline always felt that if one bothered employing servants, they might as well look the part.

"Be a dear and bring my new trinkets," Caroline instructed, floating to the settee and sliding out of her shoes. What with the murder and the funeral and the chaos it all wrought, she hadn't had time to open her rite-of-spring luncheon gifts. "Oh, and Jennie," she called out, "please remove the cemetery dirt from my navy Ballys." Caroline rarely referred to her shoes as pumps or stilettos or slip-ons. Instead she called them by name, as if they were pets or children. Bally, Jimmy, Lulu.

Chloe, of course, did the same, because everything Chloe did mirrored her mother.

Caroline plucked at the gold choker that haloed her neck. For all the things she'd done wrong, for all the pain it had cost to shield the things that needed shielding, she had, at least, raised Chloe right.

Now twenty-four, Chloe was engaged to Lee Sato, an Asian man, which was where everyone knew today's money was: technology, minerals, most of America's manufacturing. What was wrong with outsourcing a love life, too?

When he had proposed, Chloe whined ("Mummy, he says I'll have to live in Kyoto for a year or two"), at which time Caroline gently explained that a good marriage often meant compromise, that even she—even Caroline Davis Meacham—had begun her married life in Connecticut, hadn't she?

Then Caroline told Chloe she'd be able to use the sacrifices as leverage in later years when she wanted a country house, a year in Europe, or separate bedrooms.

Life, after all, was just a game, and winning was everything. Sometimes the prizes came as trinkets, like the ones that Jennie now rolled in on the dessert cart. Caroline smiled because the cart was so apt.

"Sit down and help me open my goodies."

Jennie sat and oohed and aahed while Caroline undid the bows, pulled off the lids, and extracted one bauble after another: a small Steuben piece from Katherine Ramsey, whose husband was chairman of Ramsey and Potter; an Orrefors nut dish from

Vera Stanley, married to Richard Stanley of the Newport Stanleys; a Correia perfume bottle from Meredith Gibson, wife of Jonathan Gibson, president of Freedom Securities. The most fun, of course, were turquoise boxes from Tiffany's because something fabulous was guaranteed to be inside.

Not that Caroline threw parties for the trinkets.

But like chairing the committees for the hospital gala in spring, the library fund-raiser in autumn, and the holiday museum ball, it was more fun to keep the façade alive than to look in the mirror each morning and glimpse who she was when the spotlight was off.

"Oh, look," Jennie said, "this one's from the new Mrs. DeLano."

It was a ceramic wall plaque shaped like a duck. *Friends make life ducky* was painted on its wing.

Caroline looked at Jennie.

"Well," Jennie said, because even Jennie had more sense than Yolanda, "it's the thought that counts. And besides," she added, "while she was at your party, her husband was being murdered." As if that had anything to do with any of this.

Caroline sighed. She did not want to think about Vincent. It had been too painful to stand at his funeral and stare at the ground and not at the mourners for fear she'd lock eyes with the only true love that she'd ever known.

The only real love.

The only honest lover.

The only person for whom Caroline Meacham had almost given up everything.

She did not want to think about it because it made the ache worse.

Without a word she set the duck back in its box and handed it to Jennie. Then she stood up. "I can't do this right now," she said, tossing aside the papers and the ribbons. "I must rework the seating charts for the gala."

She left the music room, her trinkets forgotten, her mask safely back in its place.

It wasn't until Bridget had stopped at Dean & DeLuca's to pick up dinner (her cook Lorraine worked only Monday through Thursday) and wheeled into the garage at her own mini mansion, that she was struck by a bolt of inspiration.

"My God," she shouted in English, not French, because no one was around. "Why didn't I think of that before?"

Snapping off the ignition, she started to laugh, because if it hadn't been for Caroline, Bridget might never have figured out the answer to all—well, some of—her problems.

At times like this Dana wished she had never quit smoking.

As Grand Central Parkway merged into I–278, she barely watched the road while she ransacked the glove box. Finally she located a stick of old gum. Unwrapping it quickly, she shoved it into her mouth.

Chomp, chomp.

She had her cell phone but not her headset, and in the great State of New York one wasn't allowed to drive while holding the phone. If she'd been in her own car, she could have called Bridget and shocked her with Lauren's confession.

But she wasn't in her own car because she'd driven Steven to LaGuardia after the funeral and the luncheon because he was headed for Cleveland, on the road again.

Of all her friends, Dana figured she was the one with the most time and opportunity to have an affair.

But Lauren?

God, she'd helped raise—was still raising—Bob's kids; well, a good part of them. Forget the moral and emotional parts, how had she handled the logistics?

"It was like magic," she explained to Dana. "You know how that goes."

No, Dana didn't know how that went.

Then, as if someone had pulled the plug from Lauren's mouth, she spewed forth too much information.

He touched me in places no man ever touched me!

He entered me from the front and the back and once upside down!

He loved to bury his face between my legs. Imagine! He did that for me!

Dana refrained from commenting that now Vincent was buried again, this time in another damp, unfamiliar location.

She hadn't listened to the blah-blah of the remainder of Lauren's verbal marathon. Instead she closed off her ears and studied her friend, the way her lips curved and curled, the way her slate-colored eyes twinkled like glitter, the way her body lilted and swayed as if she were reenacting one sexual foray after another.

She probably thought it was safe to disclose her secret now that Vincent was dead and it would be her word against no one's.

But when she said he really had been an Italian Stallion, Lauren's eyes glazed over and her body stopped lilting and she started to sob. "It's not fair," she cried. "He shouldn't have left me for her."

Mistress or not, the woman was scorned.

"I'm sorry," Dana said, after an awkward minute of solace. "But I must get Steven to the airport." She kissed Lauren's cheek and departed the ladies' room, feeling guilty that she was grateful to escape from a friend in distress.

She didn't tell Steven about Lauren's confession.

And now, driving up the highway, she thought about Vincent and his flagpole of a dick. And about the fact that he'd left Kitty for Yolanda, though he hadn't left Kitty for Lauren. And that Lauren—despite her timid, saccharine veneer—was mightily pissed.

Dana rolled the gum around in her mouth and decided that, on her way home, she must stop at the New Falls police station. If they knew another woman had once slept with Vincent, they might not be so quick to judge Kitty.

Besides, Dana reasoned as she exited onto Route 87 North, they couldn't force her to tell them Lauren's name.

❧ Ten

Bridget started in Randall's dressing room.

She yanked open one built-in cherry drawer, then another:

socks,

socks,

socks,

briefs,

briefs,

briefs.

How much of this *merde* did he have, anyway? How much did she? Did either of them really need several dozen sets of silk undergarments?

Consumption, she thought. So American. Like the society pages that triggered this frenzy. It had been the thought of those pictures—lousy, grainy photos—that made Bridget think about passports.

Were there any worse pictures than those pasted on passports?

Then another thought sparked: Her husband would soon need his passport when he—not she—went to pick up Aimée.

She spun from the drawers to the solid teak,
hand-carved,
velvet lined,
twelve-drawer
jewelry chest.

Did men who lived outside New Falls have such opulent places to harbor their treasures?

Certainly not Luc.

She poked. She pried. She rummaged around.

A tie pin from St. Andrew's in Scotland.

Silver cuff links from Tiffany's that she'd given Randall on their tenth anniversary, bought with his money, which was also an American way.

A small gold bracelet he'd worn in the eighties when men were trying out that sort of thing.

But where was the ruby pinkie ring she'd given him when he'd agreed to let Aimée go to school in France?

And where was his grandfather's Patek Philippe watch?

And where, *mon dieu*, was his passport?

The safe! her brain or *mon dieu* suddenly exclaimed.

Without wasting a second, she raced downstairs to Randall's den. She flew to the Rubens in the gilt frame on the wall (Rubens was one of Randall's favorites, a fantasy he lived out through Bridget's full breasts). She pulled back the right side, spun the dial right, left, right, then tugged at the handle.

And there it was: the navy blue, pocket-size folder with the word "PASSPORT" hot-stamped in gold on the cover.

With a wide, happy smile, Bridget extracted the document. Then she closed the safe slowly, replaced the painting, and realized she needed to restore Randall's dressing room to its neat, anal order before he returned from the club.

In the meantime she'd find a perfect spot to hide his passport. What a pity he wouldn't be able to leave the country without it. And she would have to get Aimée after all.

Dana had been in the New Falls police station once when Michael was twelve and had stolen pumpkins from Mr. White's garden and pitched them into the Hudson to see if they'd float, which, according to Michael, they did.

It didn't look like the old brick police station where she'd gone the night her father had been arrested.

In New Falls the station was built out of limestone and had peculiar sharp angles that mimicked the library and the town hall.

"I'd like to speak with the investigator in charge of the Vincent DeLano case," she said to the officer who sat at the welcoming desk.

The cop eyed her like a glazed cruller.

"About what?" he asked.

She realized she was still wearing her funeral clothes that exposed her as a New Falls wife—one of *those*. "About who might have killed him."

Her point had been made; he picked up the phone and called an extension. She was quickly escorted to Detective Glen Johnson's office, a square glass cubicle with a desk and no windows.

"We have the killer," Johnson said, standing up. He was a tall man, angular like the building. He leaned against his desk and folded his arms. "A neighbor called and reported hearing a gunshot. When we arrived, the killer was standing there, holding the gun."

"Please," Dana said. "The woman you've arrested is my friend. And I don't know if she killed Vincent or not, but I do know someone else might have had a motive."

He studied her face.

She shifted on one foot.

"Vincent DeLano was a ladies' man," she said, wondering if that were an outdated term. "Before he married Yolanda, while he was still married to Kitty, I know that he had at least one affair."

"With . . . ?"

"Well, I can't tell you that."

"But you know this because . . . ?"

"Because I was told."

"By a reliable source?"

"Yes."

He unfolded his arms, tented his fingers. "That woman wouldn't have been you, I suppose?"

"Me?" Good grief, she hadn't thought he'd accuse her. "Look, Officer, I'm trying to help. Kitty is my friend and I didn't sleep with her husband, but someone else did. Which means that at least one other person might have wanted to kill him."

He nodded and said, "By the way, where you were at eleven-thirty that morning?"

"Eleven-thirty? Why?"

He raised an eyebrow. She got the message.

"Eleven-thirty," she repeated. "Well, I was having my manicure for Caroline's luncheon. Caroline Meacham."

"We know about Ms. Meacham and her spring party. We might not be Manhattan's Twenty-seventh Precinct, but we know what we're doing."

Apparently Detective Johnson was a *Law & Order* fan, too.

She sat down on a nearby metal chair. "Why do you care what I was doing in the morning?"

He circled his desk and pointed to his computer screen. "We have new information. The medical examiner has set the time of death earlier than we first thought."

"You're kidding!"

The eyebrow lifted again.

"So Kitty didn't do it!"

"I didn't say that. But further examination showed that rigor mortis had begun to set in, so it had been a few hours. We're thinking eleven-thirty."

"Could it have been suicide?"

"No. The trajectory of the bullet was all wrong for that."

"So anyone could have shot him."

"Any of many."

"Like people you'd already ruled out."

"Bingo."

"Like all of the women at Caroline's party?"

He sat down and lodged his eyes on her. "Not all of them, maybe. But one, anyway."

* * *

"Help," Dana said when Bridget answered her door a few minutes later. "Is it possible Lauren killed Vincent?" She'd been heading home when, halfway there, she took a left not a right, because she knew this was something she could not figure out for herself.

"Why on earth would she?" Bridget asked as she let Dana into the house. "Did he beat Bob at golf?" She poured wine without asking.

Dana collapsed on the couch, then told Bridget about the Helmsley and the flagpole and the rest of the stuff.

Bridget made no comment.

"Aren't you shocked?" Dana asked.

"Actually," Bridget replied, "yes. I am."

They toasted each other and took a quick drink. Then Dana said, "I feel like our world is falling apart."

"It might not be a bad thing. Maybe we were getting—how you say—too big for our pantaloons."

It would have been nicer if Bridget weren't right.

"It's hard enough to think that Kitty was capable of killing Vincent. But Lauren?" Dana asked.

"Maybe she was afraid he would tell Bob about the affair."

"I wonder if Bob would leave her."

"Doubtful. He's an old man. And she raised all those kids."

"Like they were her own."

"But they aren't."

"Neither was Vincent."

They thought. They drank. They sat, thinking some more, black hair and silver, big boobs and little, Franco-American.

"Kitty is our friend," Dana said. "But Lauren is, too."

"We should warn her."

"I'll drive."

They set down their wineglasses and Dana found her keys and they opened the front door to leave. Unfortunately, on the other side of the door, stood Detective Glen Johnson and three other officers.

He asked where Bridget had been at eleven-thirty the day Vincent was murdered and if she'd had an affair with the man.

Bridget said she'd had a massage from eleven until noon and then stopped by her stylist's for a blow-dry. She pronounced "massage" as if she were in France, and "blow-dry" like a proposition.

Dana figured she'd done that on purpose just to anger the cops who had no doubt followed Dana to Bridget's. The Sherlocks of New Falls must have deduced that Dana would run to the woman whose name she hadn't disclosed.

She must remember to call Lauren, not pay her a visit.

Bridget then told the police if she were to have an affair, it wouldn't be with a man from New Falls. "Gossip, darling," she said, sounding more like Zsa Zsa Gabor than Marie Antoinette. "It can *keel* one in a town such as this."

No one suggested that gossip—or the fear of it—might have been what had *keeled* Vincent.

They asked the names of Bridget's masseur and hairstylist.

Bridget cooperated, then invited them to come back if there was anything else they needed. The men stared at her boobs, then reluctantly left.

The door barely closed, Bridget flew to her cell phone and began punching numbers.

"Thomas," she said breathlessly. "It's me, Bridget. Pick up. Please. *Peeeeeck up the damn phone.*"

Dana watched as Bridget drained what was left in her glass and in Dana's, too.

"Oy vey," Bridget said then, having morphed into Golda Meir. "Pick up, pick up, pick up."

When Thomas did not, Bridget said, "Listen, this is important. The police *weel* ask you about me. Tell them I was at your place the morning Vincent DeLano was *keeled*, that I was there from eleven to twelve. If you don't, I *weel* have your balls for my dinner."

She hung up, stared at Dana, and said, "That little bastard better remember I gave him five hundred for Christmas."

"Bridget," Dana said, "what are you doing? Did you lie to the police?"

"*Mais oui*," she said. "What else could I do? Tell them I was at my doctor's? That I was arranging for my chemotherapy?"

Dana reached for her wineglass, realized it was empty. "Make some sense, please."

With a casual shrug, Bridget said, "Chemotherapy. For my cancer. Didn't I tell you about that?"

Half a bottle of wine later Bridget had decanted the details and dumped the sediment in Dana's lap: She had cervical cancer. She'd had surgery. She'd had radiation. And now they wanted to inject her with poison, *mon dieu, quel ennui*—what a nuisance—that will be.

Dana was as stunned as when she'd learned Vincent had been murdered and Kitty had been arrested and Lauren had slept with him, too. "Bridget," she said, "how can I help? Why didn't you tell me?"

Then Bridget explained that she'd told no one, not even Randall, not Aimée.

"They should know," Dana said.

Bridget threw her a mind-your-own-beeswax kind of look.

"Bridget," Dana protested, then Bridget held up her hand.

"Stop harassing me," Bridget said. "Stop before I call the police."

It wasn't very funny, but Dana laughed anyway, then asked, "What are you going to do?"

"First, I am making you promise to keep my secret."

Dana supposed if she promised, she could ask for more wine, so she did both. It was, after all, not an appropriate time to comment that her mother had died of cancer, not cervical, but ovarian, "in that woman's place," her father had told her when Dana was eighteen and she was living on Long Island and hadn't been told until her mother was dead.

She supposed she hadn't forgiven him for that, either.

Bridget poured and Dana drank.

"I'll have chemo soon. When Aimée has gone back to school after her holiday."

"But that's two weeks from now."

She shrugged again. "I don't think it will kill me."

It was a poor choice of a word, whether accented by English or French.

"Besides," Bridget added, "I don't want to miss Caroline's *partie magnifique*."

Partie magnifique. Well, that was one way of describing the hospital gala. "I think the whole thing will be awkward," Dana said. She set down her glass because she was drunk.

Bridget sipped again, then said, "But everyone will be there. Maybe even the person who really killed Vincent."

"Don't change the subject. I want to talk about your cancer."

"And I, *s'il vous plait*, do not."

Eleven

Dana should have called the Hudson Valley Red Cab to drive her home, but her house was only a few blocks away, and it was still daylight, and she wasn't *totally wasted* as her boys called it. She'd wait, however, until she was safely home before calling Lauren.

"The police want to question everyone," she would warn her. "They know Vincent had an affair, but they have no way of knowing with whom."

It seemed plausible, she thought as she turned into her driveway, lost control of her car, and promptly drove up on the lawn and through the euonymus that Mario had planted last week.

She decided her driving skills hadn't been impaired by the

wine but by the fact the twins' Jeep Wrangler was parked in the driveway and Steven would be angry if one of them had dropped out of college.

The mudroom was a landfill of big-footed sneakers and laundry bags. She traversed it and went into the kitchen, where Sam stood, head in the refrigerator.

"Hello," Dana said, and when there was no answer she knew she must be competing with his iPod. "*Samuel!*" she shouted this time, and the kid jumped, banged his head on the deli bin, and spun around. There was no trace of headphones.

"Jesus, Mom, you scared the shit out of me."

When her boys came home it always took a few days for Dana to clean up the frat house lexicon. She smiled. "That would be 'Gosh, Mom, you scared the wits out of me.'"

He laughed.

He stepped toward her, she toward him. He lifted her into a six-foot-one hug. "Hi, Mommy," he said.

She laughed that time, then wriggled from his arms and touched the top of his head. "Does it hurt?"

He waved his hand in front of his face. "Whoa. Not as much as your breath. *Gosh*, Mom, how much did you drink?"

"Probably not enough. But I'll make tea while you tell me what you're doing here and where your brother is." She filled the tea kettle.

"Ah, well, I can start by saying my twin brother—Benjamin is his name—is upstairs in his room probably crashing from our four-and-a-half-hour trip home. I can then continue to express that the reason we're here might have something to do with the fact it's spring break."

"Oh," she said. "Well, I *knew* that. I just lost track of the time. There's so much going on."

He rolled his eyes as if to say, *Sure, Mom.* Sam was a straight-arrow-looking boy, the younger of the twins, who took after his father the way that Ben took after her, as if one twin had received all Steven's DNA, the other one got all of hers. Michael, the lone birth, the first, resembled them both, the egg correctly having conjoined the sperm. "Aren't you boys going to Cozumel or somewhere?"

"Ben's leaving tomorrow." He shuffled back to the refrigerator, grabbed a Coke, popped the top. "I'm staying here. I want to help you solve Mr. DeLano's murder."

"What?" Dana asked, her head sliding into hangover mode.

"I want to study the law, jurisprudence, remember?"

"And you'll be home for how long? Ten days? You think you can solve it in ten days?"

"Maybe we can if we try." It was so like him to want to help.

"What makes you think I don't have better things to do?"

"You were a journalist."

Dana laughed. "That was a long time ago, honey. Now I'm a housewife. I'm a mother." She'd always believed that her penchant for putting together pieces of a story rivaled her father's powers of deduction when he'd been a cop. Her sons didn't know about him, though: All they knew was he'd left and her mother had died.

Sam wrinkled his nose.

"Besides," she continued, "the hospital gala is a week from tomorrow. I thought I'd help Caroline with her last-minute plans." It wasn't exactly the truth, but even the gala would be preferable to having one of her kids get too close to this mess. "And you should be with your friends. Doing college-age things."

"I think murder is more exciting, don't you?"

The whistle blew. She steeped her tea.

"Not to mention I can use this for a sociology paper."

Dana had always helped the kids with their homework. It had been more fun than tennis or golf. But there was the nonsense with Lauren . . . how much would she want Sam to know? Then she thought about Ben. "What about your brother? Will he go without you?"

"A whole bunch of kids from school will be there, Mom. Besides. He's a big boy now. He can take care of himself. Me, too. Please, Mom?"

"Oh, honey," she said. "I don't know." What she did know was that Ben was the party boy and Sam, the stay-at-homer, the quiet, shy one, who never cost her any sleep. "Well," she said, "Maybe . . ."

He took that as a yes and pulled out a stool from the breakfast bar. "So, did she do it?"

Dana sighed. "Kitty? No. She says not."

"Who else then?"

She could have told him about Lauren but she really was too tired to get into that now. It was bad enough she hadn't called Lauren yet and the police might have showed up at her door. "There's a chance Vincent had at least one mistress," she said.

"A mistress? Cool."

"Not to his wife."

"What about her? The new wife? Has anyone checked her out?"

Dana held the tea mug to her lips and stared at her son as if he'd just asked if she'd walked on the moon. "Yolanda?"

"Well," he said, "she's probably the one who gets the life insurance, or at least a bunch of money from his estate. Like everyone in New Falls, Vincent's probably loaded, so it makes sense, doesn't it?"

"Detective Johnson from the New Falls Police Department. Are you Lauren Halliday?"

Luckily Lauren had seen the cruiser pull into the driveway. She'd ducked behind the six-panel, early nineteenth-century Chinese screen with the soapstone inlaid artwork of cranes and pine trees and other images that symbolized long life in the Asian culture. Her husband had shipped it home from Canton as part of his efforts to deny his oncoming mortality.

"Mrs. Halliday is not available." Florence had been around since before Bob's first wife died. When it came to protecting the family, she was tougher than a pair of big-toothed sentry dogs.

"We'll wait," the detective said.

Silence followed. She pictured Florence, hands on square hips, eyes narrowed and glaring.

More silence.

Could they hear Lauren breathing?

Perspiration rose on her forehead. She remembered the time when she'd been a kid, trapped in the closet of her aunt's bedroom at the house on Nantucket. She'd been hunting for her sandals; she'd thought her cousin Gracie had borrowed them. (*Stolen* was more like it.) But when she'd heard voices Lauren had closed the door. How was she supposed to know Uncle Raymond and Aunt Clara would choose that very moment in the *middle of the day* to have sex on the four-poster bed? Or that Uncle Raymond really did have sex on the brain the way she'd overheard Aunt Jane say to her mother?

"Maybe she'd rather come to the station," the detective said now, and Lauren blinked back to the present and the Chinese screen and the bleak situation at hand.

She would not go to the station because that was where Kitty had gone and look where that had gotten her.

"Gentlemen," she said, propelling herself from behind the screen, the courage to do so greater than the fear of ending up in a cell. "You must excuse my housekeeper. We've had some problems with men snooping because of my husband's business. He deals with investors who are out of the country." She knew it made no sense, but it was the best she could do. "Florence was merely doing her job."

"If you have problems," the detective said, "you should call the police."

She smiled, but did not say she'd call. "How may I help you?" she asked, her Boston–Palm Beach–Nantucket upbringing usurping her terrified self.

"We'd like to know where you were at eleven-thirty in the morning the day Vincent DeLano was murdered."

She tipped her head to one side as if she'd heard incorrectly.

Eleven-thirty.

Vincent.

Murdered.

The tiny squirt glands in the back of her throat suddenly spurted and she knew the next thing that would happen was that she would throw up.

"She was here," Florence said. "Having a bath."

Lauren turned to Florence. "Was I?" she asked, because she didn't want to remember that day and because of course Florence would lie; she already had.

"Were you?" the detective asked.

"She was," Florence added. "You were getting ready for Mrs. Meacham's luncheon. I remember because I was laying out your ensemble. You wore your Mikimotos."

Lauren's hand went to her throat. "Yes," she said. "I believe that's correct."

The phone rang. The little group paused. Eyes ping-ponged around.

"It's okay, Florence," Lauren said. "Answer the phone."

The woman hesitated, then left the foyer with several looks over her shoulder.

"Is there anything else?" Lauren asked as if fully cooperating.

"Just one thing," the detective said. "How well did you know Mr. DeLano?"

Lauren's private school posture faltered only a second. Then Florence called out, "Mrs. Halliday!" and waddled back to the foyer carrying the cordless. "It's for you. I believe it's Shanghai."

It wasn't Shanghai; it was Dana.

"This is the first chance I've had to warn you," Dana said in a rush. "The police might show up. Don't tell them anything."

"Yes," Lauren said, "that's wonderful news. Thank you so much for calling." She clicked off the phone and asked the detective if they were finished. He repeated the question about Vincent, and Lauren simply said, "Well, he was Kitty's husband, if that's what you mean."

❧ Twelve

Dana decided Sam had a point—had anyone thought of Yolanda? Greed could be as much of a motive as a woman being scorned, couldn't it?

The questions had kept her awake most of the night—that and the fact that Bridget had cancer.

All things considered, Dana would rather not be reminded about her mother.

In the morning she took one more trip to LaGuardia, this time with Ben, who was overloaded with sunscreen and jibes for his brother who would "rather hang out with old people."

Sam told him to shut up and Ben told him to make him and Dana tuned them out, an art she'd perfected.

Sam had wanted to go with her to see Kitty, but Dana had

said no, she didn't think Kitty would be comfortable with that.

He'd argued that Kitty had two kids of her own, even though he thought both of them were kind of fucked up.

Dana had thrown him a look.

"*Screwed* up," he said, amending his words. "Marvin and Elise. Marvin's the biggest nerd on the planet; Elise is so hot she's got her own calendar. Boob shots and everything."

Dana didn't need a translator to know what "everything" meant. "Do you have one?" she asked because of the small smile that turned up Sam's mouth.

"One what?"

"One of her calendars?"

He hesitated long enough for a blush. "A couple of guys have them at school."

So it was hot Elise, not a sociology paper, that was the real motivation behind Sam's interest in the case: If he helped out the mother, he might wind up with the daughter.

How could Dana say no to her little boy who always had stood in the shadow of his more outgoing, get-all-the-girls brothers? How could she tell him that Elise, hot or not, would probably not be around?

She decided not to burst his testosterone bubble, so they now trekked to Tarrytown to the two-bedroom apartment without having called first because Sam said it would be best not to tip Kitty off that they were coming.

Dana didn't know whether he was right, but she'd always been proud that her sons were smarter than she was.

Kitty was home.

"Come in," she said, then quickly closed the door from the daylight that had leaked in with them.

"Kitty," Dana said, "you remember my son Sam? One of my twins?"

Sam said, "Hello, Mrs. DeLano," and Kitty blanched and told him to please call her Kitty.

Dana explained that Sam wanted to be a lawyer and would like to help out if he could.

Kitty said she didn't care, which, by the looks of her place and herself, pretty much now covered everything in her life.

"Have a seat," she said.

They cleared magazines off the couch and sat down. Sam's knee landed too close to Kitty's; he squirmed.

"Kitty," Dana said, "there's been some good news."

"Yolanda's dead, too?"

"Not that I know of. But according to the medical examiner's report, the time of death was long before you were found at the scene." It was hard to understand how Kitty could be wearing a bathrobe that was so old and threadbare. Dana averted her eyes.

"How early?"

She told her.

"Well," Kitty said, "doesn't that beat all."

"Do you have an alibi for eleven-thirty?" Sam piped up.

Dana cringed.

Kitty laughed. "My only plan for the day was to meet Vincent at the house with the rug dealer. Other than that, I was home. Alone. That's a good alibi, isn't it?"

Dana cleared her throat. "Well, the time difference means the police will investigate others. For instance, everyone at Caroline's party who might have had . . ." She stammered there, and wished that she hadn't. "Who might have known Vincent."

"Yolanda included," Sam said. "She should be a prime suspect."

"Yolanda," Kitty said again, as if it were a name she could never get used to.

"She could have done it for the money," Sam said.

"What money?"

"His investment portfolio. Life insurance. The value of their house."

Kitty laughed. "According to my divorce lawyer, Vincent didn't have any money."

She could have said the sky was green or the lawn was blue or her shabby apartment was going to be featured in *Architectural Digest* and it would have been more believable.

"But he bought her a house . . ."

"That wasn't decorated yet."

"And they planned to go to the gala. He'd bring a check . . ."

Kitty shrugged. "It hadn't happened yet."

"So?" Dana asked. "Is that proof he was broke?"

"No, but it explains why I'm living like this," Kitty continued, sweeping her arm around someone's idea of a home. "It is proof that my lawyer couldn't find Vincent's stash."

"But do you believe it?" Sam asked.

Kitty sighed. "Vincent lost a few clients. But he knew how to make money. Besides. Look how Yolanda dresses. And pink diamonds? Pretty pricey, even for Vincent."

The dim light settled in, cloaking the tale with a more dismal shroud.

"So it's probably true," Sam said. "Yolanda could have killed him for the money." Then he hemmed and hawed, the same way Steven did when he was thinking. "Yolanda might know where Vincent hid his fortune. She could have known he was going to meet you. She could have shot him. She could have set you up, Mrs. DeLano."

"Yes," Kitty said, "I've wondered about that."

Dana closed her eyes.

Once, she had hoped they'd accept her as Mrs. Vincent DeLano. They'd liked her, hadn't they? Back when she'd scissored their hair and got rid of their gray and listened to their troubles, which, compared with hers, were a teeny piss hole in the snow?

She'd been good enough for that, but not for the rest.

Yolanda wiped a tear with her left hand as her right hand kept busy with a small can of spray paint.

She sniffed as she worked. She missed him, her Vincent. It hadn't been her fault that he'd loved her more than he'd loved his wife, Kitty.

Kitty had been mean to him, or so he'd said. She'd hated sex: She said it was dirty. She hated that their son and their daughter were so successful, while she had no job or career because she'd gone to college only with the intent to find a rich guy, which she'd done.

Ha! Yolanda thought as she swirled a daisylike flower around the letters she had written. *College won't help Kitty now.* Yolanda, of course, never had gone. She'd been raised in the Bronx, on the wrong side of most things, and had been lucky, real lucky, that her brother joined the army and sent money home for her to enroll in beauty school, the Big Apple School of *Esthetology*.

Her mother had gasped when she'd heard that word. "Well,

aren't you something?" she said when Yolanda got her letter of acceptance, which pretty much only meant the school had received her tuition deposit.

They never dreamed that ten years later, Yolanda would do a wash and set on a woman who lived in New Falls and was in the city for somebody's funeral. It turned out that the woman (who'd been cursed with coarse hair) was so impressed with Yolanda's work that she found her a job in the classy-ass town.

So, like the famous TV family George and Louise Jefferson, Yolanda Valdes moved on up.

The wives of New Falls didn't know if she was black or white or Hispanic. Vincent once told her if they knew her real history—that her father had come from Cuba on a raft—an honest-to-God, freaking *raft*—they would take pity and stop giving her crap with their tips. He said they would love her like he did.

But she'd been too embarrassed to tell them.

Then Yolanda got pregnant.

She figured he'd offer to pay for an abortion though she wouldn't have one. She was thirty by then, and most men around there didn't want a woman whose skin was darker than theirs and whose family had lived in a ghetto.

Besides, Yolanda had always wanted a baby.

The best she hoped for was that Vincent would pay her rent until she could go back to work.

She never, ever imagined he'd leave Kitty and ask her to marry him.

But he went to Vegas, and six weeks later they married, and three weeks after that, Yolanda miscarried.

Vincent said they could try again. He really did love her, she guessed.

She dabbed a big dot in the center of the flower, then wiped another tear because no matter how hard she'd tried the women laughed at her, had wanted to laugh right out loud when Kitty showed up at the funeral and made a fool out of her.

Loosening the wide, sparkly belt on her shocking pink minidress that, as Vincent once said, "leaves nothing to nobody's imagination," Yolanda studied her artwork on the back window of the dark green Jaguar that, like everything else, had once been his but now was hers.

R.I.P. Vincent DeLano, the artwork read. It was tacky and tasteless and would make the women all loco as she drove through their town, taunting them as they'd taunted her, taunting them, as they deserved.

And if that didn't work, she thought, hands on her hips, one foot skating in and out of its high-heeled sandal, she would tell the whole world all the secrets she knew, and watch the wives of New Falls come undone.

🍃 Thirteen

Michael came home for dinner, and though the head count was three, not five, enough of her family had gathered together to make Dana feel whole and alive. She supposed that was part of her recent dis-ease, that her role as the cog in the wheel of her family was not as vital as it once was, which certainly sucked, to borrow a word from her boys.

She plunked a bowl of rice pilaf on the table.

"Wine?" Michael asked, but she shook her head.

Sam held out his glass while Michael poured, and Sam said, "Maybe she didn't know."

"Maybe who didn't know what?" Michael asked.

"Maybe the new Mrs. DeLano didn't know that her husband was broke."

"He was broke?" Michael said as he sat at Dana's left, "his seat" at the table. It didn't matter how many of them were or weren't home, they always sat at the places they'd sat most of their lives, as if changing chairs would give them bad karma.

"We don't know if that's true," Dana said. "It's what Kitty was told during the divorce."

"Then maybe no one shot him after all," Michael said. "Maybe Vincent DeLano killed himself."

"No," Dana said. "The trajectory of the bullet would have been different if it were self-inflicted." The boys looked at her blankly. "The police told me that," she added.

"Well, if it's true he'd been sleeping around," Sam continued, "it could have been somebody's husband."

"Absolutely," Dana agreed. "Except your father. It couldn't have been your father, because I was not involved with Vincent DeLano."

"Thank God for that," Michael said, raising his glass in his left hand and crossing himself with his right.

Dana suppressed a small grin.

"I think we should see Mrs. Meacham," Sam said, lifting the platter of salmon and helping himself to a good-size fillet. "She knows everything and everyone in this town."

"*The* Mrs. Meacham?" Michael asked. "Don't you need an invitation for that? Like having an audience with the queen? Or getting blessed by the pope?"

"Michael," Dana said, "that's enough."

"Well, she's pompous, Mom. I never understood why you and Dad hung around with them. The pompous Meachams. It's not as if his fund is even doing that well."

"He sold it," she said.

"Well, I know that." And of course he did, because Michael had been at Pearce, Daniels three years now and was doing quite well for himself, with a bonus this year of six figures.

"Let's go tomorrow," Sam said.

Dana smiled. "Tomorrow is Sunday." Sunday was family day in New Falls, when most folks stayed close to home, reaping and sowing quality time with their own, unless something more interesting came up. Caroline and Jack would no doubt be with Chloe and Lee, perhaps planning the grand and glorious wedding, scheduled for next year, wedged between Caroline's other high-profile commitments. A visit from Dana and Sam would not be considered more interesting.

"See?" Michael remarked, "I knew you'd need an invitation."

"Well," Sam said, "we'll go Monday then."

"Monday I'm going with Kitty to meet her attorney." She did not tell him the retainer had been paid by Caroline.

"I need to go with you," Sam said. "Well, I'd like to anyway. You might need a male's perspective."

"No," Dana said firmly. "It will be too difficult for Kitty. She will not need an audience."

"But Mom . . ."

"But nothing," she said, hating to daunt his spirits, but knowing this time she was right. "Of course," she added, "there's no reason you can't go to Caroline's without me."

"To the Meachams? Alone?"

"You've known them all your life, Samuel. They don't bite, no matter what your brother says. Besides, you could practice your interviewing techniques on Caroline."

"Yeah," Michael added. "Like, 'Gee, Mrs. Meacham, is

your daughter really as uptight as you are?' And 'Gee, Mrs. Meacham, do you think Vincent DeLano was boffing half of New Falls?'"

Dana shook her head, resigned to the grim fact that she had three raucous boys, not prim little girls.

Sam threw his napkin at his older brother and Michael threw it back at him, then Sam flung a roll and Michael ducked and it grazed the Lalique orchid bowl that stood on the sideboard. They all held their breaths and waited for the crystal tremor to abate without breakage, then they shuddered and laughed and Dana pretended to be upset, but the truth was, all was now right in her slightly dysfunctional world.

Bridget and Randall sat at the dining room table that had been crafted of Zimbabwean teak and expertly carved in Vietnam. It was part of Randall's effort to rise up and be global, to display "Christian forgiveness" that his brother had been killed in the jungle, Tet, 1968, while he'd been protected, a sophomore at Avon Old Farms. Unlike Randall, his father and mother had not leaned toward absolution, but had both died too young of broken hearts that masqueraded as cirrhosis and colon cancer respectively, and had remained angry with Lyndon B. Johnson right up until the end.

"The police changed Vincent's time of death," Bridget said, slicing the pork tenderloin that she'd cooked herself because Randall said she was the best.

"What?"

Her eyes moved from the pork to her husband. "Vincent was shot earlier than they'd thought. So maybe Kitty didn't do it after all."

When Randall was surprised his eyes seemed to narrow and his head seemed to shrink and his toupee looked too big for his skull. He reached for the plate that Bridget passed to him and said, "That's ridiculous. Who else would want to kill Vincent?"

For a bright, *global* man, Randall could be awfully naïve. She handed him a bowl of turnip au gratin. "I cannot imagine," she said. It would be best not to tell him about Lauren and Vincent because when it came to matters of the emotional kind, Randall preferred make-believe to the real world.

They chewed, they ate.

"Dottie made my reservations for Marseilles today," he said, because, after all, the issue of France was there at the table whether Bridget liked it or not.

Dottie was the woman at Randall's Wall Street office in charge of his business appointments and travel arrangements. She worked five days a week and half a day Saturday and should have retired several years ago. But Dottie had no family and few friends because she'd been wed to the firm.

Bridget nodded, helped herself to more Cabernet.

"I'll leave at seven-thirty tomorrow night, get to Paris by nine, Marseilles by noon." His fork clinked on the china.

"Have you packed yet?" she asked. He was one of the few New Falls husbands who never expected Bridget to pack for him. He always took care of his personal needs, like his shaving kit and his socks and, of course, his passport. She swallowed her worry that her scheme wouldn't work.

"I won't need much," he said. "I'll only stay one night."

He would not stay a whole week as Bridget would have. Provence, after all, had been her home, not his. She would have spent the first part of Aimée's holiday right there, ushering her daughter to visit old friends, Madam Buteux from the market, Mademoiselle du Paul whose mother had been best friends with Bridget's, and Monsieur Luc LaBrecque, who sold horses now. She tried not to say his name too often, but, like a lover, Bridget was sometimes compelled to repeat it, to taste its magic on her tongue.

Luc.

She wondered if Lauren had been that way with Vincent.

"Do I have fresh shirts?" Randall asked.

"*Oui*," she replied quietly, "the cleaners delivered them today." Thankfully they had separate closets, so Randall wouldn't know she'd already packed her own suitcase. She wondered when he'd notice that his passport was missing and how she'd stay composed until then.

"Aimée will be surprised," Randall said, "to see me, not you." Then his eyes moved from Bridget toward the entry hall. "On the other hand," he said, his head shrinking again, a grin quickly widening his mouth, "it appears our young lady has beat us to the proverbial punch."

With a perplexed scowl, Bridget's gaze followed her husband's, then alighted on their daughter, or on someone who looked a lot like their daughter, who was now in the dining room instead of Provence.

Aimée?

Everything in Bridget decelerated: her sense of comprehension, the flick of her eyelashes, the beat of her heart. Her jaw went literally, figuratively, anatomically slack.

Aimée?

Randall stood up, went to the girl, and gave her a big hug. "Hey, kiddo," he said, "you came home on your own."

Was it true? Was it she? Was she here and not there?

But no! That was not Bridget's plan!

"Maman's horse friend needed to come to New York."

"Monsieur LaBrecque?" Randall asked before Bridget had a chance to process what Aimée had said, before she could absorb the fact that Luc's name had been spoken by Randall, not her.

"*Oui.* He has a business trip the same time as my holiday," Aimée said. "He offered to save Maman a trip. Escort me back and forth, you know?"

"Hey. Great." The words still came from Randall, because Bridget could not speak.

"His wife came, too. Their daughter goes to my school."

His *wife.* Their *daughter.* Words Bridget detested.

"But your ticket . . ."

"Dottie arranged everything. She said she'd keep it a surprise."

"Ha!" Randall chuckled, draping his arm around Aimée now and turning toward Bridget as if the girl were a showpiece and he, the proud owner. "So Dottie held out on us, eh? I'll bet she never even booked that flight for me."

"No," Aimée said with a smile.

"Well, let's look at you, girl," Randall said. "No worse for wear."

As if any fourteen-year-old, with raven hair and azure eyes and a complexion the color of Mediterranean sand and the texture of cream from a Camargue farm, could look worse for *any* wear.

"You must be starving," Randall continued, taking her suitcase and setting it in the hall, then leading her toward the table. "Pork tenderloin tonight. One of your favorites."

Aimée sat down and looked at her mother. "Maman," she said, "aren't you going to say hello?"

It had probably been less than a minute since Aimée had appeared in the doorway, yet it seemed an eternity, a slow-motion scene, a classic depiction of perfect film noir. Bridget stood up because she knew that she must. "*Ma petite chérie*," she said, moving toward her daughter in a measured, lumbered motion and planting right- then left-cheek kisses. "Forgive me. I was startled, that's all."

The *petite chérie* laughed and Randall said he'd get her a plate and Bridget returned to her seat.

She placed her napkin back in her lap, though she was damned if she remembered removing it in the first place. She took a hefty gulp from her wineglass. "I did not realize Mr. LaBrecque had business in New York." It was amazing to Bridget that her voice sounded so steady, so nonchalant.

"Something to do with the horses," Aimée said.

"Oh, *mais oui*," Bridget replied. "And did they drive you here? Mr. LaBrecque and his wife?"

"No. He got me a limo. I said that would be fine."

"It's too bad they didn't come with you," Randall said, returning with a place setting of everything. "We could have asked them to dinner."

If she hadn't been drinking from her sturdy Waterford Lismore, Bridget's grip might have snapped the stem.

Fourteen

Brunch.

For the eighteen years Lauren had been married to Bob, Sunday meant a gathering of the Halliday clan: seven children plus a few spouses now, and six grandchildren at last count with another due any day, Dory's first. It hurt now to remember that when Dory got married Lauren had been sleeping with Vincent, well not at the exact same time or even on the same day, but Lauren clearly recalled when she'd watched Dory inch down the aisle, her thoughts had been completely on him.

What would it be like to be married to Vincent, to have sex every night, every day, all the time?

The thought still sparked a warm rush all these months later, even now though he was dead. She wondered how long Vincent's memory would linger in her mind and in her vagina, and if even the clamor of Bob's children would ever be loud enough to quell the loss.

"Should Florence prepare more eggs Benedict?" The question came from Dory, who poked her head into the garden room where Lauren stood, daydreaming in silence away from the brood who apparently remained in the dining room awaiting more food.

"No," Lauren said. "There's been enough for one day, don't you think?" She meant, of course, that there had been enough visiting as well as eggs Benedict.

Dory stepped into the room. She sat down on a white wicker chair and rubbed her quite bulbous belly. "Agreed," she said. "At least it's quiet out here." Of all of Bob's kids, Lauren felt closest to Dory. They both were size fours and were blue-eyed blonds and were only eight years apart. Like Lauren, Dory wore her hair tied back in a demure ponytail. On occasion they'd been mistaken for sisters.

"I've never grown used to all the commotion," Lauren said. "It's not that I don't love everyone . . . it's just that, well, you know."

Dory nodded. "There are too damn many of us, that's the problem."

Lauren rebuffed the truth. Like memories of Vincent, some thoughts were best kept to herself. "But tell me, dear. How are you feeling?"

"Like I'm too old to be having a baby."

"Nonsense." Not that Lauren would know. "Besides," she said with her best effort to be cheerful, "it's a little late for that, isn't it?"

Dory looked at her, paused a short moment, then burst into hormonal tears. "I hate my life," she sobbed. "I hate everything about it, especially Jeffrey." That would be Jeffrey, as in her husband.

"Oh," Lauren said, going to her stepdaughter, crouching in front of her, taking her small hands in hers. "Oh dear."

"Yeah, 'oh dear' is right. What am I going to do, Lauren? I don't want this baby . . . I want a divorce!" That's when Dory's water broke, straining through the wicker, dribbling onto the floor.

Lauren screeched and promised Dory that later they'd talk about Jeffrey and what she should do, but that right now Dory needed to breathe in and out.

She wondered if there was a Lamaze technique for ridding her own mind of Vincent.

Dory whimpered.

Lauren stood up, shook off her despair, stepped over the puddle, and raced from the garden room, deciding that Sunday brunches had, indeed, become too traumatic, and she must tell Bob that, from now on, she'd be sleeping in.

Bridget had lost faith in God years ago, the day they'd buried her tiny Alain. But she supposed she should try and find it again, now that she had cancer and all. Besides, it wouldn't hurt to say a prayer or two that she would see Luc before he went back to Provence.

If only she knew where he was staying.

She'd wanted to quiz Aimée last night, but Randall had monopolized the girl, asking about her friends and her studies, then showing off the media room he'd had renovated since she'd gone back to school after Christmas. He'd popped in a movie—Ben Affleck's latest—and they settled in front of the giant new screen until Aimée fell asleep with jet lag.

Bridget had downed a Lunesta and gone straight to bed.

Over breakfast, Randall announced he wanted to go to the twelve-fifteen Mass, which was the most crowded. As the three of them strolled up the long sidewalk to the big stone church now, the bright sunlight bounced off Randall's broad smile and spun a proud glow around his cherished Aimée.

Then one of Randall's cronies pulled him aside and Bridget seized the opportune moment.

"Aimée," she whispered while grinning at the passersby who were accustomed to seeing Randall at church but not her. "I thought about what your father said regarding Monsieur et Madame LaBrecque, that it would be nice to invite them for dinner. Did they give you a number where they could be reached?"

"Oh," Aimée said, "It's not them, Maman, it's only Monsieur. His wife went on to Houston where she has family."

Only Monsieur? Only Luc? Bridget wanted to shout, *Thank you, Jesus,* but held herself back out of respect for the time and the place. Instead she said, "Well. Did you get a number?"

"Aimée, dear," Randall suddenly said as he turned back toward them and scooped an arm around the girl's waist. "You must say hello to Mr. McNaughton. He hasn't seen you since your first Communion."

Mr. McNaughton was older than dirt and probably didn't

remember who Randall was, let alone Aimée. Bridget set her jaw into a clench.

"And my dear wife," Randall said, and Bridget stepped forward and murmured *bonjour*. Then she took Aimée's elbow and guided her away.

"You were saying," she said, "about Monsieur LaBrecque."

"Oh. Well, no, I didn't get a phone number."

Bridget longed for the old days when one wore a hat and a short veil to church, when one could conceal unfettered emotion.

"Who didn't get what?" Randall asked, having jogged to catch up with them now as they ascended the steps of St. Bernadette's.

"Monsieur LaBrecque," Aimée said. "He didn't leave me a number so Maman could call him."

Bridget wanted to gulp the sunshiny air. She didn't dare look at her husband, for fear he would see the hope of infidelity dance in her eyes. "I liked your idea. To invite them for dinner." No sense in Randall knowing that the *madame* had gone on to Houston.

"Well," Randall said. "Yes."

They went into the narthex, which was dark and quiet and emoted more guilt than Bridget thought she deserved. At least the priest she'd paid off long ago was now in another diocese.

"But it doesn't matter," Aimée quickly whispered. "I gave him the house number and he said he will call."

Organ music and incense rose up to greet them. Bridget clutched her purse.

He said he will call.

She wanted to ask *when* Luc would call, but decided to

temper her interest for the sake of both her husband and her guilt.

Checking her watch before she genuflected, Bridget and said a short prayer that Luc wouldn't phone before they were back home at one-thirty, two o'clock at the latest.

Caroline leaned against the antique writing desk in her morning room even though it was past noon. She stared at the large banquet table in the center of the room and the four-by-eight-foot sheet of plywood that rested on top. It was a model floor plan of the Hudson Valley Centre where the gala would be held, and had been crafted by the hospital maintenance department exactly as Caroline had instructed, with a matching sheet covered with velveteen and fashioned to scale, and miniature tables strategically set. Around each table were ten die-cut slots where Caroline could insert tiny name cards. It was an idea she'd picked up from Windsor Castle, which had made entertaining a proper science.

She looked at Chloe and Lee's name cards. The thought of seating them at the coveted table of Meachams and Hallidays and Fultons and Hayneses had waned this morning: They'd not showed up today, Sunday, the day the Meachams typically, historically, without fail, went to the club, had been going to the club on Sundays since before Chloe was born. When Chloe had been at school, Caroline and Jack had gone alone. Mount Holyoke (and Northfield Mount Hermon before that) was an acceptable excuse. A finicky fiancé was not.

"We can't make it today," Chloe said. "Lee isn't feeling well."

Not well, indeed. He didn't like Caroline, it was now apparent. Didn't he know how hard she was working to sculpt Chloe into a perfect wife for him?

It was bad enough Chloe had left the rite-of-spring luncheon early because "Lee had made other plans," and that she hadn't been there for the post-party "review" as Caroline liked to call it. It was tradition, wasn't it? For Caroline and Chloe to curl up on the sofas and talk about everyone who'd come and what they'd worn and what they'd said or done to whom? Why else had she bothered having a daughter?

But tradition had been broken this year, because Lee had "made other plans." Would he make last-minute plans the night of the gala? She wondered how bad it would get once he and Chloe were married, once they lived together full-time, not just when he was in town and wanted Chloe in his bedroom at his beck and call.

"How about if we drive up to the Adirondacks?" Jack, her husband, asked now as he came into the morning room wearing a frown.

Caroline looked up from her work. "What on earth for?"

He shrugged. "Something to do." He, like her, did not want to go to the club, just the two of them, with no acceptable excuse for Chloe's absence. It was best if people thought they were all out of town, that no one suspected their absence was a hint that the Meachams and their future son-in-law did not get along.

"I don't think so," Caroline replied. She'd rather stay there than pretend to enjoy a road trip with Jack. "Why don't you watch a movie? Or practice on your putting green?" He'd had the green installed last summer so he could finesse his game without leaving home.

Without offering an answer, Jack left the room. Caroline sighed. She was no longer a good wife, so what? It wasn't as if Jack would divorce her. It was far too late for that.

She looked back at the seating chart, thought about Vincent, and wondered if she should have done away with her husband when she'd had the chance.

Dory wouldn't let Jeffrey into the birthing room, citing that he'd done too much damage already.

"But he's your husband," Lauren argued on his behalf. "He's the father of your baby!"

Dory threw her a look of disgust, and Lauren convinced Jeffrey and the rest of the entourage to wait in the hall until she could convince Dory otherwise. Though Lauren had never given birth, she knew what it was like to feel smothered. *There are too damn many of us,* Dory had said quite succinctly.

So now Dory lay in the bed, hooked up to various monitors and beepers and other sterile-looking things. She breathed in, breathed out, every few minutes when the pains came. "They feel like cramps," she told Lauren. "Really bad cramps." She took Lauren's hand and squeezed it again—really hard—and Lauren said everything would be all right.

"No," Dory said. "It won't."

Lauren stroked the younger woman's hair, knowing that whatever she said, it would not be as meaningful as if she'd been Dory's real mother, as if Dory's real mother had never been hit by a bus and this inadequate substitute had stepped in. It occurred to her that was where the term "stepmother" came from, that it referenced the person who "stepped in" and took over when the real one was dead or otherwise disengaged, *unable to fulfill her term*, as they used to say in the Miss America pageants.

"Your baby will be fine," Lauren said. "Jeffrey will be, too. He is a good man." She didn't say he was a "great man" because he wasn't. He was only a landscape engineer (they used to be called gardeners), but he seemed to like Dory and he at least married her, unlike Nelson, the jerk Dory had lived with for twelve years. Once Dory passed forty, it had looked as if her "chance" had passed, too, until Jeffrey came along and planted new hope where the old bushes had been.

"I can't stand him," Dory replied, then squeezed Lauren's hand again and uttered a groan bigger than the last. When the cramp subsided she added, "He's so much like Dad."

With all the time Lauren had spent with Dory, or with any of Bob's children, Lauren never would have suspected that even one of them did not worship the ground Bob Halliday strolled around on. She stroked the younger woman's forehead again. "You don't mean that, honey."

"Yes, I do."

The room was silent; the monitor beeped.

"Your father is a fine man," Lauren said, because he was her husband.

"He's a control freak, Lauren. Everything has to be his way or no way. I don't know how you've stood him for so long."

Lauren didn't answer, because what could she say?

"Didn't you ever just want to leave him?" Dory asked.

It would not be appropriate to mention Bob's limp noodle or her foray with Vincent, so Lauren just said, "Honey, life is give and take. Surely you know that by now."

"But didn't you ever just want to follow your passion, strike out on your own? Didn't you ever just want a man who's exciting? Someone like Vincent DeLano? Word is all over town that he screwed around."

This time a cramp gripped Lauren, not Dory. Her knees buckled, her face grew warm, her vision blurred. She grabbed the edge of the bed just as Dory cried out again.

Fifteen

Dana backed out of her driveway at ten-fifteen the next morning, plugged in her headset, and speed-dialed Bridget, who answered on the first half ring.

"I'm on my way over," Dana said.

"Over here?"

"Ah, yes." Silence followed. "The meeting with Kitty's attorney is this morning." Pause. "I thought you wanted to go."

"Oh. Right. Actually, I forgot."

She sounded agitated, as if Dana had interrupted. "You forgot?"

"Well, first I was going to France and then I was not and then I was and now Aimée is here. And I really must get off the phone, I have so much to do."

"Bridget, I have no idea what you're saying."

Bridget quick-breathed again. "I know. Forget it. Tell Kitty I'm sorry."

"Are you okay?"

"I'm fine. But Aimée is home. I really must get off the line."

Dana turned right at the end of her street toward Tarrytown instead of left toward Bridget's. "Before you hang up, I wanted to tell you that Lauren and Bob have a new grandson. His name is Liam." She didn't suppose Bridget was much interested in that, either, that Caroline had called last night to relay Lauren's family news. Lauren to Caroline to Dana to Bridget. The chain that no longer had Kitty as a link.

"Just what Lauren needs," Bridget said. "One more person to take care of instead of herself. I really must go now."

Bridget hung up so quickly that Dana might have called her back, but a big truck was bearing down on her bumper. She pulled off her headset and slowed to let the truck pass. Riding on his tailwind, a dark green Jaguar blew by her, too, then cut in front. Dana leaned on her horn.

The Jag stopped at the light; Dana did, too. That's when she noticed the spray paint on the rear window: *R.I.P. Vincent DeLano.*

The car, she realized, had been Vincent's.

R.I.P. Vincent DeLano? Good grief, what was Yolanda doing? Didn't she know such a public *display* was inappropriate in New Falls? Didn't she know that, without Vincent, it was going to be hard enough to blend her culture with theirs?

Then again, how would Yolanda know if no one told her?

Without another thought, Dana secured the gearshift in

park and got out of the Volvo. She walked up to the driver's window of the Jag and briskly knocked on it.

"Yolanda," she called. "Yolanda, is that you?"

The window slowly opened. Yolanda turned her face to Dana without removing her large sunglasses.

"Mrs. Fulton," Yolanda said coolly. "How nice to see you."

"Yes. Well." Dana hadn't expected such a greeting. She reminded herself the girl was twenty years younger than the rest of them. "Yolanda, dear," she said, "it's about the paint on your back window."

"It's a nice memorial, don't you think?"

"Well, actually, I don't know how to say this, but . . ." But what could Dana say? That Yolanda wasn't entitled to mourn the way she wanted?

Before Dana could continue, Yolanda smiled, without removing her sunglasses. Then the light turned green and Yolanda stepped on the accelerator, leaving Dana—Mrs. Fulton—standing in the street, with several cars honking in concert.

They sat in Paul Tobin's office, Kitty's hands folded in her lap, ankles lightly crossed, eyes staring straight ahead. The man sat across from them, his gray-haired head bent to the papers on his desk, seemingly unaware that his secretary had escorted Kitty and Dana into his office and that they sat there now, waiting. Dana had an urge to lean across his desk and shout, *HEY, YOU!* into his ear. For Kitty's sake, however, she folded her hands, too, and looked around.

The room was tired, with paneled walls and a single, grimy window that wore yellowed Venetian blinds. A trio of framed diplomas hung on the wall behind Paul Tobin's desk; Dana could not discern their heritage from her chair. On the adjacent wall, facing the window, hung a print of Edvard Munch's *The Scream*, which Dana thought in poor legal taste for a criminal attorney.

She shifted on the wooden chair that might have been posh leather if Caroline had retained a lawyer in Manhattan. She wondered how many accused murderers—guilty or innocent—had sat in the chair where she sat now.

"Mrs. DeLano," the man suddenly said with a quick, upward jerk of his head that revealed an unfortunate mole next to his nose that really ought to be removed. His eyes were dark and small and landed squarely on Dana.

"No," she said, gesturing to Kitty. "This is Mrs. DeLano. Kitty."

His head swiveled toward Kitty. He did not ask who Dana was or what she was doing there.

Kitty said hello.

"I understand you were arrested for killing your ex-husband." Well, Dana thought, at least he got that right.

"I'm innocent," she said.

He grinned a slow, unhappy grin. "Yes. Of course." Then he launched into a well-seasoned monotone that addressed procedures and legalities in accordance with "the great State of New York."

"Are you going to find out who really killed Vincent?" Kitty asked when it seemed he was finished.

"Probably not. All we need to do is prove reasonable doubt. Surely you know that."

Dana shifted again. "We were hoping for something more

concrete," she said. "'Reasonable doubt' might work for a jury, but unless the real killer is found, Kitty will remain under suspicion." She didn't add, "Of all her friends in New Falls."

"I've been retained as Mrs. DeLano's attorney. If you want me to work as an investigator, there will be an additional fee."

"I don't have any money," Kitty said.

Paul Tobin made no comment.

"What if I know who might have killed him?" Kitty suddenly said. "Would you care about it then?"

Startled, Dana sat up straight.

Kitty turned to her. "About six months ago, when Vincent said he was leaving me, I was given the name of a man who might 'help me out.'"

"Help you out?" Dana asked. "What on earth are you saying?"

"You know," Kitty said. "I was given the name of a man who would shoot him. I'd have to pay, of course. But I still had money back then . . ." Her thoughts appeared to drift, the way they'd been drifting since Dana first saw her in jail.

"Do you know the man's name?" Paul Tobin asked.

Kitty shook her head.

"Think, Kitty," Dana prodded. "Was his name ever mentioned? Or some clue about who he was? Maybe someone we know? A pool man or a handyman or someone's house painter?"

Kitty started to cry. "At first I thought it was a joke. But then I wasn't sure."

"Who gave you his name?" the attorney asked.

"One of my friends," she said.

"One of *our* friends?" Dana asked with horrified surprise. Kitty lowered her head.

"This might be important," Dana said. "Kitty, who was it?" She paused a moment, then said, "It was Caroline."

The Scream seemed to open its mouth even wider. "*Caroline?*" Dana asked.

"Yes."

"Surely you can't mean *our* Caroline." A thought flashed through Dana's mind: Caroline had known Kitty would be cold in the jail. She also knew the name of a killer? Was there a connection?

"Caroline knows everyone," Kitty continued. "Like Mr. Tobin here."

The lawyer fixed his eyes on Kitty, but did not reveal his thoughts.

"But why?" Dana pressed. "Why would Caroline kill Vincent?"

"I can't imagine. Maybe she didn't like it when he married Yolanda. Maybe she saw it as a threat to our perfect social world."

"Did you tell the police?" the attorney asked.

"No. I was afraid they'd find a way to use it against me. That knowing the name of a hit man would give me more of the means to kill Vincent."

"Well," Tobin said, closing the file on his desk. "Six months was a long time ago. I doubt there's any relevance. If you think of anything else, be sure to call. Otherwise, we'll review your testimony right before trial." He plucked another file and bent his head in silent, curt dismissal.

* * *

"I always get you boys mixed up. Are you one of Dana's twins?" Jennie had interrupted Caroline from her breakfast of a solitary scrambled egg and dry rye toast—the same breakfast she had every day after her morning run and workout with light weights and her rubdown from Thomas, the best masseur from here to Canyon Ranch.

"I'm Sam," the young man in the entry said. He took off his Mets baseball cap as if he might bow next. "And, yes, I'm one of the twins. Ben is the other one. He calls us wombmates."

Caroline was reminded she should be grateful that Chloe had found a man like Lee who was a global player, not a New Falls townie. "All right then, Sam. May I help you with something?"

"Do you have a minute to talk to me? About the day Mr. DeLano was murdered?"

Dana always said what was on her mind. Apparently he'd inherited his mother's aplomb. "Well," she said, "I don't know how I can help. I was busy hosting a party."

"Which is why I thought you might unknowingly know something. Because someone who was here might have been involved."

She studied him. "Are you with the police?"

He shook his head. "I'm home on spring break. I'm trying to help my mom. She's trying to help Mrs. DeLano."

"Kitty."

"Yes. Kitty."

She'd rather send the boy away but something told her he'd be back, maybe with Dana, maybe, good Lord, with Kitty, which wouldn't please Jack. Jack had, however, just left to play golf, so she might as well get it over with. "Of course, Sam," Caroline said, "please, have a seat." She sat on one of the silk Queen Anne chairs that flanked the Louis XV table. She motioned Sam to the matching one. No sense bringing him into the music room or sitting room and have him misunderstand that it was okay to stay more than a courteous minute. "Now," she said, smoothing her ocher crepe skirt. "How do you think I might help?"

"First of all, I wondered if you heard the rumors that Mr. DeLano was broke." He folded the brim of his cap. He had clear skin for a boy his age, with rosy cheeks that might indicate he was nervous. At least he wasn't taking notes.

She set her mouth into a smile. "I've always made it a point never to meddle in anyone's business, especially their finances."

"Well," Sam said, his cheeks growing pinker. "I didn't mean . . ."

"Vincent was not a bad man, Samuel. It's been a while since he and Kitty were divorced. If she'd planned to kill him, I'd guess she'd have done it a long time ago."

Before he could comment the back door banged, and what followed was a bone-rattling scream.

❦ Sixteen

Sam leaped from the Queen Anne and bolted through the foyer toward the commotion that had come from the kitchen, toward the scream that sounded as if it had come from Chloe.

Caroline chased after Sam, but by the time she caught up, Chloe was crumpled on the floor and Sam was cradling her head.

"Can I help?" he asked. "Can I do anything?"

Chloe sobbed.

Caroline loved her daughter but despised theatrics, which Chloe tended to employ, a vice from Jack's side of the family. She resisted telling her to stand up and stop acting like a baby. But Sam was there: She couldn't let him run home and tell

Dana that Caroline might be a great fund-raiser but she was an uncaring mother. So she stooped in an unladylike manner, jeopardizing the lifespan of her hundred-dollar French hosiery.

"Chloe, darling," she said, nudging Sam out of the way. "What's the matter?"

"Oh, Mommy, it's awful."

Caroline also hated that Chloe sometimes still called her Mommy. It sounded so juvenile.

She turned to Sam. "I need you to leave now."

"But can't I . . . can't I do something?" he asked again, rising to his feet.

"Kill him," Chloe sputtered, her green eyes—Jack's eyes—turning dark, her thin lips—Caroline's lips before plumping—growing narrower, tighter.

"Now, now," Caroline said, "no one is going to kill anyone."

"You might change your mind when you know what's going on."

"Sssh, sssh," Caroline said, then looked at Dana's son again. "Sam," she said, "thank you, but please leave."

Chloe wriggled from her mother and stood up next to Sam. "You can only leave if you promise to kill the bastard," she said.

"There are a lot of bastards in the world," Sam replied while Caroline tried righting herself without a zip or pull.

"This one is named Lee," Chloe spit out the word. "Lee Sato. My *formerly* intended. He just broke our engagement."

Caroline sucked in a loud breath that probably could be heard in the next room and down the street and into the next county.

"He's been *cheating* on me. He says he's in love with another girl. A *Russian* girl, of all things. She doesn't even speak English."

Caroline didn't mention that Lee barely did. "Is this girl . . . wealthy?"

"Her father is an international businessman. He has *piles* of money, Mommy. Much more than we do."

And that, Caroline knew, said it all.

"I don't care what that lawyer says," Dana seethed once she and Kitty escaped Paul Tobin's office and were safely ensconced back in the car. "The fact that Caroline asked if you wanted a hit man is relevant, Kitty."

Kitty shrugged. "He's right about one thing. It was a long time ago."

"Kitty! Think about it! How many of our friends do you know who would even think such a thing?"

"True. But Jack is still alive. She obviously didn't have him bumped off."

Hit man. Bumped off. *Lawyers.* Dana turned onto the main road back toward Tarrytown, wondering how their quiet lives had come to this, and hating that the disruption was so reminiscent of Indiana. "But how the heck does Caroline know a hit man?" she asked. "He probably isn't in one of Jack's foursomes."

"She didn't say. She just gave me his name."

Dana debated whether she should tell Kitty that Caroline had known it was cold in the jail.

A Jaguar passed. Dana cringed. Thankfully the car was navy, not dark green, and no memorial to Vincent graced the back windshield. *Oh God*, she thought, *what should I tell Kitty?* Would she meet up with Yolanda at a traffic light one day? And what if she learned about Vincent and Lauren? *How much should you tell a friend when you know it will only cause pain?*

On the other hand, Dana thought, she'd learned from her father that, sooner or later, secrets make their way to the surface.

She took a deep yoga breath. "Kitty," she said, "this attorney isn't going to help you. He has no intention of conducting an investigation. He probably doesn't think what you said is relevant because it's about Caroline. She paid him, don't forget."

"Do you think they're in this together? Do you think Caroline killed Vincent and this lawyer knows it and that they're in cahoots to frame me?"

Dana recoiled at Kitty's *cahoots*. "I don't know, Kitty. I can't imagine why Caroline would want to kill Vincent. But I do know two things. First, we are going to the police. Detective Johnson has to know about this."

"You don't think it will hurt me?"

"Kitty! It's the truth! The truth can't hurt you because you didn't kill him!"

Kitty silently stared out at the street. "What's the second thing you know?"

Dana gripped the steering wheel more tightly. "You need another lawyer."

"I can't afford one, Dana. I have no money, remember?"

In all the years Dana and Steven had been married, she'd never once asked him for anything. Oh sure, he'd given her free rein over the household expenses and let it be known that she could spend some on herself whenever she wanted. She certainly hadn't gone without. But Dana was from a cop's family, where collars were blue and left unstarched, where dining out meant Friendly's on Friday nights, where grocery shopping was supplemented by coupons. No, she'd never asked Steven for anything.

"I have plenty of money, Kitty," Dana said suddenly, as if waiting would make her change her mind. "I'll get you another lawyer. A good lawyer."

"But your husband . . ."

"Let me worry about Steven." She smiled a small, wry smile and wondered if she could convince him this would somehow help Sam get a high mark at school.

Caroline jumped into a cart that was parked outside the clubhouse and took off down the cart path toward the second tee. She did not remember getting into her car and driving over there. She did not remember what she'd said to Chloe after the girl's announcement. She only knew she must find her husband and get him off the goddamn golf course and put him to work. He had to fix this. No one else could.

Lee Sato, she seethed.

How dare he?

She pushed her foot on the accelerator. Ten fucking miles an hour? Didn't this thing go any faster? It was bad enough they wouldn't allow cell phones out on the course, as if one ringy-dingy would break the concentration of some fucking spike-shoed genius.

The cart wobbled up an incline, past Tee Number One. Four men whose wives had been at her luncheon were lining up their balls. *God,* she thought, *don't any men in this town work for a living?*

She gave a short, disinterested wave and jerked the wheel, nearly tumbling the cart onto the pavement. She didn't care if the men were watching or not. She couldn't look as ridiculous as they did in their spring greens and blues, shivering to death because for godssake it was only April and this was New York, not Palm Beach.

Around another corner, up another hill. But Tee Number Two was vacant; they must be on their second shot.

Without another thought, Caroline yanked the wheel to the left and sped (sped? ha!) up one side, then down the other of the embankment, then straight onto the fairway where she gained momentum and was flat-ass flying now.

Then she saw him.

"Jack!" she shouted above the tick-tick of the toy motor. "Jack!" Shouting, like cell phones, was not allowed on the fairway. In fact, on this particular dogleg, carts were forbidden, too.

The men were sprinkled this way and that depending on where their balls had landed. Four men and four caddies. All of whom stood still, eyes directed at her.

She spotted the pale aqua cashmere she'd bought at Myrtle Beach and given Jack last Christmas. "Jack!"

He detached from his caddy and took a step toward her. "Caroline? What in God's name are you doing?" The other men formed ranks and moved in close as if needing to protect Jack Meacham from his wife.

Bob Halliday was there, of course. And Richard Stanley. And Jonathan Gibson. Men whose money had wound up in

Jack's investments, had helped buy their house, helped send Chloe to Mount Holyoke, where she'd met Lee Sato, who had been enrolled at Amherst.

"It's that piece of shit!" She shouted though Jack was only six or eight feet from her. "He was your choice. I hope you're satisfied." She switched off the ignition and pulled herself from the cart, preferring to stand with both hands on her hips.

"Caroline," Jack said. "Perhaps we should go somewhere to discuss this . . ."

"There's nothing to discuss! Just get your ass into Manhattan and find that slimeball Sato. He's broken their engagement and he's broken Chloe's heart!" The part about the heart slipped from her mouth just as tears sprang to her eyes. "*Now*, Jack!" she cried, then climbed back into the cart before the men might notice that her hands had started to tremble and her dark mascara was running down her cheeks, before they might suspect that Jack's in-charge wife, *the* Caroline Meacham, hated her goddamn life.

Seventeen

"*You should have been there,*" Bob said to Lauren. "I have never seen Caroline Meacham quite so . . . emotional." He chortled as he sat on the edge of their big bed where night after night Lauren slept on one side and he on the other, far enough apart so no warmth from either body could drift over the mattress and stir fruitless longings.

"I can't believe Lee broke the engagement. What will Caroline do?"

"Well, for starters, she seems determined to make Jack talk some sense into the boy."

"She should leave well enough alone. If it's not meant to be, no amount of prodding will make it a happy marriage."

Bob's white eyebrows rose. "Careful, my dear. I might get the impression that you're talking about us."

Lauren ignored him. "I went to see Dory while you were at the club. The baby is adorable, but she's having some hormonal problems."

This time his chortle sounded more like a snort. He meandered into his closet. "The girl overreacts."

Lauren bit her lip and moved toward the window seat, the one place in the gargantuan house where she could safely tuck herself away and curl up into her thoughts.

Bob returned with a pair of lightweight navy flannels that he happily stepped into. They were too short, but Lauren didn't mention it. Sometimes she was tired of being his mother and his keeper as well as his wife.

"Audrey never had hormonal problems," he remarked. "Not once, not with any of the seven."

He stuffed his shirt into his pants, then clipped on his suspenders. Lauren wondered what it would take to strangle him with them, and if the elasticity would render the action worthless. "Audrey wasn't forty-one when she gave birth."

"True, but she was only forty-three when she was run over by the bus." He snapped one suspender onto his shoulder, punctuating the last word, a jab at Lauren for not giving birth to any of his children, and for having had the audacity to live when Audrey had not.

There was no way she would share her worries about Dory. There was no way she'd tell him the only way Jeffrey got to see his son was by peeking into the nursery, that Dory refused to let him into her room, that Lauren had spent half the morning trying to convince him that pain meds sometimes did strange things and that Dory would come around. "In the meantime," she'd said over and over, "you have a very handsome baby boy!"

No, she would not share these things because Bob would not understand. He was from a different generation, planet of the old.

"I'll call Caroline," she said. "I'm sure she'll want to talk about what's happened to Chloe."

Bob nodded because the men liked it when their women stuck together. Caroline's "upset" at the club would soon be forgotten and forgiven: She was Caroline Meacham, after all, and Caroline Meacham mattered for the funds she raised and the society she wrought and because, Lauren suspected, most of the men were more than a little intimidated by her.

Lauren knew that, sadly, Dory would only matter that much—even to her father—if she'd married an investment banker instead of a gardener.

If Bridget didn't get to see Luc now, her next chance might not be until August. By August she might be dead.

So there were worse things, she supposed, than sitting at home, waiting for the phone to ring, because Aimée had given Luc the house number and not the number of her cell.

There were worse things, like having the chemo that she'd start tomorrow. As long as Bridget couldn't be in France, she'd decided she might as well get it done. How could she have predicted they'd give her an appointment so soon? That's what she got going to the hospital in New Falls not New York, for figuring that any day now everyone would know anyway so she might as well save the train fare and the time.

So tomorrow she'd begin, and in the meantime she'd wait for Luc's call. She'd stay busy by moving the buttons on her lavender linen blazer, a dexterous reminder that she'd been self-sufficient before she'd turned into a snob.

She wouldn't have to move the buttons if her boobs didn't outpace her butt whenever she gained weight, which she always did when reality intruded and she buffered it with chocolate. Maybe after chemo she should have a breast reduction. Maybe Dr. Gregg would have an opening now that Caroline seemed content for the time being.

The clock struck three.

The phone rang twice.

The phone.

The phone!

The needle dropped; Bridget's blood pressure shot up. She grabbed the receiver, turned it upside down then right side up, and fumbled for the talk button.

"Hello? Hello?" Oh God, why had she said it twice?

"Bridget? Is that you? It's Lauren."

Bridget hadn't seen Lauren since Vincent's funeral, hadn't spoken with her since Dana told her about his gigantic dick.

"Hang up the phone," Bridget demanded. "Call me on my cell."

"But I only wanted . . ."

Click.

Call waiting notwithstanding, Bridget couldn't take the chance that Luc would call and she'd push the wrong button and cut him from her life.

Her cell phone rang.

"Sorry," she said to Lauren, "but Aimée's expecting a call

on the house phone." She quickly explained that the girl was home, that she'd saved them the transatlantic trip. "Speaking of kids," she added, "I heard you're a grandmother again."

Lauren said yes, but there were some problems with Dory's psyche, though what really mattered now was Caroline. She told her about the broken engagement. "I just spoke with her. As you can imagine, she's devastated. Jack needs to convince Lee to change his mind and, most of all, before the gala."

"What did you suggest?"

"Lunch, of course. Tomorrow. At the club. She needs our support, Bridget. You'll be there, won't you?"

"Well," Bridget said. "No."

"You won't go to lunch?" Lauren asked.

Bridget eyed the house phone, praying it would ring. "I can't," she said. "The people who escorted Aimée home have made plans for us in the city." Apparently she wasn't ready after all to tell the others about her cancer or her chemo. Maybe when her hair began to fall out. Or after Luc called, whichever came first.

Lauren paused, as if reassessing. "Well," she said slowly, "you will be missed."

The way you were missed at our last lunch with Kitty, Bridget might have said if she wanted an argument, which she did not.

Instead she said she was sorry, then she said good-bye.

She picked up her needle and thread again and resumed eyeballing the phone.

Elise was waiting at Kitty's apartment, sitting on a vinyl chair that once might have been white and was perched on the sagging balcony outside Kitty's front door.

Dana had planned to simply drop Kitty off, but the sight of Elise raised her curiosity. She got out of the car.

"You need to call off the dogs, Mother," Elise said, untangling her long legs and standing up, a head taller than Kitty. She pulled off her sunglasses, removed her soft, floppy hat, and shook out her mane of golden red hair.

Kitty unlocked the door, and the three of them filed in.

"I wasn't aware you knew where I live," Kitty said, tossing her keys onto the kitchen counter next to the Krups coffeemaker that seemed out of its continental element on top of the worn Formica.

"This place is wretched," Elise said, in a voice that seemed more surprised than judgmental.

"Tell that to your father," Kitty replied, and Elise winced. Elise and Vincent had been close, Dana had heard from Lauren or Caroline or someone who supposedly knew. "I'd offer you coffee but the generic brand won't be on sale until next week."

"See?" Elise said to Dana. "She wonders why I don't come to see her."

"That's hardly fair," Kitty said as she took off her jacket and sat down on the couch. "Besides, what do you expect when you greet me with an accusation about dogs?"

"Well, the police are all over town, questioning everyone as to where they were the morning Daddy was killed." She uttered the words "Daddy" and "killed" as if they hurt her throat.

Dana leaned back against the counter and studied the beautiful girl. *Boob shots and everything,* Sam had said about Elise's calendar. Dana wondered what possessed a young woman to do that, to strip herself naked when she'd been raised in a place, in a family, that was so guarded, so protective of its own.

"By everyone," Kitty said, "I assume you mean Yolanda."

"For one, yes. She went to the police station to give a statement."

Was that where Yolanda had been going when Dana had seen her this morning?

"But it's not just Yolanda. They're harassing everyone in New Falls. All of your friends, Mother. They're turning Daddy's death into a charade."

The hurt eked out again, this time when "Daddy" was linked with "death."

"First, my dear daughter, in case you haven't noticed, I no longer live in New Falls, so what do I care? Second, I'm sure that the few friends I have left won't mind the slight imposition. I'm sure they'd like to see the case solved. Because they know I did not kill your father."

Elise's glare was radioactive.

"Obviously," Kitty continued, "you don't believe that."

The girl returned the sunglasses to the bridge of her nose, which had been perfectly sculpted by nature, not man.

"I might have believed you," Elise said, turning toward the door. "But Daddy named Marvin executor to his estate. And Marvin found a paid-up life insurance policy with your name as beneficiary."

Kitty laughed. "Tell your brother to check again. I'm sure it was an oversight."

"Oh, it's true," Elise said. "The strange thing is, Daddy actually took out the policy around the time of your divorce."

Dana stood up straighter.

"I have no idea what you're talking about," Kitty said.

"Don't you?" Elise asked. "Well, the policy is for two million dollars. It would seem you would know something about that." She stared at her mother another moment, then added, "So like I said, call off your dogs, Mother. You're only hurting people who don't deserve it." With her hat in her hand and a clip to her long-legged, supermodel stride, Elise DeLano let herself out the door.

Dana had planned to go to the police and inform Detective Johnson about Caroline and the hit man. But her head was hurting from the thoughts that bounced in her brain like numbered cubes in a lottery bin, each popping up with a nice, round number: two million.

She went home.

"Holy cow, Mom," Sam said as he met her at the door. "What took you so long? I tried to call but you didn't answer your phone. Wait till you hear what happened."

Her empty nest wasn't effervescent when none of her boys was there, but right now silence might have been nice. She pressed her fingers against her temple. "Headache," she said. "I need my Jacuzzi."

He trailed her through the kitchen and out into the foyer and up the butterfly staircase toward the master suite. "But Mom . . ." he persisted, even as she waved him off, her focus on warm water and the honey-almond milk bath she'd picked up on her last trip to the spa with Caroline and Bridget and Lauren and . . . Kitty.

"Sam," Dana said when she reached the suite, "please." She closed the door in his face.

"But Mom," he said from the other side, "don't you want to know that Chloe Meacham's fiancé called off the wedding?"

She stopped, of course. Her eyes moved to the big bed, where the thick, white down comforter was waiting to bundle itself around her after a long, soothing bath.

But a broken engagement?

Chloe's?

She drew in a slow breath and leaned against the silk wallpapered wall. "Samuel David Fulton, you'd better not be lying."

If he was still there, he was holding his breath.

"Sam?" she whispered. Perhaps he'd left because he'd been only joking. It was so like her boys to joke.

"I'm here, Mom," he whispered back. "And no, I'm not lying. I even saw her cry."

Dana let out another sigh. With resignation, she opened the door. "Okay," she said. "Tell me the details. But first at least let me fix tea."

🌿 Eighteen

"So I have a theory," Sam said after he explained the scene at Caroline's ("She was defensive about both Kitty and Vincent, Mom"), said that poor Chloe was totally wrecked ("She's nice, Mom. Why would a guy do that to her?"), and told how Caroline tried to throw him out but then she took off.

"On her way out she shouted that she'd try to make Chloe's father fix everything, but not to expect much because all men are assholes."

"I doubt she used that word," Dana said, sipping her tea, her headache mysteriously gone.

Sam held up his palm. "Scout's honor."

"You weren't a Boy Scout. That was your brother Michael."

"Okay," he said. "But she said it, honest."

She sipped again. "Well, this is all very interesting, but it doesn't have anything to do with Vincent's murder."

"What if it does?" Sam asked.

Dana shook her head. "How? Other than saying hello at a few social gatherings, I doubt Lee Sato even knew Vincent DeLano."

"Maybe not. But after her mother flew out the door, Chloe made a strange comment. She said she hadn't seen her mother so angry since she'd walked in on her mother and father doing battle the night before her mother's rite-of-spring luncheon."

"What were they fighting about?"

"I asked. She said, 'I think it had something to do with some money my mother gave Vincent.'"

Dana frowned. "Why would Caroline give Vincent DeLano money?"

"An investment?"

Even to Dana, who knew little about the mechanics of investing, it didn't seem plausible that Caroline was doing business with Vincent DeLano. Wouldn't Jack—like the other New Falls husbands—be in charge of the Meachams' portfolio? "Suppose that's true. How could it be tied to Lee Sato breaking the engagement?"

Sam shrugged. "Maybe it was a bad investment? Maybe she told Lee and he lost money, too?"

"Lee is wealthy in his own right." Dana shook her head. "No, I doubt there's a connection."

Sam seemed disappointed. "You're probably right. Besides,

what would Mrs. Meacham do? Shoot Mr. DeLano, then run home and jump into her hostess clothes for her stupid party?"

Dana laughed. She looked into the bottom of her mug as if the remnants of tea leaves might hold the answer to the puzzle. Then she had a thought. "Well, if it's possible that Caroline had a motive, she might have had the means."

"Huh?"

She told Sam about the hit man.

He blinked. "Was Caroline the one who had the affair with Mr. DeLano?"

Dana shook her head. "You must keep this a secret. It was Lauren Halliday."

Sam slumped down on the stool. "Jesus, Mom. This is New Falls. Murder? Mayhem? Mrs. Halliday? Is all this for real?"

"It's for real." She was tired. She was drained from speculation and from the sudden feeling that they were in over their amateur heads. "And there's more, Sam. I offered to get—and pay for—a new attorney for Kitty. I don't know how your father will like it. Not that I even know where to find one."

His eyes lit up. "We start on the indispensable Internet," he said. "Home of every solution to every problem known to man."

But Dana shook her head. "I promised Kitty, but now I'm not sure, Sam. When I dropped her off, her daughter was there. She'd stopped by to tell her mother there's a life insurance policy and that Kitty's the beneficiary."

"Life insurance? Man, that won't help her case, will it?"

Sam, of course, was on Kitty's side because Kitty was the underdog. "The worst part is, it's a lot. Two million dollars. But Kitty claims she didn't know."

"Two million freaking dollars? Oh, Mom, what are we going to do?"

Dana set down her mug, closed her eyes, took a breath. Then she said, "We're going to tell the police. And we're going to go there right now."

"I told you we were getting too big for our pantaloons," Bridget said when Dana called after leaving the police station where she and Sam told Detective Johnson every single thing they knew, including that Lauren was the one who had been Vincent DeLano's mistress before Yolanda, and that Caroline and Jack had argued because Caroline had given Vincent some money, though no one knew how much or why. Then Bridget quickly added, "Now hang up and call me on my cell."

Dana didn't question Bridget, why would she? Right now, Bridget seemed to be the only one not connected to Vincent, the only one whose name—if it had been on a website—would not be hyperlinked to the murder.

"Do you want to have dinner with Sam and me?" Dana asked. "Steven's in Chicago until tomorrow."

"I'd love to, but I can't. I'm expecting an important call."

"Forward it to your cell. Come with us, please. Sam and I are going crazy with all this new information. We need you to help us sort it out."

"But Aimée is home."

"Oh. Right. I forgot. I don't expect you'd want your fourteen-year-old to know all the New Falls dirt."

Bridget laughed. "No. But if you want to talk, you could go with me tomorrow afternoon."

"Go with you? Where?"

"To chemo. One-thirty. I haven't told Randall or Aimée, and I could use the company."

Dana said she'd pick her up at one o'clock.

"Who was that?" Aimée asked as she sauntered into the family room and plopped down next to Bridget. "And what are you doing?"

She was young and bright and oh so *trés* grown up. But Dana had been right: Aimée should not be exposed to the New Falls dirt. "That was Dana Fulton, and I am moving buttons." Since the lavender blazer, she'd moved the buttons on half a dozen other jackets, two dresses, and three cardigans. "Your *maman* is getting fat." She lifted her eyes and scrutinized her daughter. "And you are getting so pretty." Aimée had spent the day with Krissie, her longtime childhood friend. Unlike Aimée, Krissie was homely.

"Daddy always says I'm beautiful."

"Your papa spoils you." Bridget smiled. How could she help but smile? Her daughter really was a beauty, with softer angles that promised sweetness in a body, not like the severe angles of Elise DeLano, who, until Aimée, had been the best-looking girl New Falls had generated.

"What did you do all day, Maman?" Aimée asked. "Practice being a seamstress, a couturier?"

"Working with your hands creates a rich soul." She couldn't say she'd been waiting for Luc's call that still hadn't come.

"Shall I work with my hands when I'm grown up? I was rather thinking about becoming a physician. A pediatrician, maybe."

This was the first Bridget had heard her daughter wanted

to be a doctor. "Whatever suits you best," she said. "Just don't count on a man to support you. Every woman needs her own career." She smiled again. "Even a spoiled woman such as yourself."

"Or you, Maman." Aimée laughed.

"Or me."

Aimée seemed to think about that for a moment. Then she asked, "Are you sorry I'm an only child?"

Bridget stuck her finger with the needle, muttered, "Oh, shit," excused herself in French, then said, "Such a child you are. Another could hold a dozen candles, but it would not be you." Her heart hurt as she said it, as if the needle pierced the place where Alain lingered. Once she'd planned to tell Aimée about him; hell, she'd always planned to tell Randall. But time and life had always gotten in the way, and now an admission would seem strangely belated. Besides, if Randall and Aimée thought Luc was merely an old family friend, it was better, it was better, she'd told herself over and over.

"I guess that means you love me."

Bridget set down the needle. "*Mon dieu, quelle question!* Now tell me, what did you and Krissie do today?"

"Went to Bloomingdale's. Hung out. You know."

"Did you spend your papa's money?"

"*Oui. Un peu.*"

Bridget smiled again. She loved to hear her daughter speak French. It made it easy to picture her in Ste. Marie de la Mer, the sea breeze lifting her luscious hair, the warm sun tanning her perfect face. She wondered what Alain would have looked like at fourteen, if he would have become as wonderful as Aimée.

"Maman," Aimée said, lowering her voice, "there's something I must tell you, but I don't want to upset you."

The first thing Bridget thought was that Aimée had a boyfriend, then worse, *mon dieu*, that she was pregnant. Squeezing the needle tightly, Bridget forced a look-at-me-I-am-calm kind of smile. "You can tell me anything, *ma petite chérie*, you know that."

Aimée closed her eyes. "I don't want to go back to school in France, Maman. Please, don't make me go back."

Being pregnant would not have been the worst thing after all.

Lorraine grilled lamb chops for dinner. It was a good thing it was Monday and she was there, or the Haynes family would not have been fed.

Bridget took her place at the Zimbabwean teak, unfolded the linen napkin, and spread it casually across her lap, as if the last thing on her mind was screaming her head off.

She couldn't let this happen. She couldn't let Aimée drop out of school because then she wouldn't have a reason to go home. She wouldn't be able to place wildflowers on the stones in the churchyard that marked where her mother and father and Alain were at rest. And she would never see Luc again.

She passed the peas.

"Papa, I spent some of your money today," Aimée said as she scooped the vegetables onto her plate.

"Well, good," Randall said with a chuckle. "I count on my girls to keep my credit revolving."

In all the years they'd been together, even when Randall was angry with her for not wanting another child, he had not deprived Bridget of anything she'd wanted, not a dress, not a spa weekend with her friends, not a Mercedes, though her current one was smaller than his and was alabaster, not silver.

Dana had said Vincent might have been broke. If he'd kept his "credit revolving," would he still be alive? And why was Bridget thinking about Vincent now? God knew she'd hear plenty tomorrow: Dana seemed obsessed to find his killer. Dana was a good friend—to her, to Kitty, to everyone. Maybe Bridget should tell her about Luc. About Alain. And the other lies. But could Bridget purge her past as easily as chemo would surely purge her cancer?

"Isn't that right, Maman?" Aimée was asking.

"What? I'm sorry, I was thinking."

"I told Papa I think you've decided to stop shopping and become a couturier. That things change sometimes. Like how we work or don't work, and where we live and where we go to school. Isn't that right, Maman?"

It was apparent Aimée wanted her mother to tell Randall her request about school. If Bridget refused, she might lose Luc anyway and her daughter, too. Bridget sighed. "Randall . . ." she began.

"Papa," Aimée interjected, "I don't want to go back to France. I want to be near my friends. Like Krissie. And the others."

"You don't like the school? But are you sure?" He acted surprised, but his toupee stayed in place. Perhaps he'd been praying for this every day at St. Bernadette's.

She said she was absolutely, positively sure, then Papa and *petite chérie* began to biopsy the alternatives.

"As long as it's a good school," Randall said excitedly. "Where did the Halliday kids go?"

"Or Chloe Meacham? Didn't she go somewhere in Massachusetts?"

"Deerfield, I think. Or somewhere near there."

"As long as it's not that place in Springfield, Papa. There is nothing to do in Springfield."

"How about Loomis-Chaffee? That's in Connecticut. You could come home every weekend. That would make you happy, no?"

Blah blah blah, Bridget thought. *Blah blah, blah blah blah*. She stabbed her lamb chop as if it were her broken heart.

"We can ask someone to pack your things in France," she then heard Randall say. "Perhaps Monsieur LaBrecque and his wife."

"What?" Bridget interrupted, a little too loudly.

"Monsieur LaBrecque," Randall repeated. "He and his wife might agree to pack Aimée's things. Save us a trip."

"Oh no," Bridget said. "That would be an imposition. I'll go in a few weeks." She couldn't say she'd wait until her chemotherapy was over. Why had she been so *stupeeed* to have scheduled it now? Was it too late to cancel?

"I won't need help, Maman," Aimée said. "I packed everything before I left. All Monsieur LaBrecque would have to do is arrange for the shipping."

Again Bridget had been thwarted. Was destiny telling her to leave things alone? "Well," she said, "I suppose I could ask him. If he ever calls. Did he give you any idea when he might?"

"*Non*," Aimée said. "But he's staying at the Pierre. You know, that big hotel near Central Park."

Sometimes Bridget hated that her lovely daughter was fourteen and was too wrapped up in *self* to communicate like the adult she pretended she was. "I thought you said you didn't know where he was staying?"

"I said he didn't give me the number." She shrugged. "But he did say he would call. You can ask him when he does."

"He's at the Pierre?" Bridget repeated.

"Your Maman must have put her peas in her ears," Randall said and Aimée laughed, and again Bridget wanted to scream.

Nineteen

"What do you mean you'll pick me up at midnight? And why on earth are you whispering?" Dana had finally had a chance to languish in her bath, and now she was stretched out on the chaise in the bedroom, wearing a soft terry robe, her legs wrapped in an afghan her mother had made when Dana was twelve and had contracted the Hong Kong flu.

She'd been reading Sam's textbook titled *The Criminal Mind* when Bridget called.

"Just be ready. Please."

"It's after eleven, Bridget. Are you feeling okay?"

"I'm fine. But I need you to go somewhere with me."

"Don't be ridiculous!" Dana said with a laugh.

"Please, Dana. Don't make me beg. Or worse, don't make me call Lauren. Or Caroline."

"Now that's a threat."

"It's only because there's somewhere I must go, and it's not a good idea for me to go alone."

"Where?"

"Into the city."

"New York City?"

"Well. Of course."

"Bridget . . ."

"Please, Dana. I know Steven's not home."

"But Sam is."

"So, leave him a note."

"If this has something to do with Vincent's murder, he'll want to go."

"It doesn't. It's all about me."

Dana paused. She rubbed the back of her neck that had stopped aching but now threatened to start up again.

"I'll drive Randall's new Mercedes," Bridget said.

"You'll stand out like a beacon."

"I don't care. I'll feel safer."

"You're insane," Dana said.

"I know. But I'll make it worth your while."

"How?"

"I'll tell you a secret too juicy for you to believe."

"Oh, Bridget."

"Oh, Dana."

"Oh, for godssake, all right."

145

* * *

Lauren didn't know why Bob always fell asleep so quickly, why his snores kicked in with the first refrain of the white noise machine that he kept by the bed.

It must be so he wouldn't have to think about having sex. Or about not having sex, as was more the case.

She lay on the warm sheets—"Audrey only bought eight-hundred count," Bob announced shortly after their marriage, so, for eighteen years, Lauren had done the same. It hadn't mattered that she preferred cool cotton percale, the kind that reminded her of Nantucket nights, when salty breezes blew and buoy bells rang in the foggy distance and life had been simple and safe, well, relatively safe, if one discounted Uncle Raymond.

Lauren hated that things had changed, that time had raced by too quickly while Bob's kids were growing up, while he was growing old, while Lauren was trying so hard to please. In the end she pleased Vincent but only for a short time.

Sliding out of bed, she slipped on her white satin robe and matching mules. She padded from the room, into the hall, and down the wide marble staircase. Unlike for Bob, sleep rarely came easily for Lauren. And now, with Chloe's engagement crisis added to the New Falls mix, how could she think about sleeping when Caroline was so upset? When next week—of all weeks—was the grand hospital gala! Now, more than ever, Caroline needed her friends. Too bad Lauren was the only one who seemed to care.

She moved into the den with its semicircular wall and its bank of wraparound windows that gave a perfect view of the town. It was Bob's favorite spot in the massive house, the place from which—if Caroline had allowed it—he could practically steer the New Falls ship.

He's a control freak, his daughter Dory had said. *Didn't you ever want to just leave him?*

Guided by the moonlight, Lauren made her way to the bar. She removed the crystal stopper from the Courvoisier decanter and poured a snifter more than half full. She supposed that in order to be such a successful banker, any man would have to be a control freak. Or any woman, if she wanted to work.

For a brief period, in between marriages, Lauren had considered having a career. She'd envied her cousin Gracie, who was riding the wave of women's lib, the feminine tsunami set in motion by Friedan, Steinem, and Bella Abzug in her hats. Gracie had gone to law school—law school!—then clawed her way up from the cesspool of poor relations. Lauren suspected that when she and Bob were on Nantucket and the opportunity arose, Gracie still stole small, inconsequential things from her—a bottle of suntan lotion, a notepad from Lauren's purse, a simple gold earring. It might have been from habit, or a need to feel in control.

Like Bob, had Gracie ended up with a negligent sex life?

Meandering to the window, looking down on the quiet neighborhood, Lauren swirled the brandy in her glass. She wondered if Dory would stay married to Jeffrey and if sweet little Liam would have a happy home. Then she wondered why neither Bridget nor Dana would have lunch with Caroline:

"I have to go into New York," Bridget had said.

"I'm sorry, I must bring my son to an appointment," Dana

had said, had lied, more than likely, when Lauren had called her that afternoon. Dana had been so distant since she'd told her about Vincent, about their affair. *Friends*, Lauren thought, *could be such a disappointment.*

She tasted the slow burn of the brandy, then stopped halfway into her swallow. At the bottom of the hill, where the front lawn met the road, Lauren saw headlights. They swept this way and that as the vehicle maneuvered the winding road, traveling with purpose, going too fast for this late at night.

She kept her eyes on the vehicle. Who on earth could it be? From her bird's-eye position, she recognized the style—a big Mercedes, not unlike so many in New Falls. But where other big ones were black, this one was silver. Silver, the same color Mercedes that Randall Haynes drove.

Was it Randall?

And if so, where was he going?

It was almost midnight.

Should Lauren call the Haynes house and make sure everything was all right?

✿ Twenty

'*Twas the night before chemo and there Bridget* was, traversing the back roads of New Falls, having waited until Randall and Aimée were sound asleep, having sneaked from the house and into the garage. She'd put the transmission of Randall's S–600 into reverse and quietly rolled it out to the sloping driveway, then down to the road, without turning on the engine or even the headlights. And now she was headed to Dana's, so they could tiptoe into the city and find Bridget's lover, or rather the man Bridget had once slept with and had made love with and now only *wished* were her lover.

God, she thought, *I am pathetic.*

Dana was standing at the foot of her driveway, wrapped in

her long red down coat, because Dana had become such an animal lover lately that she wouldn't even wear faux, though for some oxymoronic reason, she saw no problem donning the down. How that irritated Caroline! Not to mention the local furrier, who still did a brisk business in New Falls.

"Talk about the car being a beacon," Bridget said as Dana climbed in. "Your coat can be seen from here to Long Island."

"It's freezing out. It's midnight."

"We'll stop and get coffee." She paused while Dana buckled her seat belt. "You're a good friend to do this, Dana."

Dana rolled her eyes. "Well, I couldn't have you going off and getting into trouble. It seems I have enough friends there already."

Between New Falls and the Upper East Side, Dana filled Bridget in on Caroline's hit man and Kitty's supposed insurance windfall. (They didn't discuss Lauren and Vincent because that was old news by now.) Then Dana told her what Sam had said about Chloe's broken engagement, and Bridget told her what Lauren had said. It wasn't until they'd merged onto FDR Drive that Bridget revealed their destination.

"We're going to the Pierre," she said, sipping the last of her Dunkin' Donuts coffee that had cooled off in the forty-minute trip. "I need to see my first husband."

Late night traffic slipped by them. It always amazed Bridget that so many people here in the States always had somewhere to go, day or night.

"I didn't know you had a first husband," Dana said quietly.

"*Non*," Bridget replied. "No one does. Not even Randall."

* * *

"You're sure you want to do this?" Dana asked after the valet took the Mercedes and they went into the lobby.

"I must see him one last time," Bridget replied. "I want to tell him in person about my cancer." She'd already told Dana that she and Luc had been childhood sweethearts, that they'd married too young, that they'd divorced. She did not tell her about Alain (to speak his name would be too painful) or that she still loved Luc, that she'd never stopped loving him, all these years (not that Dana wouldn't figure out that part by herself). As they stepped up to the front desk, Bridget said, "Luc's my last link to my home. I'm sure you know what I mean."

Dana said she didn't know much of anything lately, except that her friends seemed to be having lives far more interesting than hers.

A clerk promptly appeared.

"Monsieur LaBrecque," Bridget said, "Monsieur *Luc* La-Brecque."

"One moment please."

Bridget tapped her foot in time with the tap-tap of the clerk's fingernails on the computer keyboard. Dana still clutched her coat as if it were January and New York were Fairbanks. Together they resembled two spoiled housewives on a dubious mission.

"I'll ring him now," the desk clerk finally said.

Bridget grasped her new Kooba handbag in one hand, Dana's arm in the other. She hoped Dana couldn't tell she was holding her breath.

The clerk turned his head and said a few words into the phone, then a few more.

They waited.

He spoke again.

They waited some more.

Then he turned back and, with a small smile, said, "Mr. LaBrecque will be down momentarily. The Pierre bar closes at one, so may I suggest you wait in the lobby?"

"Bridget."

The sound of his voice—the sound of his voice saying *her name*—brought tears to her tired eyes.

"Luc," she replied. When she'd seen him last fall it had been years. He'd been thinner, older, yet then—as now—she had still seen the boy who had ridden the white horses alongside her father, who had woven a wreath of flowers for her hair on the day they were wed, who had proudly held their son on the day he was born.

Luc.

He always seemed like the happy, vibrant boy who did not need a wheelchair.

From the corner of her eye, Bridget saw Dana blanch. *Right,* she thought. *I forgot to mention the wheelchair.*

"This is my friend Dana Fulton." Dana said hello, then discreetly excused herself and crossed the trompe l'oeil muraled lobby, where she sat out of earshot, friend that she was.

"Bridget," Luc said as he rolled next to her. "Why are you here? Is everything all right? It is so late."

He was so close to her now, his heat and his being and his body that she once had so loved, that her tears could not stop, her tears could not stop.

"Come," he said, "*asseyez-vous.* Sit."

She followed his lead as she always had. He guided her to a chair in a dimly lit corner. She sat.

He touched her arm. "*Mon dieu,*" he whispered. "*Quel est erroné?* What's wrong?"

"*Mon coeur,*" she said, touching her chest. "It breaks when I see you. *Je suis désolé.*"

He leaned toward her; she leaned toward him. He held her; she cried softly.

"You look wonderful, *chérie.*" Then he pulled away. "And yet you are . . . sad."

"*Non,* not sad," she said. "I am happy to see you. I will always be happy when I see you."

He touched her cheek. "I was going to telephone tomorrow when my business is finished. Why have you come tonight?"

"We need to talk," she said. "Aimée is not going back to school in France. I'm afraid I will never see you again."

"She told me her plans," he said, lowering his voice. "It is for the best. Your home is here, Bridget. It has been for years."

"My home is with you, Luc."

"*Non.*"

"*Je t'aime,*" she said.

He put his fingers to his lips. "*Non,*" he said. "It would not work. I have a different life now. I love my wife."

There is a certain sensation that comes with loss that Bridget remembered from the day Alain died. It begins in your throat as a soft, gentle puff, a "lump," people called it, though nothing was there. Whatever it was, it was in her throat again now and had started to travel to her head and her heart.

I love my wife. Could he have been more clear?

"But . . ." she said, "but I have cancer."

He blinked. "What?"

She didn't respond, which she supposed was mean, but he had rejected her, so did it matter?

"Bridget," he said, touching her arm. "Is it bad? Is it true?"

Her eyes dried; her ache lessened. "Tomorrow I begin chemotherapy. I only wanted you to know. Just in case. Because if I do not survive, there will be no one to put wildflowers on the graves of my family, the grave of our son."

Then she stood up.

"Bridget," he said, "*Non. Ce n'est pas possible.*"

"*Oui,*" she said, then turned to look for Dana. The word "cancer" had certainly gained his attention, but suddenly it did not feel so well, *she* did not feel so well. She had wanted his love; she did not want his pity.

"Then is this the reason?"

"Reason?" she asked. "What reason?"

"Is this why that man came to my home asking many questions? Bothering my wife? Bothering my daughter?"

She stood still, perfectly still. "A man?" she asked. "What man? What questions?"

"He asked questions about you. About when we were young. Does it have anything to do with you having cancer?"

A wave of dread rose like a groundswell. It was cold and damp and a shiver ran through her. She swallowed air. "You should have called me," she said.

"I am sorry."

Sorry? She doubted he was sorry. He'd obviously been more concerned about *them*, his wife, his daughter. She closed her eyes. "What did the man look like?"

"It was a month ago. Maybe more. He was an American."

"Was he old? Was he young?"

"He wore one of those *stupide* baseball hats Americans love. I don't know which team. But he had gray hair. And a mole. Yes. He had a mole right here." He pointed to the side of his nose. "He frightened my daughter. I warned him not to return."

She pulled her coat more closely around her. "If he comes back," she said, "tell him I said to contact me." Then she closed off her pride and her emotion, said *au revoir*, and went to find Dana.

"All these years I have thought I still loved him," Bridget said when they were back in the silver Mercedes, heading north.

"But you stayed here with Randall?"

"When I tried going back, Luc had another."

"I'm sorry," Dana said.

"It was my fault. He was my life and I let him go."

"Perhaps it was not meant to be. Perhaps you were both meant to be with other people."

"Perhaps," Bridget said, and then they rode in silence back to New Falls, her love and her thoughts all tangled together like the brush in the marshes back home in Provence.

Twenty-one

"*I can't imagine where she was going,*" Lauren whispered to Caroline the next day as she poured lemon water at the table at the club. "I called the house. I woke Randall up. He thanked me for calling, but said everything was fine."

"And so you did what?"

"I was worried, Caroline. Ever since Vincent's murder a pall has come over this town. I slipped out of the house. I drove past Bridget and Randall's. The front lights were off, as if no one was expected." She'd wanted to creep up to the garage and peer in the window to see if both the small and the big Mercedes were there. But Randall might have a security system, and how would she have explained if a siren went off in the night?

Caroline shook her head. "Bridget has been acting oddly, that's for sure."

Lauren nodded, glad that this luncheon had begun on such a melodious note. There was nothing like another friend's troubles to take the edge off your own. "Now," she said as tenderly as she could, "let's talk about Chloe. It's not permanent, is it?"

"The breakup? Not if I have anything to say about it. If she doesn't get married, what will she do?"

"What was her major in college?"

"I don't remember. It didn't seem important, once she'd met Lee."

They toyed with their glasses as if they held wine.

"He's been cheating on her, for godssake. There was a time when that sort of thing was handled with tact. Now everyone seems to feel they're entitled to be happy. No matter what they screw up in the process."

"Or who they hurt," Lauren said, thinking of the many times she hadn't been thinking about Bob, when she'd been consumed by the fervor of the friction of the sheets in the Helmsley. "Caroline," Lauren continued, "is there some way I can help?"

Caroline gazed out the expanse of windows toward the first hole. "Well, if Jack can't get him to change his mind, someone will have to send back the engagement presents. I won't have the stomach for it."

Thankfully most upscale stores now sent only cards and not gifts, which saved so much trouble in case of duplicate or unwanted presents or in situations like this. Lauren had helped Dory navigate nearly three hundred gifts, so she was well-versed in the system.

"Consider it done," Lauren said. "Though we'll first pray that Jack can set things straight."

"Thank you," Caroline said, her amber eyes lowered in rare humility. "At least I have one friend I can count on."

They fell into silence, Caroline somber, Lauren with thoughts turned to Dana and Bridget. It would be nice if they'd help with the gift returns, if they'd soon grow weary of assisting poor Kitty, if life could go back to the way it was, when what mattered most had been shopping and lunch.

Just then a scuffle erupted at the door.

"She's *lunching*," the maître d' insisted, his voice rising in a how-dare-you tone.

Then Bob's favorite caddy shoved the maître d' and rushed into the dining room, his forbidden spikes puncturing the high gloss of the hardwood floor. It took a moment for Lauren to realize he was rushing toward her.

"Mrs. Halliday!" he shouted. "Your daughter said you were here! Mr. Halliday collapsed on the seventh green! An ambulance is on the way!"

Her life would be better if Bob were dead.

How many times had Lauren pondered that? And was this her penance for such evil thoughts?

She sat in the VIP waiting area off the Emergency Room (Caroline had insisted—how could she say no?) toying with the brass grommets on the teal leather arm of the chair. She knew she should call the children, Bob Jr. and Marcia and Dory and the rest. (Had Dory been the "daughter" the caddy had spoken with? Was she at Lauren and Bob's house with the new baby, and if so, why?) But Lauren didn't want to think about Dory or any of the broadband of Hallidays right then. She told Caroline she'd wait to notify the others until the doctor brought news, until a diagnosis or prognosis or some kind of *osis* had been delivered.

What Lauren really wanted was time alone to savor the possibility of freedom.

She had a trust fund with money left from her parents (it was rather small—sadly, they'd had more status than money), that Bob had supposedly added to over time. As for him, he had investments and plenty of them. But how much would be hers, how much would go to his offspring if he died? She'd tried asking him once. It was Vincent's idea.

"Sooner or later, the old guy's going to kick it," Vincent had said. "Are you sure you're protected? Are you sure there's enough?"

Bob laughed when she asked, called her a dim-witted woman, said of course he'd seen to it that she'd be taken care of, that his net worth was sufficient to be spread all around.

Vincent told her she should have asked for specifics.

Vincent, she thought now. If only Bob had died before Vincent had taken up with Yolanda. Maybe they could have had a chance after all.

Still, she'd be "taken care of"; Bob wouldn't have lied. But what would she do? What would be the point of staying in New Falls if she had no husband? She could buy an apartment in the city, maybe that would be fun. But she'd have no friends there, and the city could be so lonely. She had friends on Nantucket, though they weren't there off-season. They'd be older, as she was, which would mean peace and quiet. The problem was, the family house had been commandeered by cousin Gracie years ago, and she was not big on welcoming guests. The few times Lauren had convinced Bob to go, they stayed at the Jared Coffin House in the center of town.

Would Bob leave her enough to buy a cottage on the island that had grown so pricey?

Before Lauren finished sorting her options, Caroline returned, bearing a bottle of Pellegrino. "Plastic," she said, holding up two cups. "Hospital regulation."

On the way to the hospital, Caroline had said it would be better if Bob had a heart attack than a stroke. "All that rehabilitation," she'd said. "And even at that, who knows what you're left with?"

So far, no one was saying exactly what happened, exactly what, if anything, Lauren would be left with.

Caroline poured water, handed a cup to Lauren.

"How long will it take?" Lauren asked as if Caroline knew more about the hospital than its fund-raising.

"I've pulled out all the stops. The best team is with him." The best team no doubt meant the most expensive, the physicians who were indebted to Caroline for her work on the gala, and were surely looking forward to the event this coming Saturday night.

This Saturday night? Good Lord, would it be appropriate for Lauren to go if Bob were dead or dreadfully infirm?

She sipped her water, swung her feet back and forth under the big leather chair, and tried not to think about the pale peach Karl Lagerfeld hanging in her closet. She'd bought it last month to wear to the gala and make Vincent regret that he'd chosen Yolanda.

"Bob's always taken such good care of himself," Caroline said over Lauren's thoughts. "This seems rather unfair."

Lauren didn't answer. They both, after all, knew there were many more things in the world less fair than Bob Halliday dropping dead.

Suddenly her feet stopped swinging. "I had an affair," Lauren said abruptly. "I told Dana."

Caroline was nonplussed. "It's not the end of the earth, Lauren. Plenty of people have affairs."

"Maybe. But not everyone's ex-lover is shot to death." She hadn't meant to tell her. Or had she?

"Please don't tell me you're talking about Vincent DeLano."

Lauren didn't answer.

"Oh God, Lauren. What were you thinking? That man was despicable."

Before Lauren could explain what she, indeed, had been thinking, a man dressed in green scrubs appeared in the doorway. "Mrs. Halliday?" he asked. "Your husband is going to be fine."

Lauren's eyes darted from the man in scrubs to Caroline, then back to the man again. "Fine?"

Caroline stepped forward. "Fine?"

The doctor nodded. "It isn't his heart. It wasn't a stroke. All his vitals are perfect. We'll run a few more tests, but right now it looks as if he had an anxiety attack."

"An anxiety attack?" Lauren and Caroline asked simultaneously.

Then Caroline added, "Well, that's impossible. What does Bob Halliday have to be anxious about?" Neither woman suggested that perhaps he'd found out about his wife and Vincent.

The doctor smiled and looked back to Lauren. "If you'd like to see him now, he's been asking for you."

Twenty-two

Bridget wore a ruby red silk camisole and matching capri pants with geisha girls hand-painted in rich, vibrant colors. Her outfit was accented by black marabou feathered slip-ons and topped with a black burnout velvet shawl. She camouflaged everything under a long belted trench coat in case she ran into Randall or Aimée while coming or going, then gave Dana a peek when she climbed into the car.

"If I have to have chemotherapy," she said, "I might as well do it in style." She didn't add that her attire was most conducive to managing hot flashes that plagued her on the hour, every hour. She didn't add that being a bit silly helped take her mind off Luc.

It wasn't until they were in the treatment room (*infusion*

room, the nurse corrected, to which Bridget said, *Quoi que, whatever*), and Bridget was in the recliner with an IV needle stuck in her hand, that she said, "I was thinking I could use a pedicure."

Dana laughed. "A pedicure?"

"Yes. Now."

"Now? Ah, excuse me, but you're rather busy at the moment."

"Actually, I'm not. All I have to do is sit here for what will seem like days. Which is why I brought my cuticle oil and my creams and my clippers and my polish."

Dana smiled with one side of her mouth. "And . . . ?"

"And do you feel like giving a pedicure to a cancer patient?"

Dana laughed again. "I guess it would be better than reading an old *People.*"

"Great. Everything is in my bag. It will divert me from picturing my head without hair, or from the fact that I'm scared to death."

Dana closed her eyes. "Bridget . . ." she began, but sudden tears clogged her throat, so all she said was, "Yeah, well, I would be, too." Then she moved to Bridget's bag, dug out a clear vinyl pouch filled with pedicure things, and tried not to wonder about her mother, and whether she'd been scared, too.

It was hard to believe that just eight days ago Caroline had been welcoming those who were her friends (and those who wanted to be) to her rite-of-spring luncheon. Now Lauren was right—ever since Vincent's murder, a pall had dropped over the town.

Before leaving the hospital Caroline decided to stop by the community relations office and check on last-minute reservations: She had to give the final head count on Wednesday, even though the gala now seemed rather trivial.

Trivial?

Totally, she was mortified to admit to herself.

Taking the elevator to the third floor, she began to navigate the maze of corridors with the confidence of a person who'd never feared hospitals, never winced at illness, never fainted when she'd seen blood. *Fainting shows weakness*, she'd once said to Chloe, though now she wondered if Chloe ever listened to anything her mother told her, and if so, how on earth she'd lost Lee.

Bypassing radiology, Caroline sidestepped a nurses' station and took a short cut through oncology. She might not have noticed Bridget if the ruby red pajamas had not caught her eye. But there she was, in Infusion Room Six, with a tube snaking from her left hand.

Caroline halted. "Bridget?" she asked. "What are you doing here?" As she stepped inside the doorway she saw Dana, frozen in what looked like a clumsy curtsy, crouched at Bridget's feet. But Dana wasn't curtsying, she was painting Bridget's toenails. "Good Lord," Caroline exclaimed, "what are *both* of you doing here?"

A quick pause elapsed, then Bridget said, "Hell of a place for a pedicure, *n'est-ce pas?*"

Like the rest of them, however, Caroline hadn't been born yesterday. It took her only a few seconds to figure it out. "*Cancer!*" she suddenly cried without an effort at nonchalance.

"Cervical," Bridget replied.

"So much for HIPAA," Dana added, a remark that Caroline did not find amusing.

"Well, good heavens, Bridget, why didn't you tell anyone?" Then she looked at Dana. "Well," she added, "I guess you did."

The foursome that had once been a fivesome, when Kitty was still married to Vincent, now seemed to have been cut to a twosome, a pair, which annoyed Caroline as much as the fact that she hadn't been told.

She supposed she should ask if Bridget was all right, so she did.

"I will be," she answered. "Dr. Wolfe is my doctor."

He was a Manhattan oncologist with privileges at New Falls. He was a generous donor, so Caroline said, "Well, you're in good hands then. I'm sure you'll be fine."

"I'll be at the gala, if you're concerned about that."

Naturally it had crossed her mind, but she said, "Oh, Bridget, the only thing that matters is that you get well."

"I intend to. For one thing, I want to be around to help Dana solve the mystery of Vincent."

"Mystery? Between us girls, I find the matter already quite tedious."

Then Dana said, "Speaking of which, Caroline, did you give Vincent money before he died? A loan perhaps?"

The IV pump beeped.

Caroline laughed. "Give Vincent money? Why would I do that?"

"I don't know. But your daughter mentioned something to my son . . ."

Straightening the shoulder chain that held her Dior bag

neatly in place, Caroline said, "Oh, *that.*" Was that why she'd been slighted? "Well, yes," she began with the story she'd concocted. "Vincent had asked Jack to invest in a new venture, but Jack turned him down. I didn't think that was fair. With or without Kitty, Vincent had been a friend many years, hadn't he? And now he had Yolanda, and I thought it was important to be supportive. It was also why I invited her to my luncheon, an act which none of you commented on, but I now gather several weren't pleased."

"It was your party," Dana said.

"You could cry if you wanted to," Bridget added, but Caroline sloughed off the remark.

"I hope I've answered your question," she said to Dana, narrowing her eyes in a slight glare. "Now I must get back downstairs. Bob Halliday is in Emergency. He had an anxiety attack. Good heavens, it seems as if everyone is falling apart." She wished Bridget good luck, then scurried out to the hall, away from the women who had once been her friends.

Dana didn't get home until late afternoon. As soon as she entered the house, she remembered that Steven would be home for dinner, and she hadn't planned a thing.

Sam greeted her with a smug smile.

"Please tell me you've whipped up a casserole and put it in the oven," Dana said. When the boys were young she'd had help. But now Dana ate most meals alone and did not need a cook to nuke a Lean Cuisine.

"Sorry," Sam said. "We can order pizza. How were things at the hospital?" he asked. Dana had told him about Bridget. In the absence of her husband, Sam had become a confidant.

"Fine." Then she related what Caroline had said about the money she'd given Vincent. "I don't know if it's true, but that's what she said. Now tell me, what have you been up to?"

"Me?"

"You." She dropped her bag and headed for the tea kettle, deciding to wait for wine until Steven arrived.

"Oh, nothing much."

He stood and watched as she filled the water, picked out a mug, dropped a tea bag in.

"Mrs. DeLano called," he said.

"Kitty?"

"She wants you to go with her tomorrow to visit her mother in Hyde Park."

"Well, I'm not going to do that."

"Why not?"

"Because I was away most of today and tomorrow is Wednesday and your father will be home tonight and I don't know his schedule and besides, I'd really like to spend time with you before you go back to school."

"So we can solve the murder."

"No," she said with a mother's smile, "so I can spend time with you."

"Maybe I have other plans."

"Like?"

"Like it's going to be a nice day and I'm planning to ask Chloe Meacham if she'd like to go for a walk."

"Chloe?" She did not ask what happened to his fantasy about Elise.

"Strictly business, Mom. Maybe she'll be more inclined to tell me stuff her mother won't."

"Such as?"

"Such as . . . well, come into the family room and see what I've done."

She turned off the burner under the kettle because she knew with Sam this could be an ordeal. Secretly, however, she'd rather have him home than doing the things his twin brother was no doubt doing in Cozumel.

With warm, motherly thoughts, she followed Sam into the family room, then quickly saw why his smile had been smug.

Twenty-three

"Samuel David Fulton, what in God's name have you done?" Dana peered around the room at the giant, easel-size sheets of paper that clung to the walls, the windows, and the drapes, that masked the montages of photographs of when the boys had been kids, that transformed the space she'd spent considerable time and a small fortune redecorating when the twins first went to college. The room now resembled a cross between a classroom and an interrogation site. On the sheets, notes and arrows and numbered lists had been neatly printed in different colored markers.

"Samuel?" she repeated because he was too busy smiling to respond.

"Isn't it great? Look, I have a system. The black ink signifies a before and after timeline of when Vincent was killed. It shows us everything that's happened. Then I used a different color ink for each potential killer and everything we know about them."

The first giant sheet covered images of the vacation in the Hamptons, 1993. It was scribed in red marker and was titled:

CAROLINE MEACHAM

"The luncheon began at twelve-thirty," Sam said. "We assume she was at home at eleven-thirty, but has anyone checked this out?"

He pointed to the word "ALIBI," which was followed by three question marks.

Then came "MOTIVE," along with the words, "*Gave money to Vincent?*"

The last line read:

MEANS — *Connected to a hit man?*

"Lauren Halliday," Sam continued, skipping over a few sheets to one printed in blue. Beneath Lauren's name he'd written:

ALIBI — *???*
MOTIVE — *Vincent was her lover.*
MEANS — *A close friend of Mrs. Meacham.*
      Hit man?

Dana glanced around. A poster for Bridget had been penned in green, Kitty in yellow, Yolanda, purple. Each commentary included added notes:

> BRIDGET HAYNES — *Cancer (is this connected?)*
> KITTY DELANO — *Inheritance (a surprise?)*
> YOLANDA DELANO —

Dana quickly noted that Yolanda necessitated big "???'s" from top to bottom.

The display was well-structured though a bit overzealous.

"Good grief," Dana said. "Why is Bridget a suspect?"

"She lied to the cops, Mom."

The fact that Bridget said she'd had a massage when she'd been scheduling chemo hardly seemed qualified to count as a lie. Dana skimmed the sheets for Rhonda and Georgette and a dozen or so others who'd been at the luncheon. "Well, at least you've been doing your homework."

"Pretty cool, huh? I'm missing a bunch of women, I know. I'm hoping Chloe will give me her mother's guest list."

"Samuel," Dana said, closing her eyes, choosing her words, opening her eyes again. "I applaud your efforts, really I do. But I don't think you should have all this . . ." She waved her hand as if conducting the New Falls Symphony, which, on second thought, perhaps she was. "All this *information* out here in the open as if it's an *exhibition*. These women are my friends, honey. I'd hate if they thought we're spying on them or, good grief, accusing them."

"But I figured they don't come over very often, and even

if they do, you don't entertain them in the family room, do you?"

It was true: When friends got together they sat in the kitchen for tea, the formal living room for wine. In New Falls, no one but family used the family room. One exception had been when Dana and Kitty had sat in the sunroom and the tree had come crashing through and Kitty had saved Dana's life.

Like most things, there were always exceptions.

"But other people come and go, Samuel. The cleaning people. Sometimes your father's business associates . . ."

"Well, can we leave the stuff up while I'm home?" Of the three boys, Sam was the least spoiled. Which was probably why he didn't pout long. "It helps me think, Mom. And I'll be back at school next week. Can we close off the room until then?"

He'd gone to so much work, it would be a shame to take it down.

She looked around again, studied the clues assembled in the room. Detective Johnson might do well to have a look at this. "So do you think I should go with Kitty to Hyde Park tomorrow?"

Sam shrugged. "Sure, why not? While I'm interrogating Chloe, you can work on her."

Dana dropped down on the couch that faced Yolanda's purple name. "We should focus on Yolanda, shouldn't we?"

"We should focus on every one of them, Mom. I know they're your friends, but it's pretty obvious one of them is a killer."

* * *

Caroline told Jennie she'd be in her bedroom and please do not disturb. No phone calls, no visitors, no matter if the entire hospital gala went up in smoke.

She was depressed.

After stripping off her Austin Reed pleated trousers, she pitched them onto the floor. The people in community relations had already known about Chloe and Lee. How had they found out so quickly? And what made her think she flew above the radar screen just because she was who she was?

This wasn't, of course, just about Chloe, and whether she, like her mother, seemed to be destined to live a loveless, unhappy life.

No, it wasn't just about Chloe. It was also about Caroline's friends: Lauren, Bridget, Dana. All the women who had come to her luncheon, who would be at the gala (the number of reservations had escalated since Vincent's murder; even the nobodies now wanted to chew on the New Falls social pie, no matter what it would cost them).

It was about all the women whose lives were *gentler* than hers, who had a friend who would give them a pedicure if they had cancer. Women who had husbands, lovers, some with both. Hell, even Lauren, sweet, timid Lauren, had danced under sheets that weren't hers, all in the name of passion, of love. All the while pretending to be Bob's perfect wife.

Caroline, of course, was a pro at pretending. She'd learned when she'd been young, whenever Mother had been stricken by a "sick headache" (translation: when Mother had ingested too many martinis), and Father had relied on Caroline to accompany him to the symphony or the gallery opening or the

charity event, or when he needed her to host dinner guests
Mother had invited then forgotten she had. Caroline had become a pro at pretending to be everything but herself.

God, she'd become such a cliché.

Moving to the windows, she pulled the drapes, shutting
out the leftover light of day. She went to the bed—the wide,
king-size bed that was just like the one Jack slept in, had
been sleeping in, down the hall in the guest suite for the last
dozen years. She peeled back the fluffy comforter, crawled
beneath it. She wished she had a small dog to cuddle against,
to feel its breath rise and fall, to feel its warm belly curved
against hers.

But Caroline did not have a dog and did not need one now,
any more than she needed a husband in her bed.

The simple truth was, Caroline needed a woman.

There, she told herself. *I admit it. I need a woman, damn it. But
not just any woman.*

"Elise," she whispered into the room.

More than Caroline wanted the gala to be a huge success;
more than she wanted her picture in *Town & Country* or the
Times or any of those; more than she wanted life—at least, her
life—Caroline Meacham wanted Kitty's daughter.

It was the real reason, of course, she could no longer be
friends with Kitty, the real reason she'd alienated Bridget and
Dana. Things had become so complicated; what else could
she have done?

If only she could go back to the beginning . . .

"My mother doesn't understand me," Elise had said one
summer afternoon before Vincent left Kitty. She strode

around Caroline's pool, a gin and tonic in one hand. Her other hand was planted on the shorts that rode too low on her slender hips, that rose too high up on her supermodel legs. Each time she tossed back her thick red hair, her firm, full breasts peeped from her too-tight spandex top as if searching for someone who might be interested.

At first Caroline averted her eyes, too startled that the young woman had aroused—yes, aroused—such primal thoughts.

How old was Elise anyway? Twenty-seven? Twenty-eight? Certainly it was sick for a woman over fifty to love, to lust, after a twenty-eight-year-old. (Not that anyone had questioned Vincent when he'd taken up with Yolanda, double standards being what they were.)

While Elise had talked and strode, Caroline focused on the age difference, not on the goddamn elephant in the goddamn backyard, the fact that the twenty-eight-year-old was a *woman*, for godssake, not a man.

Hello?

But when Elise claimed to have something in her eye and she straddled the chair where Caroline sat, bending close enough for Caroline to breathe her breath onto her breasts, to feel her ready sex radiate from between those silky thighs, Caroline decided it didn't matter if this was man or woman, beast or beauty.

She moaned a soft moan now, then stuffed a pillow between her legs, wishing Elise were there.

They'd fucked that afternoon. Hot. Fast. So wet that Caroline thought she'd expire from dehydration. It was the first time in her life that she'd lost control.

After that, once a week (God, only *once*), they met at Elise's apartment in the city and spent several hours doing what they did.

It was love, well, Caroline knew that. Beyond that, it made no sense at all.

She hadn't been there since the holidays, since she'd given Elise a diamond "E" from Tiffany's wrapped in a silver bow, since they'd talked about arranging a January respite in the Bahamas.

She'd left Elise's apartment feeling warm and alive. But as she'd stepped out of the elevator and began to cross the lobby, a gray-haired man approached. He had small eyes and a mole next to his nose. He brushed a light layer of snow off his worn nylon coat.

"Vincent DeLano is one of my clients," he said. "He's in search of some capital for a new venture. So he hired me to find out if you have any secrets—the kind your husband might not want let out of the bag. The secrets of the wives are usually far more enticing—and valuable—than those of the husbands. Don't you agree?"

She did not say a word, just stood like a Degas, poised between steps.

He smiled, or rather, he leered. "I didn't expect the mother lode. To find out that you're not only cheating, but that your lover is my client's daughter." His mole quivered along with his smirk. "Which I think changes the parameters of who should pay whom."

She made the deal, paid him for his silence.

Then she'd broken things off with the love of her life, to

protect Elise, to protect Jack, and more, to protect herself and her place as champion over her world.

And now Caroline's cheeks were wet with tears. She ached for love; she ached for *her*. Why couldn't they be together, now that Vincent was dead?

Twenty-four

They were back, but this time Lauren couldn't breathe. Maybe she was having an anxiety attack the way Bob had. Thank God the doctor had wanted to keep him in the hospital overnight. Thank God Bob wasn't there.

"We understand you had an affair with Vincent DeLano," Detective Johnson repeated as they stood in the foyer, predator facing prey.

She cursed herself for telling Dana. Dana must have tattled. Lauren had told Caroline only that afternoon, and no one else knew.

"Mrs. Halliday?" the cop next to the detective asked. "Is it true?"

Florence told them to get out.

The detective said, "If we leave, Mrs. Halliday will come with us."

Lauren tightened the ribbon around her ponytail. The ribbon was pink today, a perfect complement to her spun silk dress that had been crisp that morning but, like her, was tired now.

The cop turned back to Lauren. "Would you like to call your lawyer?"

Her *lawyer?* Her lawyer would be Bob's lawyer. No, of course she wouldn't like to call him. "Florence," she said, "Get Mrs. Meacham on the phone." Caroline would know what she should do.

"Is Mrs. Meacham your attorney?" the detective asked while Florence hustled away.

"I don't need an attorney," Lauren said. "I did not kill Vincent."

"But you're friends with Caroline Meacham."

"Well. Yes. Of course."

"Did Mrs. Meacham ever give you the name of a hit man?"

In spite of the tremor now tremoring all through her, Lauren laughed. "Excuse me?"

"A hit man. You know. Someone who is hired to murder someone else."

"I know what a hit man is, Detective. And no, Caroline didn't give me a name. I didn't need one, and I doubt she'd need one, either. Mrs. Meacham would not kill anyone any more than I would." Once again, her words sounded surprisingly steady, strong, convincing.

"Did Mrs. Meacham have an affair with DeLano, too?"

She paused.

She paused some more.

She tried to swallow his words, but they regurgitated.

Caroline?

And Vincent?

Florence saved the day, or at least a few seconds of it, when she waddled back into the foyer. "Mrs. Meacham is not available," she said.

The detective nodded. "Would you like to come with us now?" he asked Lauren matter-of-factly. "Or shall we wait until your husband gets home?"

Just then Dory appeared in her bathrobe and bare feet, little Liam suckling her breast. "I'll go with you," Dory said, and Lauren didn't stop her because this whole ordeal had just become too much for her to bear alone.

"All right, it's true." Lauren sat on a cold plastic chair in the interrogation room that really was the lunchroom because how often did the New Falls police need to interrogate?

They'd allowed Dory to sit at the far end of the room next to the vending machines. She did not flinch at Lauren's confession.

"It was over months ago," Lauren continued, her voice now small, the way she felt. "Then he started seeing Yolanda." She touched the Formica table, then withdrew her fingers. Criminals, after all, must have left germs.

"Were you upset by the breakup?"

"It was my idea." There was no need to say that he'd started seeing Yolanda before he'd stopped seeing her.

"Why?"

"It was morally wrong, Detective. I am a married woman. He was married, too."

"To the first Mrs. DeLano."

"Kitty," she said. "Yes." She sat there another intolerable moment, anticipating the question: *And Kitty was your friend?*

Instead he cleared his throat and asked, "What do you know about Mrs. Meacham's relationship with Vincent DeLano?"

She forced her lips into a smile. "I didn't know she had one."

"She never mentioned that she'd like to see him dead?"

"No. She thought he was despicable, though I really don't know why." If Caroline had slept with Vincent, she deserved some of this torture, too.

"What about anyone else? Has anyone you know been acting strangely since the murder?"

She wriggled, trying to get comfortable. But the cold plastic chair now felt like a big pile of resentment. Why had she been singled out just because she'd been in love? "This is a small town, Detective," she said. "What's considered strange in other places isn't always thought of as strange here."

The cop didn't reply.

"Take last night," Lauren continued. "Bridget Haynes was driving around in her husband's silver Mercedes. It was nearly midnight. I called to ask if everything was all right. Randall lied and said yes. Don't you think that's strange?"

The man didn't answer, but simply said, "You're free to go for now." He motioned to another cop, who stood up, scraped the metal legs of his chair across the floor, then escorted the ladies from the room.

* * *

"Dory," Lauren said on the drive home, where they would go together because Dory and the baby seemed to live there now without Dory's husband, "I hope you'll forgive me."

"Forgive you? For what? For having a little fun in your life? You had fun with Vincent, didn't you?"

Lauren smiled a half smile but held back the raunchy, heated details. "I'll have to tell your father now. In case everything comes out."

Dory shifted Liam to her other breast. Lauren felt a twinge of envy for the mother-baby love of which Bob had deprived her.

"Can I be there when you tell him?" Dory asked. "Can I please watch my father fall apart?"

Lauren said no, that would not be appropriate. But she felt secretly vindicated, pleased that at least one person seemed to be on her side.

After chemo, Bridget had made it into the house undetected. She was exhausted from stress, exhausted from worry, exhausted from the fact she'd barely slept the night before thanks to the man she'd once loved.

She'd been so exhausted she'd forgone the stairs that led up to the bedroom and lay down on a wicker sofa on the back porch, trench coat and all. The next thing she knew, Randall was gently shaking her shoulder.

"Bridget?"

She awoke to see his face shadowed by Detective Johnson. Quickly she sat up, blinked a few times, then tried to tuck the marabou-feathered slip-ons under the couch.

"I guess you remember Detective Johnson?"

"*Mais oui*," Bridget replied, extending her hand, remembering what she wore, and praying no one would offer to help her take off her coat. "*Qu'est que c'est?* I am sorry. I was napping." She fluffed her curls, moistened her lips. "You have more questions?" she asked with her best imitation of a coquette.

"Only one," the detective asked. "Where did you go last night?"

Bridget laughed. "*Moi?* Why, I was home last night, wasn't I, *chéri?*" She threw Randall a sunny, confident look.

"Actually," he replied, "I believe you went out around midnight. Your friend Lauren called because she'd seen my car. She wanted to be sure everything was all right." He sounded more bewildered than angry.

Still, she might have killed him if the cops weren't there. Then again, maybe she should kill Lauren. Would Caroline still have the name of that hit man?

She laughed again, her thoughts awhirl as if trapped in the spin cycle of a washing machine. "How forgetful of me. The truth is, I did step out for a few minutes."

Detective Johnson and his partner and Randall simply stared.

"Shall we go into the living room, *messieurs?* I've had a *trés terrible* day, and we can sit more comfortably there." It was twenty paces into the living room, twelve more to the couch, not nearly enough time and space to conjure a good excuse. "Please, everyone, sit down. I'm sure we can clear this up *vite, vite.*"

They waited for the truth. Luckily she had an option.

"Randall, *chéri*, sit next to me." She patted the cushion; Randall sat. Detective Johnson sat across from them; the other cop stood by the door, in case she tried bolting, she guessed.

She cast her eyes down to the hardwood floor. "I did go out last night, but not because of Vincent or his murder, if that's what you think."

"We're following up on anything that indicates unusual behavior," the detective said.

"*Oui*. I suppose in New Falls it is 'unusual' for a woman to go out at midnight and leave her husband home." She waited for the silence to heighten the drama. Then she raised her eyes in search of pity, and prayed that Randall would forgive her for what she was going to do.

"I have cancer," she said.

Ba-boom.

The announcement blew like an unexpected mine during peacetime.

"What?" Randall shouted, though perhaps he didn't realize that he'd shouted.

She closed her eyes and prayed again that if there was a God, He or She would allow her this teeny, manipulative transgression. "I have cancer," she repeated, taking Randall's hand. "Forgive me for not telling you, *chéri*. I did not want you to worry." But her prayer went unheeded: His toupee looked enormous.

She turned back to the cops. "It's cervical cancer. I've had surgery and radiation and my family has not known. Today I began chemotherapy."

"At midnight?" Randall asked. He was confused, of course.

She shook her head. "I went to see my good friend Dana Fulton. She's the only one who knew. I'd told her because her mother had cancer, too." She lowered her eyes again. "I was anxious about the chemotherapy. I could not sleep; I went to Dana's. She drove around with me."

It seemed convincing, even to Bridget.

Detective Johnson stood up. "Well, Mrs. Haynes. I'm sorry about your trouble. But I'm sure you understand we're investigating a murder. So we'll just go check out your story with Mrs. Fulton."

Bridget jumped—too quickly?—to her feet. "Are you going right now?"

"Well. Yes."

She nodded. "Good. Then I'll go with you. Let's get this over with once and for all so you won't have to trouble us any more."

Twenty-five

Bridget didn't have a clue how she would be able to signal Dana about what she'd told the cops. She only knew she must keep Luc's name out of this. She'd already hurt Randall enough.

Randall followed the police car, and Bridget rode with him.

"Is it true?" he asked.

"*Oui.* It is cancer, Randall. But I will be all right."

"I wish you'd told me sooner."

She looked at him, at the tears that now coated his eyes. It was impossible not to feel love when someone loved you so much.

"*Je suis si désolé,*" she said quietly. "I was trying to protect you." She stared back out the windshield at the taillights of the police car and hated that she'd been such a fool.

"You're the only one who knew," Lauren said to Dana. "I *trusted* you, Dana. I trusted you and you *told* on me." Her hands were on her hips, her small, oval face thrust forward, her cheeks pink, mottled with fury. She looked like a high school cheerleader whose boyfriend had gone to the prom with her best friend.

"Lauren," Dana said, "please try to understand. Someone killed Vincent. The police need to know anything that might be pertinent. Doesn't it bother you that his killer is still out there?"

"The only thing bothering me is that my friend betrayed me."

"Lauren, I'm not the only one who knew about you and Vincent. Steven knew."

"Steven? Your Steven?"

"Yes. That's how I found out. And there must be others. Plenty of our neighbors go to Harry's Bar when they're coming or going from the city. Plenty of our neighbors could have seen you at the Helmsley."

The doorbell rang. Dana rushed toward it. If Sam emerged from the family room where Dana had sequestered him when Lauren arrived, someone might catch a glimpse of his giant posters, his confluence of clues that pointed fingers all over town.

Good Lord, it was the cops.

And Bridget.

And Randall.

Dana smiled a tight smile. "Greetings," she said. It was too bad Caroline and Kitty weren't there, too. Maybe they could fill in some of the question marks in the other room.

They went into the living room. Dana closed the French doors.

"Mrs. Halliday," Detective Johnson said when he noticed Lauren.

"Detective."

Dana offered wine. Bridget was the only one who accepted.

After everyone but the cops had taken a seat, Detective Johnson asked, "Where were you last night, Mrs. Fulton?"

"Last night?"

"It's okay," Bridget interjected. "He knows about my cancer and the chemo. He knows I came to see you because I was upset."

"You have cancer?" Lauren asked.

Detective Johnson held up his hand. "Please, ladies. Allow me to ask the questions." He pitched a look at Bridget. "And please, don't answer for Mrs. Fulton." He turned back to Dana. "Last night," he repeated. "Where were you?"

Dana shrugged. She did not know how their trip to Manhattan could relate to Vincent's murder. It was Bridget's private business, after all. Already too much of their privacy had been leaked. "Bridget came to see me, just as she said."

"Because of her cancer?" Lauren asked. "Why didn't I know about it?"

"No one knew," Bridget replied. "Not even Randall."

Randall nodded.

"Did you know about Vincent and me?" Lauren asked suddenly.

Bridget smiled. "Of course. Everyone knows about you and Vincent. Really, that's old news." She sipped her wine, set down her glass, and stood up. "Thank you for clearing up my whereabouts for these nice gentlemen," she said to Dana. Then she turned to her husband. "Randall? I'd like to go home now and get out of these decadent clothes." She unbelted her trench coat and revealed the ruby silk pajamas, distraction, of course, her intent.

The cops, indeed, were distracted.

Randall stood up and said, "Okay, let's go."

That's when Steven opened the French doors. Instead of announcing, *Hi, honey, I'm home*, he asked, "What the heck happened to my family room? And why is it that every wife in New Falls seems to have murder on her mind?"

He thought it was a joke, of course. Steven had no idea what Dana and Sam had been doing while he'd been away; he had no way of determining if these were facts of the real crime, or notes for a criminal justice paper. He also didn't know that the people in the living room had not gathered for friendly cocktails.

"Murder is my business," Detective Johnson said as he stood up. "Glen Johnson with the New Falls Police Department," he said, shaking Steven's hand. "You must be Steven Fulton."

Steven shook, nodded, then turned his eyes to Dana, who did not know what to say. Sam stepped in behind him and said, "Sorry, Mom. I couldn't hear what was going on from the family room. I snuck outside and listened at the window." He pointed to the window at the far end of the room that had been opened to the fresh spring air. All eyes swung toward the window, then back to Sam. "I guess that's when Dad came home."

"And I guess this is when we are leaving," Bridget said, with a flourish of her trench coat as she attempted to cover the silk.

"I'm right behind you," Lauren said, "and I want details about this cancer before you get into your car." She rushed out after the Hayneses and shut the front door.

"Well," Steven said, "apparently I know how to clear a room. Gentlemen? Will you join me in a bourbon?"

"Thanks, but no," Detective Johnson said. "I think your wife has seen enough of us for a while."

"On the contrary," Dana said, because it seemed there were no more secrets, except where she'd gone last night with Bridget, and she would not tell them that. "You might be interested in seeing the data our son has compiled."

❧ Twenty-six

Hyde Park, New York, was famous as the birth-place of Franklin D. Roosevelt and as the "Summer White House" while he had been president. It was also known for the Culinary Institute of America, the Vanderbilt mansion, and the Clinton Vineyards, no relation to the other president. Three hospitals served the area, three newspapers, two libraries (plus the presidential one), and fourteen churches, only one of which was Catholic.

Ordinarily Dana would not be thrilled about a visit to a nursing home. Her father was close to eighty now—if he were still alive. He could be in a nursing home, but she didn't know about that, either.

No, she thought as she parked the car and followed Kitty toward the door, ordinarily she would not be thrilled to be there. This time, however, she was glad to have left town and the speculation and the yak-yak about Vincent's murder.

Kitty's mother was napping in the solarium, but they were welcome to wake her up, the nurse's aide at the front desk reported.

The corridor was wide and cheerful and carpeted. It was not littered with drooping-headed people in wheelchairs as Dana had expected, but was decorated with pastel still lifes of spring flowers and hazy landscapes of the Hudson Valley. If Dana's father were in a nursing home, it would probably not be this nice.

"Mom?" Kitty called out, and Dana followed her into a pleasant room that had been painted soft peach and was adorned with lush plants and a baby grand piano in the far corner.

"Mom" sat on the piano bench, the lone person in the room. She looked up and waved.

"I'm over here!" she shouted happily. "I see you've brought a friend."

Kitty kissed her mother's cheek. "Mom, this is Dana. Dana, meet my mother, Muriel Dalton."

It occurred to Dana that until then she hadn't known Kitty's maiden name. Then again, no one in New Falls but Steven knew she'd once been Dana Kimball and the subsequent burden that held. She took the woman's hand and smiled. "Hello, Mrs. Dalton." The woman was small and thin, the way Kitty had become in recent months. She wore a pretty blue-flowered dress and smelled like baby powder.

"Thank you for coming," she said to Dana, then dropped her hand and turned back to Kitty. "How are the children?"

"Fine. They send their love."

Apparently Mrs. Dalton didn't know the "children" barely spoke to Kitty.

"And Howard? How is Howard?"

Howard? Had she meant to ask about Vincent? Didn't she know they were divorced? Didn't she know the rest?

"Howard's fine, too, Mom. He would have come, but he's so busy with the nightclub."

Dana stopped herself from asking who the heck Howard was and what "nightclub" she meant. Maybe Kitty had a brother—the way Dana had a father—that she never spoke of for family-secret reasons.

"The aide said you were napping."

Kitty's mother waved her hand and laughed a whisper of a laugh. "When I'm not playing the piano they think I'm napping. That way they won't bother me."

Dana joined Kitty in a nod as if they both understood.

"Would you like me to play now?" Mrs. Dalton asked. "Would your friend like my Glenn Miller rendition?" Her eyes twinkled from either excitement or medication.

"That would be nice," Dana said before Kitty had a chance.

Mrs. Dalton smiled again. She lifted her hands over the keyboard, then began to play. "Moonlight Serenade," she said, but the sounds emitting from the piano were nothing like the classic, nothing, in fact, like music at all. The gnarled fingers plinked and plunked and struck one mis-chord after another.

Dana glanced at Kitty, who averted her eyes, folded her

arms, and walked to the window. Dana sat down and waited for the time to pass.

Later, back in the car, Kitty thanked her for being kind. "I should have warned you," she said. "My mother's mind is gone."

"But she seems so . . . so normal."

Kitty nodded, her eyes filling with tears. "She thinks I'm my sister, Alice."

"Alice? I didn't know you have a sister."

"She lives in Baton Rouge. She married a musician that my mother adored."

"Howard."

Kitty nodded. "Alice hasn't been in touch for years. She's dead, for all I know."

Well, that was something Dana could relate to. "It's a nice place, though, where your mother is. It must be expensive." The last sentence popped out like a cold sore.

"It is," Kitty said. "But Vincent was paying for it."

Vincent?

"It was part of the divorce," Kitty added. "In lieu of alimony, he was ordered to pay my mother's long-term care."

"But I thought he was broke . . ."

"Men like Vincent are never completely broke."

Dana mulled that over as if she were Sam. Did any of this make sense? If Kitty needed Vincent to support her mother, why hadn't she told the police? Wouldn't it help prove her innocence?

With both hands on the wheel and her eyes on the road,

Dana thought back to something she'd learned from her father: Examine the pieces of a story before trying to put them together.

She reverted back to the beginning. *The former wife of futures trader Vincent DeLano was found standing over the corpse, a trickle of blood oozing from his left ear, a gun slack, still smoking, in Kitty's right hand.*

She thought about Kitty's explanation, about the rug dealers who supposedly had been coming from Newbury Street.

And then Dana had an idea.

"Kitty," she said, "not to change the subject, but I've been thinking of doing Michael's room over now that he has his own place. I remember what you said about the Newbury Street rug dealers. Maybe I'll give them a call. What's the name of the shop?" She thought she sounded believable. She didn't expect Kitty would cry.

"Well, this is just great," Kitty said. "You think I killed him."

"What?" Dana asked. "No!"

"Yes you do. Why else would you ask about the rug dealers? You want to check out my story. You want to see if they exist, if they were really coming that day."

"Kitty . . ."

Kitty shook her head. "Never mind. Just take me home. God, Dana. If you don't believe me, who will?"

Dana sighed. "Well, you have to admit . . . between your mother and the surprise of the life insurance . . ."

"I knew about it, all right? I knew about the insurance. The truth is, I *insisted* on it. For my mother's care if he died. I didn't tell anyone because what would they think? The police? My kids? The whole freaking town?"

"You won't believe this, honey, but Chloe didn't really like Lee Sato very much. She was only going to marry him because her parents wanted her to."

Dana dropped her pocketbook on the kitchen counter and looked at her husband. They'd stayed up too late last night, reviewing Sam's charts and facts and contemplating theory after theory with the police, who revealed there simply was no evidence—no latents, no hair, no fibers, nothing that would do *CSI* proud. The ballistics report, which wasn't yet complete, seemed to be all they might have to go on.

Steven had told them this was way more fun than working or being retired like his father in Boca Raton.

He handed her a glass of wine though it was only three o'clock in the afternoon. She took the glass, kicked off her shoes. She wanted to ask Steven if he thought they should track down the rug dealers, but she was too tired of all the nonsense now. So instead of asking about rugs, she asked about Sam.

"Believe it or not, he had a date."

"A date? With whom?" She didn't know why she asked. She always hated when Sam's brothers teased him for being more into books than girls.

"He only said it was undercover work. I asked 'under whose covers?' He said I wasn't funny." Steven grinned. "I think I was, though."

Dana sat down at the kitchen table and didn't ask if he

thought the date might be with Chloe. Steven leaned against the counter. She never would admit it to the feminist movement, but she felt better balanced when her husband was at home, as if he were the ballast of the ship that was their house.

"Kitty's mother lives in a pretty fancy nursing home," Dana said. "Paid for by Vincent's money."

"Who's paying for it now?"

"The insurance money will. As soon as Kitty receives it."

Steven swirled the ice cubes in his bourbon. "Honey, are you sure Kitty didn't kill Vincent?"

Maybe the real reason Dana hadn't mentioned the rugs was that she didn't want Steven feeling as doubtful as she did now. Kitty, after all, had saved her life once with the tree in the sunroom and the CPR. "Well, to be honest, I'm not sure. But I do think she deserves a fair trial. A competent defense."

"And?"

"And this loser Caroline hired is not going to help."

"I'd be a little nervous about that anyway. What with the hit man and all."

"The 'alleged' hit man, Steven. Good grief, these women are our friends. Listen to the way we're talking about them."

Steven laughed. "Our friends have always been entertaining. It's funny, though, I never trusted DeLano. I think that spilled over onto his wife. Sorry."

"You never trusted Vincent?"

"No. I always thought he was sneaky, and I thought Kitty was too needy. I know you think she saved your life, but the truth is, I'm sure you would have come to on your own. As for Kitty and Vincent's kids, Marvin is a dork and Elise is a hottie, but they're both a little strange." He grinned again because, unlike many men, Steven was happy. "Now if you'll excuse me, I'll go add the nursing home to Kitty's growing list of motives on her chart."

Dana sipped her wine. "Wait," she said. "There's something I want to mention."

He waited.

"A lawyer," she said. "For Kitty."

"What about it?"

"I'd like to help her. I'd like to find someone capable. Wasn't Michael in school with someone whose father is a criminal attorney? Remember? We saw him on the news once, in a high-profile case."

"I'm sure he charges a small fortune. I didn't think Kitty has money anymore."

"She doesn't. I'd like to pay his retainer. She can pay me back when the insurance money comes through."

He really laughed that time.

"Honey," she said, "I'm serious. I think Kitty would do it for me if the situation were reversed."

"You mean if you murdered me? Now you're scaring me, Dana." Still, his laugh didn't abate.

"I'm serious, Steven. You know what I mean."

"Yes, I do. And I'm sure you'll know what I mean when I say that you'll pay for Kitty's attorney over my dead body, not DeLano's."

She was about to debate him when Sam walked in the door, apparently finished with his date with whomever. "Are you guys expecting a visitor?" he asked.

Steven said, "No, why?"

"There's some guy in our driveway who asked to see Mom. I would have invited him in but we have steps."

"Sam," Dana said, "What are you talking about?"

"We have steps. He couldn't get up them in his wheel-chair."

Twenty-seven

Good Lord, it was Bridget's first husband no one knew about. His wheelchair was parked in the driveway, a gypsy van idled at the curb, a short metal ramp angled from the side door to the pavement.

Dana asked Steven and Sam to wait inside.

"Dana Fulton," he said. "I'm so glad it's you." His English was better-enunciated than Bridget's when Randall was around.

"Monsieur LaBrecque," Dana said as she shook his hand. It was large, cool, dry. "How did you find me?"

"I remembered your name. I knew Bridget lived in this town. It's not hard to find anyone."

The indispensable Internet, as Sam had called it.

In the late day sun, shadows sketched his face like thin, charcoal-like lines. It was apparent that he'd been great-looking once; he was good-looking still. He had a thoughtful smile and sincere eyes. Traces of muscles that had been robust formed the shoulders covered by his jacket. "I'd invite you inside . . ." Dana began.

"*Non,*" he said. "I do not intend to stay. I only want to ask about Bridget. She said she is sick."

"Yes."

"Will she be all right?"

"I don't know. I hope so."

"And other things?"

"Other things?"

He paused as if to collect his thoughts. "I told her about the man who came asking questions. She did not want to talk about it. But it left me with a bad feeling."

A cloud of discomfort draped itself over Dana like a delicate stole. She folded her arms. "Monsieur LaBrecque. How may I help you?"

"I have known Bridget almost all of my life. When a man asks questions, I worry. I worry for Bridget. And for our daughter."

"Your daughter?"

"Aimée. She is my daughter."

Dana didn't know what to say.

Luc LaBrecque nodded. "Ah. I see Bridget hasn't told you. She hasn't told me, either. But the truth is, Aimée looks just like my mother." He smiled with soft recollection, then said, "A long time ago, my life with Bridget became crowded by pain and loss. We both were empty. Still, we needed to be loved. And so we found others to love us when we had no love left inside us . . ." His sentence stopped before it was completed.

"I think Bridget will understand that. In time."

He smiled almost sadly. "How do you say it in English—life goes on. Things happen, but life always goes on."

Dana stared long after he had stopped talking. In a few short moments he had shared more of Bridget than Bridget had in the years she'd known her.

But was Aimée really his daughter, not Randall's?

Then Luc handed her a small card. "Please. If something happens, please contact me. I will always care about Bridget, but I cannot be there for her the way she might want. Tell her I am sorry for that. And tell her I will tend to the wildflowers, the way I've been tending to them for years." He turned his chair around and wheeled back to the cab, drove up the small ramp that the driver unhitched, then slid the big sliding door closed.

Yolanda was tired. She'd spent most of the day scrubbing *R.I.P. Vincent DeLano* off the back windshield of the Jag because her plan had backfired. Instead of feeling satisfied, she'd only been embarrassed.

"It's about the paint on your back window," Mrs. Fulton said when she banged on the window. "I don't know how to say this, but . . ."

But nothing. The red light turned green and Yolanda had floored it before Mrs. Fulton (wouldn't you know it had to be the nicest of the New Falls bunch?) could see that Yolanda's complexion had gone from bronze to pink. She was no match for those women, no matter what Vincent had thought.

"Marvin spoke with our attorney today," Elise said as she entered the family room and flopped onto one of four microfiber chairs that Yolanda had picked up at Raymour & Flanigan in Poughkeepsie. They were supposed to have been temporary, until Vincent had the funds to have the whole house decorated. But money was tight, then tighter, and the chairs became fixtures, arranged as four corners, points of a square: one for Yolanda, one for Elise, one for Marvin, the fourth for Vincent that Yolanda vowed no one else would ever sit in. "The only way we'll get the two million," Elise went on, "is if my mother is convicted."

"She'll be convicted. I know that upsets you."

Elise crossed her long legs and frowned. "I'm not a kid. I'm a grown woman with a fabulous career." Then her eyes got huge and wet. "But somebody killed my father. He wasn't perfect, but he was the best father I had, you know?" Tears splashed down her face and her nose began to run. "If my mother did it, I hope she rots in hell."

Yolanda leaned forward, took Elise's hands. "She will rot in hell, Elise. I promise that. And you and your brother will get the money."

"I don't need the damn money. I'm going to give my share to you."

She shook her head. "I told you. Vincent left me some cash."

"Which you don't want to use."

That was true. Yolanda didn't feel the cash should be spent. She loved her Vincent, but the money didn't feel like hers—anymore than it had been his. She would not, however, tell Elise about that.

"Besides, you'll need the money," Elise continued, "When the baby comes."

Yolanda left her chair and moved to the gray stone fireplace that had never been used, that still had plastic packing feet on the grate. "None of them know it yet, Elise. Not the other New Falls wives. Certainly not your mother." She rubbed her forearms, feeling a sudden chill.

Elise moved up behind her, wrapped her arms around Yolanda's softly mounding middle. "Daddy wanted you to have this baby so much," Elise whispered. "I can't speak for my brother, but I'll be here for you. Daddy really loved you."

"He loved me, not your mother?"

"He loved my mother once. Then he loved you."

Yolanda patted Elise's hand and said, "I am so lucky to have you for a friend."

Elise said, "Likewise," and then she said she had to get back to the city for an evening photo shoot, but suggested Yolanda take a morning train in and they could shop for baby things, her treat.

Dana knew how to Google so that was where she started.

Oriental Rug Dealers Newbury Street Boston

A list quickly appeared; she got to work on the phone, grateful that Steven and Sam had decided to go to the practice range at the club to hit balls. She didn't want either of them—especially Steven—thinking she now doubted Kitty.

"Hello. I live in New Falls, New York, and you've been recommended . . ."

One after another said they would not go to New York, it was out of their territory, as if they were pretzel cart vendors in Manhattan and were not allowed to encroach on someone else's corner.

Bangs and Holfield was different.

"Yes, we have several clients in New York," a pleasant woman said.

Dana held her breath. "I live in New Falls," she said. "In fact, you were recommended by my friend Kitty DeLano. I believe she's been trying to sell you a number of carpets." She waited for a reply.

"I'm sorry," the woman said, "I'm not familiar with that name."

Dana hung up, tried a few more.

"We can't go to New York."

"Can you drive to Boston?"

And then, "Oh yes, Mrs. DeLano. How is she doing? We went there last week, but something terrible had happened. Police cars were everywhere. I phoned to reschedule, but she said she'd have to get back to us. Perhaps we could take care of your business at the same time . . ."

Dana said, "Thanks. I'll let you know." She hung up the phone with verification that Kitty had been telling the truth.

Twenty-eight

She didn't care what Steven said.

Whether it was out of guilt because Kitty had once saved her life (would she really have "come to" on her own?), growing doubts about Bridget (of all of them Bridget was her best friend, wasn't she?), or just because Dana was angry that Steven had grown up in a functional house and didn't know what real suffering, real anguish were, Dana decided to hire an attorney for Kitty—one who might at least determine who had pulled the trigger.

The rug story had solidified Dana's resolve.

Dana, however, had never gone against Steven's wishes. Well, there was the time when she'd talked Michael into

Northwestern for grad school when Steven was insisting that he go to Wharton, Steven's blessed alma mater.

But Michael had already gone to Choate and Yale, and Dana had wanted him to get out of New England. She'd wanted him to experience life in the Midwest, close to where she had been raised, close to things that had mattered when she'd been young, museums, music, theater—not that Michael was like her.

She'd claimed victory over Steven. It cost her three weeks of cold shoulder and two years of occasional glib remarks that were out of character for him.

And now, in addition to the dollars and cents, she had no idea what this would cost her. Bridget might suggest that Dana offer a little extra sex. But she would not tell Bridget, because whom could she trust?

"Sam," she prodded the next morning after Steven left for his office and not the airport for a change. "Wake up. I need your help."

A shower and two Starbucks later Sam drove his Wrangler into the parking garage adjacent to the Wall Street building where Michael worked.

"I can't believe you just didn't call him, Mom," he said as they crossed from the garage into the building. "If he remembers the guy's name, he could have told you on the phone."

"I'm hoping the lawyer might see us if he knows we're in the city, if he knows this is important."

"If there's a fat chance he's available," Sam said with a wry smile.

The office was black and white, pewter and glass. Dana felt a swell of pride that Michael—her son!—had already achieved so much. And then he came into the reception area wearing the Armani they'd given him last Christmas. He looked so handsome! So successful!

"Mom?" he asked. "What's wrong?"

"Nothing," Dana said, toning down her smile. "Everything is fine. But I need the name of an attorney for Kitty DeLano. I was thinking about the man whose son you were in school with."

Michael folded his arms and looked at Sam, who shrugged. "You drove into Manhattan to ask me someone's name?"

"Well. Yes. Or rather, Samuel drove."

He eyed them both. "I'm really busy, Mom. Besides, do you think it's a good idea to get involved?"

She'd forgotten he was Steven's son as well as hers.

"Name, please."

He sighed an old man's sigh. "Mom," he said again. "I can't."

"All I need is for you to call him for me. Set the stage. You know?"

"No," he said too quickly.

She blinked. "No?"

"The truth is, Dad already called this morning. He warned me you might try to do this."

Someone must have turned the heat up in the room. Dana brushed the slow burn on her cheeks and leveled her sights on her eldest son. "You're telling me your father told you not to help me?" Steven, her perfect husband? Father of her perfect children?

Michael laughed with hesitation.

Sam laughed with nervousness.

Dana was so angry, she didn't say good-bye. She spun around and stomped back to the elevator. Sam caught up with her just as she stepped inside.

"Mom . . ." he tried with an effort to appease.

But Dana shook her head. She didn't want to talk to him, to any of them. For the first time in forever, Dana felt like an unappreciated, unimportant, uneverything-ed wife.

"We could stop for lunch somewhere if you want," Sam said as Dana marched toward the garage. He was such a sweet boy, Sam. If *he* had known the name, he would have shared it with her.

She shook her head again, stepped off the curb, and waited for a limousine to pass. As it did, she did a double-take. "That looks like the Meachams' car," she said, forgetting she didn't want to talk to anyone.

"Yeah," Sam said. "Maybe Mr. Meacham came downtown to plead with Lee Sato. The Sato offices are right up the street."

They crossed and went into the garage. Dana might have suggested that perhaps it was not Jack, but Caroline. Then she decided that Caroline was a lot of things, but she was above stooping that low.

Caroline couldn't believe she was stooping so low.

She'd stayed awake most of the night thinking about Elise, thinking about Chloe, and cursing Lee, because he was a man and most things wound up being their fault. She also was worried that Dana's son might try to insinuate himself onto her rebounding daughter. Sam was nice enough, like all the Fulton boys, but he wouldn't amount to anything out of the ordinary. He'd be rich, but not rich enough; he'd be connected, but not connected enough. He'd be just another New Falls kid.

He wouldn't be a global player.

Which brought her back to the cursed Lee and the need to patch things up. Because at least one thing in her life simply had to go right.

Jack had been useless. Of course, his idea of trying hard was to leave Lee a couple of voice mail messages. He hadn't called his driver and hotfooted it into the city for a face-to-face showdown for which Caroline was now prepared to stoop so low.

They made it downtown in record time despite the morning rush. Gerald knew not to pussyfoot around when Caroline was perched on the backseat.

He curbed the car at the World Financial Center where the Sato family business held court.

She told him not to move in case her party was unavailable. Then, her pale aqua cape stating her presence, she clipped across the esplanade, paraded past the imposing palm trees in the vaulted Winter Garden, flashed her ID at security, and headed toward the bank of elevators as if she did this every day.

He was in the office, but tied up in a meeting, the attractive, young woman at the front desk said. Caroline wondered if Lee was banging her in addition to the Russian.

She checked her watch: "I'll wait," she said and took a seat in the reception area, where she looked out at the thirty-story view.

And wait she did.

One hour, then two, then three, Caroline waited. She sucked in her fury and her pride. She resisted tap-tapping the toes of her caramel calfskin Torrini pumps, or sliding out of her cape in an effort to get comfortable. She sat and waited while one suit after another strode past her. The men nodded, the women didn't. They all were young. They all acted as if they were important.

At one-twenty-three Lee emerged from wherever he'd been hiding.

"You're still here," he said.

She did not stand as he approached. "I won't go home without an explanation."

"Your daughter has my explanation. Other than that, it's not your business, Caroline."

From the beginning he had called her that, before she'd had the chance to say, "Oh, don't call me Mrs. Meacham. Please, it's Caroline." Lee had been rude that way. Entitled via his money.

"You dated my daughter a long time. She is crushed beyond belief."

A young man armed with a BlackBerry passed. Caroline supposed she might have—maybe should have—been embarrassed to be sitting in the reception area having a private conversation, but Lee did not seem inclined to invite her to his office, and for once her mission was more important than her shame.

He sat down in the steel suede chair beside her. "Chloe is

not crushed. She's pissed. She's strong, though, like her mother. And she will go on."

Caroline stared at the marble floor. "Can't we work something out?"

"Well," he said, "I don't know what you mean."

"I mean what if I convinced Chloe it was all right for you to have other women, that it might even be good for your business, but that she is the only one you really love."

"Caroline," Lee said, "don't do this."

"She'd listen to me, Lee. She always does."

"No, Caroline."

"What if my husband's business could help you some way? He often learns things through his associates . . ."

Lee held up his hand. "If you're talking insider trading, Jack Meacham is the last person I would count on. After all, he is married to you."

She snapped her face around until it met his. "How dare you," she hissed.

He laughed.

He laughed!

"Caroline," he said again, this time standing up, "Nice try. But please go. Before you embarrass us both by offering your body as a last-ditch attempt to drag me back into your wretched fold." He turned on his well-polished heel (three inches—he was short, though that was hardly adequate consolation) and swaggered away, leaving a trail of chuckles in his wake.

"Well let me tell you one thing, Lee Sato." Caroline leaped from the chair and shook her fist at the air. *"I wouldn't fuck you if you were the last peon on the planet! You were never good enough for Chloe.*

Never!" A spray of spit spewed from her mouth. She quickly dabbed it away, then cupped her hand and shouted, *"And another thing, you jerk! She's going to keep the fucking ring!!!"*

He waved his hand without a simple glance back at Caroline. Then he turned a corner and disappeared from the lives of the Meachams of New Falls.

Twenty-nine

The worst part was, of course, that Steven had second-guessed her, that he'd known Dana would go to Michael even after he'd said no.

How should she, could she, would she deal with that? They fought so rarely, this was foreign turf.

But he hadn't trusted her! He'd gone ahead and expected she'd defy him. *How dare he!*

Well, of course, she *had* defied him.

So . . .

So she fixed some tea and resigned herself to remain perplexed just as the phone rang.

Kitty.

Oh, great.

"I won't need that lawyer after all," she said.

What?

"They've dropped the charges, Dana. They know I didn't kill him."

Was this all a dream? Was it still last night and was Dana still asleep and had this morning never happened? It would explain a lot.

But Kitty was saying something about ballistics, and how they didn't match her gun and that things were finally going to go her way.

"Now they can't deny me the insurance settlement. Now my mother will be fine."

Dana knew that last part would be a stretch.

The second thing she knew was that she had ignited a major upset in her marriage for no good reason after all.

"Yes, my wife and I were friends with Kitty and Vincent DeLano. But that has nothing to do with who killed him."

Lauren stood in the hallway outside the hospital room. She couldn't breathe again. She held her hand to her throat, wishing she had on her pearls, wishing she had something to toy with while her husband and the detective (*him* again!) conversed.

She supposed she should be grateful that the nurse had tipped her off by saying the cops were there.

"We'll decide what does or doesn't have to do with murder," the detective said to Bob.

She wondered if the detective had made a special trip to see Bob, and if so, dear God, why. She leaned against the wall.

She would have run to the stairway but didn't think her legs could carry her that far.

"And I'm telling you," Bob said with insistence, "we don't know anything about it." His mouth must be stretched white and terse, his glare arrogant and condescending.

"Do you know where your wife was from eleven in the morning until one o'clock the day DeLano was shot?"

"Why do you ask? DeLano's ex-wife killed him, didn't she?"

"As it turns out, he wasn't shot with her gun. So the playing field's wide open."

"Well, you're wasting your time here, Detective. My wife is as timid as a bird."

"Humor me."

"Okay. Well, I don't know where she was at eleven-thirty, because I was on the golf course. Where I usually am."

"And she wasn't with you?"

"My wife never got the hang of holding a club. No, I was with Jack Meacham. And Randall Haynes. Oh no, that's not right. We were going to be a foursome with Steven Fulton, but Fulton had to go out of town and Haynes canceled but I don't know why. So I was with Meacham and Lauren was not. Now, if you'll excuse me, Detective, I'd like to get dressed. My wife will be here any minute and I'm going home. Unless, of course, you bring on another anxiety attack."

Lauren could feel Bob's blood pressure rise, visualize his face, his neck grow pink then red, his one large purple vein begin to throb from his temple to his forehead. It was what happened whenever he was challenged, or when someone challenged one of his own. He might be a control freak, but at least he was loyal.

The cop let out a sigh. "Mr. Halliday, did you know your wife had an affair with DeLano?"

She didn't gasp, not really. She drew in a tiny whoosh of air that got stuck halfway down to her lungs.

Bob laughed. "You are out of bounds, Detective. If I were you, I'd be careful whose wife I accused of doing what. Aside from the fact it isn't nice, it also can be dangerous."

"Is that a threat?"

In the hall, Lauren slowly pressed her fingers to her lips to prevent herself from crying out.

"Call it advice. Financial advice, actually. Something to do with your pension. Did you know that my firm handles the pension fund of the New Falls Police Department? And those of many towns between here and Manhattan? You wouldn't believe how vulnerable those accounts are. Even in this day and age."

She knew she should stop them. She should stop Bob and she should stop the detective and she should stop everything right then and there, but she couldn't stop anything if she couldn't move.

"So I was right. It was a threat. Well, Mr. Halliday, if I were *you*, I'd be careful whom *I* accused of what. In the meantime, you might like to know that your wife admitted they had the affair."

The corridor warmed, the lights dimmed. Then Lauren's head started to swirl and she dropped to the floor.

* * *

Bridget had spent the whole morning in bed and well into the afternoon. Randall thought she was sick from the chemo. He'd offered to stay home from the office, but she'd said no, she had Aimée if she needed anything and it was Thursday so Lorraine would be there.

At two o'clock she was still staring at the ceiling, wondering what she should do next. Randall had been so kind last night, so worried about her cancer, so forgiving that she hadn't told him.

No, it wasn't the chemo that had made her sick, but the toxins of her guilt.

Suddenly there was a gentle knock on the door. "Bridget? Are you asleep? It's Dana."

Dana. Oh, *mon dieu*, could there be a better friend?

"Entrez, s'il vous plait," Bridget said. "Please, please come in." She pulled herself up, leaned back on the white satin-tufted headboard, then plumped the pillows around her as if she were lying in.

"Bridget," Dana said as she *entrez*-ed. "Are you all right? Lorraine said it was okay to come up."

"Oui, oui, I am fine. Really I am. But these are arduous days, are they not?"

Dana sat in the boudoir chair next to the bed. "Arduous, yes, that's a good word. You're not sick from the chemo?"

Bridget shook her head. "Only tired. Is that why you've come? To check in on me?"

"Yes, in part."

It was the term "in part," that made Bridget bristle, made her brace herself for what might be coming next.

"That and some news."

"Good news, I hope, for a change."

Dana shrugged. "Good news for Kitty. The ballistics report has come back from the lab. It wasn't her gun that killed Vincent."

Bridget sat up even straighter. "*Chouette!* So she didn't kill him!"

"Apparently not. The police are dropping the charges. She'll get the insurance money."

"Two million dollars. Whether her children like it or not."

"For her mother's care," Dana said, then went on to tell her about Mrs. Dalton and the nursing home and the piano.

"Maybe Kitty's kids will be nicer to her now. Or maybe she'll move to Poughkeepsie."

"Well, it still isn't over. I had hoped we could get her another lawyer, one who might find out who really killed Vincent."

"Oh," Bridget said. "*Mon dieu.* If I am sick about anything it is about hearing of that."

The room grew uncomfortably silent, uncomfortable, at least, for Bridget.

"Bridget?" Dana asked. "Do you know anything about it?"

She blinked. "*Excusez-moi?*"

"Now, please," Dana said, "don't get upset. But are you hiding something? I could tell you didn't want me to tell the police about the Pierre. And you lied to them when they first questioned you . . . and you called Thomas and asked him to lie for you . . ."

Bridget flung back the covers, grabbed her robe from the headboard, disentangled herself from the bedclothes, and yanked one arm through a sleeve that was inside-out. "*Mon dieu*," she muttered again, "I can't believe you ask me these things. To question me, as if you were the police." She dodged the boudoir chair and clomped to the chaise by the bay window that overlooked the lawn that sloped down to the Hudson. "After all these years as friends, now you think I am a *keeler*."

Dana's voice softened. "I didn't say that, Bridget. Please. I'm only trying to help you. If there's something—anything—that you need to hide . . ."

"All I was hiding was that I have *cancer*! If it were you, would you want it broadcasted? 'Dana Fulton has cancer! Just like her mother!' How would you like that, *mon amie*?" She wasn't sure if it was the word "cancer" or "mother" that made Dana pale, but Bridget nearly drowned in a new wave of guilt. "Dana," she said quickly, but Dana had stood up and was moving toward the door.

"I'm sorry, Bridget," she said. "Forgive me for being so insensitive. I seem to be saying all the wrong things these days."

"Wait," Bridget said again, padding after her, "I am the one who's sorry."

"I have to get home," Dana said as she exited the room and descended the stairs. "I'll call you tomorrow." She said it as if she meant it, but she didn't look back.

Bridget stood at the top of the stairs, her robe half hanging from her inside-out sleeve, just as Aimée came out of her room down the hall and said, "Maman! You must be feeling better."

🍂 Thirty

If Caroline's father saw her now, he would be disgraced.

"Carolina"—he always called her Carolina in honor of South Carolina where her mother had been born, the diva of Charleston and purveyor of too many mint juleps—"Carolina, why did you let that young man shame us?" he would ask. But her father had died two years ago, having outlasted her mother by a dozen.

Still, he was dead and couldn't know, could he?

Her neck was stiff and tears teased her eyes as she climbed into the limo that had dutifully remained halted at the curb.

The driver shut the door behind her, then circled around and got behind the wheel.

He cracked the privacy window. "Home, Mrs. Meacham?" to which she uttered a small "Yes," then he closed the window and she leaned her head back and let the tears drizzle down her flawlessly made-up cheeks.

The car glided into traffic, just another rich folks' limo, transporting another problem-free life of privilege. Surely no one on the outside would guess the last place Caroline wanted to go was back to New Falls, back to the whispers of everyone who now knew about Chloe, back to rearranging the seating for the goddamn hospital gala on the goddamn Windsor Castle-inspired goddamn velveteen-covered plywood.

Out of habit, Caroline reached into her purse, took out her cell phone, and checked her messages.

Rhonda Gagne wanted a gratis seat at the gala for her nephew who'd be in from Miami.

Jack said he'd be late getting home tonight in case she wondered. Sadly, she wouldn't have.

Chloe said, "Mom, you might not believe this, but Dana's son told me that the gun that killed Mr. DeLano wasn't Kitty's."

Reference to Vincent, to Kitty, only made Caroline think about Elise.

Argh.

Could she see her just one more time? Could she explain why she'd ended their affair?

Then Caroline reminded herself that Vincent had been Elise's father. Elise would not want to believe he was capable of blackmail, or, God forbid, that he wasn't without flaws.

With a small sigh of resignation, Caroline started to return Chloe's call. Then she thought of her own father, how she'd idolized him, how she'd thought he was perfect, how screwed up her life had been—maybe still was—because of it.

Then she thought, *Maybe if we want to be happy, all we must do is grow up. Grow up and live our own lives.*

Without another thought, she snapped the cell phone shut, leaned forward, and slid open the window.

"I've changed my mind," she told Gerald. "Take me to the Upper East Side."

If she could see Elise, if she could touch her again, maybe Caroline might make it after all.

"Are you feeling better?" Dory's soft voice asked now as she stood in the bedroom, next to the window seat where Lauren sat. Liam was in her arms.

After Lauren had passed out at the hospital, she'd been rescued by Detective Johnson, of all people, who'd heard the thud as she'd hit the floor. She'd been rescued, revived, then checked out by a doctor and proclaimed able to go home.

"Yes," Lauren replied now. "For the first time in years I feel as if I'm free."

"Of my suffocating father."

"Yes."

"Thank God. I thought it would never happen."

Lauren closed her eyes. "All the way home from the hospital he wouldn't speak to me. I said I was sorry. I asked him to forgive me. Still, he wouldn't speak."

"No one ever defied him, Lauren. No one ever dared."

"He will divorce me."

"Did he say that?"

"No. I told you. He wouldn't speak."

"Maybe he'll get over it."

"Not if his buddies find out. Not if they find out at the club."

"Men. They're more pigheaded than women."

"Much more." She didn't tell Dory she thought it was Dana who'd told the police. It no longer mattered. Lauren no longer needed to pretend that living with Bob Halliday was grand. If Dana was responsible for that, she should be thanked, not condemned. "I'm thinking of going to Nantucket. To get away from New Falls for a while."

The baby gurgled. Dory smiled and touched his sweet face. At least she seemed to like being a mother, if not a wife. "You'll be gone for the hallowed hospital gala?"

Lauren looked away. "I hardly think I'll be missed."

"Then I'll run away with you," Dory said suddenly. "The baby and I will run away with you."

"You can't! What about Jeffrey?"

"Jeffrey—and my father—can go to hell," Dory said. "And you and I will go to Nantucket."

"In that case," none other than Jeffrey said from the doorway where he suddenly appeared, "you might want this along for protection from the sharks." From his thumb and forefinger, he dangled a hefty-looking gun.

"*Jefffrey!*" Dory shrieked.

"*Get away! Get away!*" Lauren cried, snatching up all the pillows on the window seat and barricading them around her as if the downy innards could stave off the explosion from a thirty-eight.

"For godssake," Jeffrey said, lowering the gun, "Take it easy, will you?"

"What are you doing here?" Dory asked, her voice still pitched in a shout. "What are you doing with that gun? There's a baby here, in case you forgot."

As if on cue, little Liam began to cry.

"I haven't forgotten. I've hardly even *seen* him, Dory. Christ. Can't I at least see him?" He tried to step into the room, but Dory raised her hand like a school crossing guard in traffic.

"Don't you dare," she said.

He stopped. "Why are you going to Nantucket?"

"Why are you carrying a gun?"

Lauren shrank back against the window, watching the chess match unfold in front of her: queen; rook; little Liam, pawn.

"I found it in Caroline Meacham's water garden."

Lauren eased the pillows back. "What?"

"Gardeners find all kinds of things. Golf balls, winter gloves, snakes sometimes. Never dreamed I'd find a gun. It was caught up in a lily pad, like someone tossed it there."

"Dear God," Lauren said. "Did you show Caroline?"

"No one was home except for the maid. I didn't think I should tell her."

"What about the police?" Lauren asked. "You have to take it to them."

"Yeah, I planned to, as soon as I was finished with your lawn." He did theirs after the Meachams. Despite being "family," even Jeffrey knew that in New Falls, Jack and Caroline came first.

"Take it *now*, Jeffrey," Lauren demanded. "It could be a murder weapon."

He jerked up straight, looked at the gun with new respect. "Do you think it got Mr. DeLano?"

For a man with a college education, even one in landscape engineering, Jeffrey sometimes seemed a little vague. "It's possible," Lauren said.

The three of them stared at the gun as if it knew the answer.

"Do you think," Dory asked, momentarily forgetting she wasn't speaking to her husband, "that someone threw it into Caroline's water garden on her way into the luncheon?"

"Someone," Lauren agreed. "Or Caroline herself."

Caroline crossed the atrium of the apartment building as she'd done countless times, aware that Elise had never wanted a doorman—a "watchdog," she called it—who announced everyone's visitors and made covert notes of their personal lives.

A doorman, however, might know if Caroline would be welcomed, or if Elise had another lover by now.

Her gait slowed at the thought.

Caroline, after all, had been the one who'd broken things off—had been *forced* to break things off, thanks to that slime Paul Tobin and the two hundred thousand dollars she'd given him that he'd supposedly given to Vincent. ("He'll be pleased to know you're a lesbo," Tobin had told her. "The cash will keep him from spreading the word." An extra hundred thousand for Tobin was to "reassure her" that he wouldn't tell Vincent her lover was Elise.)

So she'd broken up with Elise to protect her—from scandal, from Tobin, from Vincent—and from having Elise learn the kind of man Vincent had become.

She stepped into the elevator, pushed the "up" arrow, and

told herself to not think about it now, because Vincent was dead and could no longer hurt them.

The ride to the penthouse was swift and unnerving. Caroline tiptoed toward the door marked "B" and nervously rang the bell.

She waited.

No one came.

She knocked.

Elise was usually home at this time, having worked three or four hours in the morning, then returned for a nap that would allow for an evening shoot—or, better, for a nightlife, a trolling of the sex clubs if she so desired.

Caroline stood there, pondering the words "Elise" and "desire" in the same sentence, when the door suddenly jerked open.

They stood there a moment, eye to eye, breath to breath.

"Caroline."

"Elise."

"What are you doing here?"

"I've come for a visit."

"A visit."

"Perhaps I should have called."

"Yes, you should have called."

A thin ridge of moisture formed on Caroline's forehead, under her arms, between her thighs. "I had business downtown. I took a chance." So it was true. Elise had another lover, someone younger, no doubt, someone more sultry. Perhaps someone she'd met in the clubs.

"But you and I have no further business together," Elise said. "You're the one who wanted it that way."

"I've changed my mind."

"Too late. The glow is gone. That's what happens when things are only about lust."

She started to protest, but a woman's voice suddenly came from down the hall.

"Elise? Do you have a guest?"

The voice sounded familiar.

Oh God, it was Yolanda.

"Mrs. Meacham?" the young woman asked after she came around the corner and practically stopped *dead*, a most apt description.

"I was in the neighborhood," Caroline said, her brain starting to stutter, her words clipped in staccato. "I'm bringing good news for Elise. The police have confirmed that her mother's gun did not kill her father."

With that, she smiled a perfunctory smile, gave a quick bow (*A bow? Oh God, had she really done that?*), swooped her cape over her shoulder, and traipsed back to the elevator as if her mission were complete.

Thirty-one

Steven was gone again, this time for a one-day meeting in Albuquerque where the parent company for a chain of resort spas was buying an "all-natural" aloe-and-shea-butter-based cosmetics business. "It seems like a perfect marriage," he said over an early dinner before he took off for the airport.

Dana said, "Oh, like ours."

They hadn't spoken about the issue of a new lawyer for Kitty. If Michael had told him that she indeed had planned to go against Steven's wishes, no one had told her.

Still, there had been a decided chill in the dining room, and she was glad he was leaving.

"I'll take the red-eye and be back Saturday morning," he said. "In time for the gala."

Right, she thought. *The freaking gala is this weekend.*

He kissed her cheek and he was gone and she retreated to the family room.

Sam was out; he'd mumbled something ambiguous about following up on a lead, though Dana wondered if he'd gone to see Chloe—the only one in New Falls over twenty-one who did not have a chart on Dana's family room walls, except Elise, but she wouldn't kill her father, would she?

Dana scanned the potential murderesses, the cast of their real-life whodunit. The evidence again suggested that Kitty hadn't done it, so who was left?

Lauren?

Caroline?

. . . Bridget?

The fact was, any of them might have.

Lauren had an affair.

Caroline knew a hit man.

Bridget had too many secrets, including if the father of her daughter was husband number *un* or *deux.*

They'd all been friends many years. Had their trust—like hers and Steven's—really been on tenuous ground? But wasn't communication between women usually more honest than between women and men?

She surveyed Sam's data, his notes, his charts. One loose designer thread after another.

She pondered this way and that, then pondered some more. Then Dana realized there was only one way left to get at the truth:

The wives of New Falls needed to do lunch.

❦ Thirty-two

They met at Caffeine's instead of the club, where the staff would be queued up to eavesdrop.

They ordered wine. When it was poured and everyone sipped, Caroline began. "Before we start, I have some news."

"Caroline," Dana said, "with all due respect, please shut up. This time, I'm in charge."

Caroline pursed her puffed lips. "That's fine, Dana. Then while you're in charge, do me a favor and ask if anyone has any idea why a gun was in my water garden."

"A gun?" Dana asked.

"A gun?" Bridget asked.

Lauren, however, remained mute.

"I was in the city yesterday. I arrived home to an entire

squadron of police tramping through my landscaping, stringing yellow plastic tape from my weeping cherries to my Japanese maples. They drained the pond that Lauren's son-in-law spent fifty-three thousand dollars digging up." She leaned forward in her chair, placed her elbows on the table, and tented her fingers. "So, if anyone has any ideas, I'm listening."

"Good grief," Dana said.

"Good grief," Bridget said.

"Was it the gun that killed Vincent?" Lauren asked.

Caroline shrugged. "Who knows. They aren't telling me anything. They're treating me like a suspect."

"We're all suspects," Dana said. "Even more now that Kitty has been cleared thanks to the ballistics."

"Don't look at me," Bridget said. "I was arranging for my chemotherapy. I doubt anyone can top that."

"I didn't kill him," Lauren said. "By now you all know about my affair. When Vincent took up with Yolanda, I was angry and hurt. I would have loved some revenge, but I'm afraid of my own shadow, and all of you know that, too." She was, of course, making oblique reference to the neck wattle she'd yet to have tightened.

"But you're running away," Dana said. When Dana had called about doing lunch, Lauren said she was packing for a trip to Nantucket.

"I'm running from Bob, not from Vincent." Her voice fell to a low octave that implored no further details.

"Well, I know I didn't kill him," Dana said. "I had no need."

"You have no secrets?" Caroline asked with a sad laugh. "Come, come, Dana, we all have secrets."

Bridget pulled out the neckline of her scoop T and used it to fan off a hot flash.

"If I have secrets," Dana said, "they do not involve Vincent. Or anyone in New Falls, for that matter."

"Then what might they be?" Caroline asked.

"Oh, stop it," Bridget interrupted. "Whatever they are, they can't be as incriminating as knowing a hit man. Caroline, why don't you tell us about that?"

Caroline fingered her glass as if it were Steuben. "Okay, if we're going to be honest, you asked for it. A while back, I considered having Jack killed."

The whole restaurant went quiet, or was it only their table?

"What's the matter?" Caroline asked. "Are you going to tell me that not once in your married life none of you wished your husband was dead?"

Dana opened her mouth to say, "No!" but realized the others had fallen silent. She said a quick amends to Steven for letting them think she agreed.

"What did you do?" Bridget asked. "Look one up in the Yellow Pages?"

She fingered her glass again, ignored the remark. "Do any of you remember Mike Dawson, the pro?"

He'd been the good-looking golf pro who'd given them a few hopeless lessons then one day disappeared, the way golf pros often do.

"He'd been hitting on me, and I let him. But I told him the only way he'd have a chance was if Jack was out of the picture. I'd been kidding, well, mostly, but Mike gave me a name and phone number. I kept it because I figured someday . . ."

The steward uncorked a second bottle of wine. Caroline's voice drifted away on its bouquet.

"I don't believe you," Lauren said.

Caroline laughed. "Well, it's true. It's also why Mike disappeared. After consideration, and *re*consideration, I changed my mind. The thought of starting over alone, or worse, with someone else, simply seemed too tiring. But after that, Mike's presence made me nervous. I decided his association with the underworld was inappropriate for New Falls. So I told Jack he'd propositioned me. The next day, Mike and his Big Berthas were gone."

They mused, they sipped, they ordered salads niçoise. Then Dana said, "I thought you knew someone in jail."

Caroline blanched. "In jail? Me?"

"You knew it was cold when Kitty was there."

She smiled a smile that seemed to be private. Then she said, "Sorry. The only one I've ever known in the pokey was my dear mother. Every so often she'd wind up in the drunk tank and I'd bail her out. My father wouldn't do it because he wanted her to stay there and learn a lesson. He figured that way she might get sober. He figured wrong."

"Oh, Caroline," Lauren said.

"Oy vey," Bridget said.

"So you're saying you didn't kill Vincent," Dana said.

"Scout's honor," Caroline replied. "Though I might as well tell you I had a good motive."

Lauren's lips puckered. "Why? What did my Vincent ever do to you?"

No one commented that he hadn't been *her* Vincent.

"Well, for one thing, he was blackmailing me," Caroline

replied. "I'd already paid him two hundred thousand dollars and I knew he'd be back for more."

Bridget gripped the enamel sink in the ladies' room where she had fled after feigning nausea from the chemo, and who could argue? Apparently Dana could, because she blew through the door right behind Bridget and asked what was really going on.

"I'm sick," Bridget said. "I don't think I'm supposed to have wine."

"Wine runs through your French veins," Dana said. "Besides, I might believe you except I saw your jaw drop when Caroline mentioned blackmail."

Just then the door opened again, and in came Lauren followed by Caroline.

"Are you all right, Bridget?" Lauren asked while Caroline took a seat on the stiff brocade sofa parked in front of a gilt-framed mirror.

"I'm terrific," Bridget said. "*Trés* terrific."

"You don't have to be sarcastic," Lauren said.

"I have cancer," she replied. "I have a right to get sick. Or sarcastic."

None of them challenged that.

Then Bridget said she was sorry. "It's not the cancer," she confessed. "The *son of a beetch* Vincent was blackmailing me, too."

Lauren's hands flew to her ears. "Stop it! Stop saying bad things about him!"

Dana's eyes flicked from Caroline to Bridget, back to Caroline again. "Why would he blackmail either of you?"

There was a fat, pregnant pause. Who would go first?

Eenie.

Meenie.

Miney.

Bridget wound up being Mo.

"*Merde*," she said, just as someone flushed, exited a stall, washed her hands too quickly, and departed the ladies' room. Bridget shrugged as if secrets no longer mattered. "Vincent found out I'd been married before. He learned I had a son who drowned in the marshes. He knew I never told Randall."

It grew quiet again.

"You had a son?" Lauren whispered. "But you didn't tell Randall?"

Bridget lowered her voice. "It would have upset him because I'd never been truthful. When I first met him, Randall thought I was a virgin. He is so Catholic, even back then. Randall is a good man, but sometimes he is naïve."

"How much did you pay Vincent?" Caroline asked.

"Same as you. Two hundred thousand."

Caroline stood up and said, "I need more wine."

They reassembled their postures, their napkins, their platitudinal smiles.

Then Bridget said, "So Vincent blackmailed us both, Caroline. I have revealed my deepest, most painful secret. What did Vincent learn about you? Was it motive enough for you to kill him? Because believe it or not, I did not."

In their absence, the salads had arrived. Caroline picked up her fork now, tined bits of olives as if they were delicate diamonds, plinked them one by one onto her bread and butter plate. "Perhaps none of you know this, but I am a lesbian."

If someone had dropped a proverbial pin, it would have echoed from New Falls to New Delhi to New Guinea then back to New York.

"Excuse me?" Dana asked as another piece of black fruit dotted the white china plate.

Caroline sighed. "So shoot me, I'm gay. Don't worry, though. I never eyed any of you in the locker room. In fact, I've only really had one female lover."

No one spoke; no one could.

Then Bridget said, "Well, I guess that tops my cancer. So Vincent found out you liked women and you paid him to be quiet."

"He found out because he had a private investigator doing his dirty work. Not an investigator, really. More like a greedy attorney."

"Paul Tobin?" Dana said, as some pieces fell together.

"When Kitty was arrested that lowlife called me," Caroline continued. "He said he needed a big case, and that he wanted hers."

"Or he would take over blackmailing you where Vincent had left off?" Bridget said.

"Worse. He'd tell the world the rest. That not only am I a lesbian, but that my lover was Vincent's daughter."

Vincent's daughter?

Vincent's *daughter?*

"*Elise?*" asked Dana, Bridget, Lauren, all at the same time.

Caroline nodded. "I sold my mother's sapphires to keep them quiet."

"And now a gun shows up mysteriously in your water garden," Dana said.

"A gun that, chances are, is connected to Vincent's death," Bridget added.

Lauren jumped up, flung her napkin on the salad niçoise.

"I'm tired of you! I'm tired of all of you! You are turning my Vincent into some sort of . . . of . . ."

"Rogue?" Caroline asked, then said, "Sorry, my dear. But I believe your Vincent did that to himself."

Tears jumped from Lauren's eyes, landing on the napkin that had landed on the salad.

Dana stood up and took Lauren's arm. "Please, honey, sit down. No one's trying to trash Vincent. We're just telling the truth."

"But I can't believe it . . ."

"Can't," Caroline said. "Won't."

"Caroline, please shut up," Dana said for the second time during the lunch. She turned back to Lauren. "We don't always know people the way that we think. It happens to all of us, Lauren."

"You don't understand," Lauren wept. "I gave him two hundred thousand dollars, too. But I thought he loved me . . ." Then she looked at Dana. "Did he blackmail you, too?"

Before Dana could answer, Bridget said, "Ha. Dana has no secrets," and, well, except for her father, that was pretty much true.

"So," Dana said, wondering what Sam was going to say about all this, "the bottom line is, Vincent blackmailed all three of you, but you say you didn't kill him."

"Not me."

"Not I."

"Not *moi.*"

239

"And there's a gun now that's no doubt connected."

"No doubt."

"No doubt."

"No doubt."

"Okay," Dana said, folding her hands in her lap. "Then I have a question, and please don't get angry. If none of us did it, what about our husbands? Is it possible one of them found out about the blackmail . . . that one of them is Vincent's killer . . . and that he threw the gun in the water garden on a whim?"

🍂 Thirty-three

Upon leaving the restaurant, Dana decided that as soon as she arrived home she'd go directly into the family room and remove each giant Post-it that covered the walls. She would stack them in a pile, gently fold them over. If Sam wanted to refer to them for his research paper, that would be fine. But the public exhibition was going to be closed.

Soon this whole mess might be over.

But first Dana was going to Kitty's. Maybe Kitty knew how long Vincent had been replacing an income in futures trading with tax-free blackmail. Maybe Kitty knew more than she'd revealed.

Dana passed through the same traffic light on the road to Tarrytown where she'd seen Vincent's Jaguar and Yolanda's custom paint job. Dana didn't doubt that the young woman had loved him. As a bona fide salesman at some point in his life, Vincent could be persuasive.

In the end, maybe he'd chosen the wrong *man* instead of woman to try to persuade.

Over crème brûlée (one serving, four forks), the women had decided to confront their husbands.

Then they promised they'd be honest with one another about it, no matter if Jack or Bob or Randall did the deed. (No matter that Bridget's "confession" had not included anything about Aimée belonging to Luc, not to Randall, but Dana was willing to allow that sin of omission, because at least she'd admitted she'd been being blackmailed.)

Steven, of course, was off the ladies' hook, because Dana had no secrets, or none that Vincent had apparently known. So while the other women grilled their husbands, Dana would grill Kitty. Between them, they might cook up the answer to who had murdered Vincent. Which would be pretty ironic for women who preferred not to spend much time in their kitchens.

Half an hour later, pulling into Kitty's less than humble apartment complex, Dana wondered how Sam could have known she'd go there straight from lunch. It sure looked like his Wrangler in the lot.

"Admit it," Lauren said as she sat on the edge of the bed, Bob bleary from an after-golf, after-lunch nap, Lauren terse and resigned and determined. "You had Vincent killed, didn't you?"

Bob rubbed his eyes. "Use your head, Lauren. Why would

I have him killed? The more he banged you, the more you'd stay off my back."

It had been months since she'd suggested Viagra. It had been months (years?) since Lauren had tried talking to Bob about his wilted penis and their displaced sex life. Displaced. Misplaced. Way*laid*.

Leave it to a man to make this about sex and not about the fact he had failed as a spouse.

She jumped up from the bed because she couldn't stand being so close to him. "He was blackmailing me," she said.

"For chrissakes, Lauren, I knew that. I knew about the two of you from day one, not to mention that when you withdrew two hundred thousand dollars from your trust fund, your attorney was on me like DeLano on your tits."

He'd set up the trust fund supposedly as hers; she hadn't known it was being monitored.

Her eyes stung. She stood at the window seat, too angry to sit. "I'm going to Nantucket for a while."

"After the gala, I presume. You can't expect me to attend that alone." His words carried an air of deservedness.

"I can't imagine why you want to go," Lauren said. "Everyone in town now knows I loved Vincent."

Bob laughed.

He rolled out of bed, straightened his boxers, and shambled over to her. He quickly grasped her wrist. "You loved Vincent?" he asked with a sarcastic whine. "How about this? You used to love this." He shoved her hand down to his crotch, to a small bulge that had formed at the fly. Then he grabbed her thin shoulders, pushed her against the window seat, ripped off her skirt and panties, and crammed his fingers into her.

"Did DeLano do this? Did DeLano like to play rough?"

His hot breath was on her. She tried to scream, but she was too stunned by this sudden monster and by the penis that was somehow erect, straight-standing, angry.

"Stop!" she cried. "You're hurting me."

He didn't stop. Then, just as he tried to shove himself inside her, he let out a mournful wail. His milky white nothing trickled onto her thigh.

He panted, spent. She pushed him away.

"You disgust me," she said, her hands quivering, her heart racing. "You disgust me like no other person has ever disgusted me." She ran from the room and down the hall, grabbing her new spring handbag on the way out.

Sam must have had a brilliant idea and couldn't wait for Dana to come home before he shared it with Kitty.

Dana knocked on Kitty's door, wishing he hadn't come there without her. Not while Kitty was still under suspicion. Then she smiled. Sam was a big boy, he'd reminded her. He could take care of himself.

The door didn't open. She must have been too quiet.

She knocked again. "Kitty," she called. "It's Dana."

There was no reply.

Dana frowned. She looked back to the Jeep, then back to the front door, then back to the Jeep.

"Good grief," she muttered with a scowl. It must not be Sam's Wrangler after all. And Kitty must be out.

Slipping her hands into her jacket pockets, Dana went down the stairs and headed toward her car. She might have gotten into her Volvo and driven away if a car hadn't pulled into the lot at that moment. As she turned to see if Kitty might be in it, which she was not, the Jeep caught Dana's eye again. That's when she noticed the small sticker attached to the back bumper.

Dana crept toward it. As she feared, the sticker read, *Dartmouth.*

Oh my God, she thought. Her heart started to pound. If this was Sam's Jeep, where the heck was he? *Where was her son?*

She twirled around and looked up at Kitty's door.

Had Kitty hurt him?

Kicking off her heels, Dana sprinted forward, raced toward the building, zoomed up the stairs.

Bang! Bang! Bang! She two-fisted the door.

"Kitty! Open up! Open up or I'll call the police!"

Three seconds elapsed. Then four. Then five.

Dana yanked open her purse, fumbled for her cell phone.

Then she heard "Don't," from the other side of the door. Suddenly it opened and there stood Sam. "Don't call the cops, Mom. Everything is okay."

Clearly, however, that wasn't the case, because Sam's hair was tousled and he did not have on a shirt, and Kitty sauntered up behind him, tying the tie of her old, threadbare robe.

When Caroline arrived home after lunch, Jack wasn't there. She couldn't recall if he'd mentioned any meetings in the city, she paid so little attention to him these days.

She ignored the yellow POLICE DO NOT CROSS tape visible from the front windows and went into the study. There, the velveteen-covered plywood sheets waited in repose, the template of tables neatly arranged on the top, the miniature name

cards precariously placed like mah-jongg tiles at a champion-
ship match.

Even if her husband had been there, she had no intention
of interrogating him as to whether he'd killed Vincent.

What would be the point?

She doubted he would have gone to such lengths if he'd
learned her secret. Besides, so what? Whoever killed Vincent
deserved a big thank-you. Their worlds were safer now, their
secrets were protected, with him dead and gone. She wished
she'd realized that before giving Paul Tobin the retainer to
handle Kitty's case. On his own, Tobin had little-to-no power.

Leafing through the phone messages that sat on her desk,
Caroline knew none would be important. Anyone who mattered would have called her cell.

Still, there was a noteworthy collection: the caterer, the flo-
rist, the linen supplier. She'd ordered light yellow linens this
year and giant yellow tulips in crystal-clear vases. Even the
china would be the palest butter color. Yellow was Elise's favorite color. When it came to anything "Elise," Caroline had
been a weakling.

She began to turn away from the desk and the messages
when one caught her eye: *Yolanda DeLano.*

Caroline snatched up the paper, checked the message: *Please
be sure her tickets are waiting at the reception desk at the gala.*

With a grim smile, Caroline thought, *So Yolanda will be coming after all.* She wondered what the other women would think
about that.

Thirty-four

"*Mom, please. I knew you'd overreact.*"

"*Overreact?* Why would I overreact when my son is sleeping with one of my friends who might have murdered her husband? Why would I do that, Samuel? Answer me!" She thought she was doing well not to shout, *Wait till your father gets home!* which wouldn't have worked anyway, because his mother was barely speaking to his father. She rubbed her fingers up and down her seat belt. When reality had registered, she'd run back to her car and Sam had run after her and Kitty, for all Dana knew, was still standing in the doorway, laughing at her.

God, she thought. Elise with Caroline. Sam with Kitty. Was none of the children safe anymore?

"I didn't expect this of you, Sam," she said, her voice dropping a level because the pain of shouting was too great. She did not add that she might have expected it of his twin brother, Ben.

He sat in the passenger seat, drumming his fingers on the dashboard, staring out the window. She wished he'd put his shirt back on.

"It's no big deal, Mom. It's only happened a few times."

A few times? You haven't been home a week . . ." He was so vulnerable. So caring and so damn vulnerable.

He shook his head. "Over Christmas. Remember when I went to pick up coleslaw for your party?"

She didn't remember, not exactly. But she did remember the Christmas Eve open house that she and Steven threw each year. And she knew the New Falls Deli made the best, to-die-for coleslaw. "What about it?" Dana asked.

"I saw Mrs. DeLano at the deli. She asked if I was home on semester break, and if I was helping with the party. I asked if she was coming. Geez, Mom, how was I supposed to know you and Dad didn't invite her? She'd been at every party I could ever remember."

Dana could explain that she couldn't have invited Kitty because Kitty was divorced, single, not a fitting position for a party. "I didn't invite Vincent and Yolanda, either." Her voice quieted, her heartstrings inevitably tugged by his innocence.

"Well, it was Christmas Eve. And she was all alone."

His skin was far too thin to live in New Falls, New York. "And so you slept with her?"

Sam winced. "No," he said. "Not then."

"But later. Before you went back to school."

"Well," he said. "Yes."

"Do your brothers know about this?"

"Sort of."

"And your father?"

"No."

He was twenty-one years old. What was she supposed to say? That he'd be better off with Chloe? Or Elise? Ha! So it had not been Elise who'd attracted him.

"Honey," she said, the word slipping out, "is this why you didn't go to Cozumel? Is this why you've been so intent on finding Vincent's killer?"

He shrugged. "It's not like an affair, Mom. But I feel sorry for her. Her husband dumped her. Her kids are never around. Her mother's sick. She has *no one*, Mom. Can you imagine what that's like?"

As a matter of fact, Dana could imagine. She could go him one better by imagining what it was like to still be a teenager, to learn of your mother's death from your father who was in jail. Yes, Dana Kimball Fulton knew all too well what it was like to have no one.

"Sam," she said, her spine stiffening, "this is neither the time nor place to talk about this. Go back upstairs and put on your shirt." Her voice broke; she hoped he didn't notice. "I can't tell you what to do, but I sincerely hope you say good-bye to Kitty once and for all. The woman is vile. She has taken advantage of you, and for all we both know she's a killer."

He paused a brief second before opening the door. And Dana closed her eyes because she could not stand to watch him leave.

* * *

Bridget sat in the living room, waiting for Randall to come home, holding a note that Aimée had stuck under the four-inch letter "A" magnet that hung on the refrigerator door.

The house was quiet: It was Friday, so Lorraine was not there, either, which gave Bridget the chance to reread the note several times.

> *Mom. Went to the mall with Krissie. Monsieur LaBrecque called. He's leaving for Texas tonight to join his wife. I told him I'm not going back. He said in that case they'll leave for France right from Houston. He told me to tell you good-bye.*

It was the last sentence, of course, that smarted the most. *He told me to tell you good-bye.*
Short. Abrupt. Definitive.
Good-bye.
She half wondered if she should have asked him more about the man who'd gone to France asking questions. Would Luc have had as much motive to kill Vincent as Randall or Bob or Jack? Was he physically capable of flying here, killing Vincent, then returning to France to come back with Aimée? But, if so, where would he get a gun in this country?

She was still sorting those thoughts an hour later when Randall came into the room.

"Bridget?" he asked. "What are you doing here, sitting all alone in the near dark?"

He sat down beside her, he took her hand. His toupee looked a little off-kilter today, but his fingers felt warm threaded through hers.

"Oh, Randall," she quietly said. "We have to talk about Vincent DeLano. I must tell you what he did to me. Then you must tell me if you killed him."

And because Randall was Randall, so kind and so caring, he sat and he listened while she told him about growing up in the Camargue, about her mother and her father and the young cowboy named Luc and the wreath of flowers he once made for her hair. Then she told him that they were married and that they had a son. She told him how bright and adorable her *petit* Alain was, and how he filled their lives with so much love.

She told him about Luc's accident and about Alain's death, and all through her talking, Randall patiently listened without interrupting, without letting go of her hand.

She did not, of course, deserve his love.

When she was finished, Bridget said, "Do you want me to continue?"

Randall shook his head. If he wondered if Aimée was Luc's daughter, not his, it seemed he did not want to know. Perhaps some old doors were better left closed.

"Vincent found out about my past," she continued. "I paid him so he wouldn't tell you." She didn't add that the money had come from the pile of cash she'd amassed over the years from the generous allowance Randall had afforded her. It had been money she'd intended to use when she left Randall and moved back to France, back to Luc, if only Luc had said he wanted her back.

"I wish you'd told me these things earlier," Randall said. "But it was a long time ago, Bridget. We have a good life here, don't we? We've made a good home for each other in spite of it all?"

Perhaps he did know about Aimée, she thought. Perhaps he had known from the beginning when she returned from her father's funeral with a new glow of pregnancy. "*Oui*, Randall," she said, and reached up and touched his loving, trusting face. "We have made a good home." Then she leaned against him because she finally knew she was safe, that this was where she really did belong. "And you did not kill Vincent?"

Randall let out a small chuckle. "*Non, ma chérie*, I did not kill Vincent. The truth is, I was afraid you were going to say that you had."

They sat there, holding on to each other, until the sun set and Aimée came in with Krissie and said, "Oh, gross, my parents are hugging," and the girls giggled and Bridget could not believe how full and happy she finally felt.

Thirty-five

Steven came in on the red-eye Saturday
morning and crawled into bed as Dana crawled out.

"How was your meeting?" she asked out of obligatory wife-
liness.

"Noisy. Energizing. It's more peaceful at home."

Ha! That's what he thought.

She grabbed her bathrobe and headed for the shower. "I
have to pick Ben up at LaGuardia."

"Send the car. Or send Sam."

Dana shook her head. "No. I need some alone time."

His cocked an eyebrow. "Honey," he asked. "Are you angry
with me?"

If she said yes she'd be admitting that she'd gone behind his back. If she said no she'd be dishonest. "Go to sleep, Steven. I'll wake you in time for you to get into your tux."

"I'm not going to sleep until you tell me what's wrong."

Maybe that was why their relationship had worked so long. They'd always been able to communicate, hadn't they? To talk things out before they reached operatic crescendo?

"I have a headache," she said.

"Then call the car to pick up Ben."

"I can't," she said. "I'm angry with you. I'm angry with myself. Worst of all, I am so pissed off at Sam, I'm not sure which one of us I'm more infuriated with."

"Come back to bed," he said.

"Why? Will sex solve my problems?"

"Yes. It always does."

"Steven!"

He patted the edge of the bed. "Come back to bed, honey. And tell me what's going on."

She hated that he was right, that orgasms could wash away more layers of tension than hours of heart-to-hearts. She hated that because he was a man, that concept came so easily to him.

"Please?" he asked. "Then I can forgive you for going to Michael behind my back and you can forgive me for second-guessing you on that one and we can have great sex and everything will be fine."

So. Michael had told him that she'd been there. Should she be angry with him, too? "What makes you think everything will be fine?"

"Because I love you. Love conquers all, doesn't it?"

"You might not totally agree. When you hear the rest."

"What 'rest'? Did you kill Vincent DeLano?"

"No. Did you?"

"No."

"Did you know that Sam was screwing Kitty?"

He paused, startled. "Ah, no. I didn't know that."

The sight of his surprise, God help her, gave her momentary satisfaction, for which she instantly felt guilty.

Then Steven said, "Jesus, doesn't the boy have better taste than that?"

In spite of everything, she laughed.

He reached out to her, then patted the bed again. "Come here."

"I can't. How can we make love when I'll only picture Sam and Kitty?"

He frowned. "That's true. You have a point."

"Steven!"

He smiled. "Come here?" This time he asked softly.

And Dana took off her robe and went back to bed, not because she was such a great wife, but because she really loved this man and sometimes love really did conquer all, at least for a while.

Lauren touched the tiny folds of skin gathered at her throat that Dr. Gregg would never repair. They would show now, she knew. Now that her Mikimotos were gone.

Caroline had told Lauren the name of the man who'd bought her mother's sapphires—Wallace Ashton, who lived in Brooklyn Heights. After Lauren had argued with Bob— indeed, after he'd tried to rape her—she'd left the house. She'd called Caroline, asked for the name, then conveyed her regrets that she wouldn't be attending the gala after all.

"For what it's worth," she'd added, "I don't think my husband killed Vincent. Tell the others I'm sorry, and that I'll be in touch."

She'd gone to Mr. Ashton's, then spent the night in an Omni hotel on Route 95 somewhere off the highway in Connecticut.

Now it was morning. She'd had a surprising appetite that she'd filled with coffee and an omelet and a blueberry Danish at the restaurant on the nineteenth floor. She even enjoyed the view—what was not to enjoy? Lauren was finally free.

She had on the clothes that she'd worn to lunch yesterday. She had a toiletry kit that she'd bought in the small shop in the lobby. She had her big Mercedes that Bob could trace, but she hoped he wouldn't. She'd even parked it in self-park for the night instead of valet, in order to save seventeen dollars.

She had those things and an envelope, that, thanks to Mr. Ashton, held three hundred and ten thousand dollars in cash. She had a suspicion she could have held out for four hundred, but she was in a hurry and did not want to quibble. She would not touch the trust fund: She did not know how much of the money had been from her parents, or how much Bob had added. It would be easier to begin anew.

Nantucket awaited. And Lauren planned never to return to New Falls.

The rest of her life would be spent on a tiny island with over eighty miles of beaches and memories of a childhood that might have been quirky, but at least belonged to her.

There was only one thing left for her to do now.

Before leaving the parking lot, she turned on her cell phone and called Dory.

"Go home to Jeffrey," Lauren said. "He is your husband, and you have a new baby. Go home and try to work something out. If you can't—if you truly can't—you'll know where to find me."

"You look lovely," Jack said, and Caroline was surprised because it had been so long since he'd said that.

"Thank you," she replied, and eyed herself one last time in the full-length mirrored wall at the Hudson Valley Centre. She was glad she'd had the facelift done in time for tonight. The facelift and the Versace had been good choices, the latter with its halter top and long slit that skimmed up her thigh. Like the surroundings, the dress was soft yellow, which seemed ludicrous if the affair had been only "lust" as Elise had proclaimed. "You look rather nice yourself."

He smiled a crooked smile, the same smile that had captured her heart a hundred years back when he'd had less money and she'd been determined. She had loved him then, she supposed.

She turned from him and surveyed the ballroom. In moments the doors would open and New Falls would step inside. The tables were set, the flowers arced perfectly in their vases, the lighting had a gentle glow. The twelve-piece orchestra had finished tuning up and sat there, violin bows poised, waiting for her cue. (She'd tried to get that little combo Condoleezza Rice played in, but was informed that "they don't do this sort of thing." Whatever.)

Along the side wall the waitstaff stood in crisp, spotless white. They held small serving trays with delicate hors d'oeuvres: raspberries and Brie wrapped in phyllo, baked feta-stuffed olives, wild mushroom pierogi with Oregon white truffles.

She'd stayed up most of last night, rearranging the damn seating. With Lauren and Bob out of the picture and Yolanda back in with whoever was her date, Caroline decided she might as well seat the DeLano party in the Hallidays' place. If nothing else, it would draw attention to their table and might give Caroline points for showing sympathy toward the new widow.

"Penny for your thoughts," Jack said because he was a geek sometimes.

"My thoughts are worth much more than that," she said with a slow smile.

"So I've heard."

What did he mean by that?

"Will she be here tonight?" he asked. "Elise DeLano?"

The halter seemed to tighten at the back of her neck. Her eyes stayed on the waitstaff. "Kitty's daughter?" Her heart beat once, then twice.

"I had a visit yesterday, from a fellow named Paul Tobin. I believe you know the man?"

She stepped away from Jack. She could not risk perspiring on the Versace, not now, not tonight.

He followed her to the door, to the place where they would stand, the king and queen of New Falls, welcoming their subjects, one and all. "I believe you underestimated the man. We need to talk, Caroline."

"Not now," she said, and motioned for the maitre d' to open the grand doors.

The music began, the waitstaff went into motion, a smile miraculously found its way to her newly plumped-up lips, the kind of smile she'd mastered when she'd been a girl and her father had needed her to act as if Mother was not in bed, drunk.

Beside her, Jack's smile twinned hers. *Hello,* he said to friends and strangers. *Hello, nice to see you.* He leaned down to her ear and whispered, "It isn't like you to be sloppy, Caroline. We'll talk about that later, too."

She couldn't tell if the music was the prelude she'd picked out. She didn't know if people were finding their place cards, if the waitstaff was circulating properly. It was as if she'd moved into a different dimension where it had become difficult to hear, to speak, to think.

And then Yolanda arrived. She wore the pink diamonds Vincent had bought her. She also wore a pink form-fitting dress—one that clung to her belly, her small but obviously pregnant belly.

"Yolanda," Jack said because Caroline had not. "You look lovely tonight."

Yolanda smiled and rubbed her belly. "I decided it was time to show New Falls that I'm going to have Vincent's baby."

"That's nice," Jack said, though Caroline half heard him because behind Yolanda was Elise—breathtaking Elise—dressed in a pale yellow gown not unlike Caroline's. She should have guessed the girl would come with Yolanda. She should have guessed they'd try to ruin her night.

"Nice dress," Elise said to her.

"Elise," Jack said as the odd couple moved down the king and queen's reception line. "My goodness, look how you've grown up."

Just then Caroline spotted Dana and Steven, Bridget and

Randall. She broke away from Jack and from tradition and moved through the crowd of people to speak with her only friends.

"They've done it to get back at me," Caroline said to Dana and Bridget, once the men went to the bar and they had a moment to themselves. "They've done it to thumb their noses."

"You mean at *us*," Bridget said. "It's obvious that both Yolanda and Elise hate everything about New Falls."

"Where are they sitting?" Dana asked.

"With us. I decided to be kind, so I seated Yolanda's date next to me."

"Oh no."

"Mon dieu."

"What's worse, Jack knows. Paul Tobin went to him. I guess Tobin is angry that Kitty is free and he won't get his trial of the year."

"This is awful," Dana said.

"Trés terrible," Bridget said.

"Where's Lauren?" Dana asked.

"She and Bob had a quarrel. They won't be coming. Oh, this is all simply dreadful."

Then the drama relocated to the front door when Kitty suddenly walked in.

Thirty-six

She was wearing a light green dress that they'd all seen before—perhaps at last year's gala, perhaps the year before.

"I'm hoping to buy a ticket at the door," she said as she boldly approached Caroline.

A chill crawled from Dana's fingers to her toes.

"Kitty," Caroline said, recovering in an instant because she was still Caroline Meacham, after all. "I can't imagine why you've come, but it's not appropriate."

"Why not? I used to live in New Falls. I raised my children here, or perhaps you hadn't heard. And I'm prepared to make a large donation. I'm about to come into two million dollars, in case you haven't heard that, either."

"*Keety*," Bridget said, and Dana might have, too, if only she could speak, if only she could look at the woman and not see big-hearted Sam's face. "You don't want to cause more trouble, do you?"

But *Keety* raised an eyebrow. "I've only come to reclaim my rightful position in this godforsaken town." Her eyes were distant, filmy, as they traveled the room. "But do tell: Has my successor come as well?"

Dana deduced that Kitty was drunk.

Caroline stayed composed. "Yolanda purchased tickets in advance," she said, then cupped Kitty by the elbow. "Now I must insist that you leave."

"But wait," Kitty said, "I see her now. She looks rather shrunken standing next to that beautiful redhead—oh, look! That's my daughter. It seems she's stolen her, too."

"Kitty, stop it," Dana said, at last finding her voice. "Get out of here before you ruin the whole event. Which, in case you didn't notice, has nothing to do with you."

But before Kitty made another sound, her eyes suddenly grew wide and her unlifted jaw went slack. "My God," she said, her voice thundering now, "is that little hussy with child?"

Like the audience at a runway show, coiffed heads rotated toward the subject at hand, who now stood in profile to them.

"*Mon dieu*," Bridget said again, "it surely looks that way."

Kitty laughed. Then she took off toward Yolanda before the wives could shout, "*NO!*"

They watched in horror as Kitty wagged her finger at Yolanda's face. "I suppose you're going to try to say that baby belongs to Vincent."

Yolanda blinked, but did not answer. She turned her back.

"Mother, go home," Elise said, placing a protective arm around Yolanda's shoulder.

"Go home? Well, my darling daughter, I don't have a home."

Her voice continued to hover above street level. The orchestra slowed, the sole focus turned to the pregnant young woman in pink, the redhead in yellow, the disheveled woman wearing last year's light green.

Caroline raced toward the musicians, telling everyone along the way to please have a good time, that everything was under control.

But it wasn't.

Kitty laughed again.

"You might fool the others, you little slut, but just so everyone knows, my husband could no longer father children. After Elise was born, Vincent had a vasectomy. A *vasectomy*. Do you know what that big word means, little girl?"

Thankfully, Dana spotted Detective Johnson, even though he wore a tux. She was grateful that, this time, Steven did not step forward, knight in shining armor that he so often was.

She signaled the detective with a plea for help.

He approached, he smiled, he whisked Kitty away, her final refrain resonating through the hall:

"That baby is not Vincent's! Vincent had a *vasectomy!* That baby belongs to some other worthless soul!"

The rest of the evening was a little edgy. Yolanda and Elise departed right after Kitty, which meant there were two empty chairs at their table after all, not counting the spaces where

Lauren and Bob should have been. Caroline acted distracted; Jack was unusually quiet; Dana and Steven, Bridget and
Randall remained out of duty. Shortly after they presented
Caroline with generous checks, the Fultons and the Hayneses
gladly left.

Randall suggested they stop somewhere for a nightcap,
but Dana had a headache and said thanks anyway. She did,
however, notice the way Bridget held Randall's arm as they
left Hudson Valley Centre. She didn't think she'd ever seen
Bridget do that.

"Maybe they had a nap together before coming tonight,"
Steven said when Dana mentioned it in the car on the ride
home. He was, of course, referring to the "nap" they'd had together, after Steven slept most of the day and woke up wanting sex again as if the first time hadn't been enough.

They'd decided make-up sex was so much fun that they
should fight more often.

In between, Dana managed to spend some time with Ben
(actually, while doing his laundry and repacking his bags for
Dartmouth), long enough to be reassured that Cozumel had
not changed him into a boy that she no longer knew, not the
way New Falls had changed his twin.

"It's nice," she said to Steven now, "that sometimes there
can be happy endings, like with Bridget and Randall." She
didn't mention that Sam and Ben had gone back to school
while Dana and Steven napped, leaving a lame note that cited
wanting to miss traffic.

Nor did she mention that she'd seen the sheets of Post-
its stacked where she'd left them, as if Sam no longer cared
who'd murdered his lover's husband.

Talking about those things wouldn't have made them go away, though it might have cushioned the surprise when they pulled into the driveway and saw Sam on the front steps.

"Hey," Sam said, standing up awkwardly. It was the first time he'd spoken to his mother since she'd told him to put on his shirt. "How was the gala?"

"Boring," Steven said. "Except that Kitty showed up. She caused quite a scene."

Dana winced.

Sam cowered. "You look nice, Mom," he said.

She glanced down at her silver Marchesa gown that looked less tired than she felt.

"Can we talk?" he asked.

"Sure," Steven said, "but I thought you boys had already gone back to school."

"Not yet, Dad. But I really just wanted to talk to Mom."

"Oh," Steven said. "Well, sure."

He went inside the house because Steven was a good dad and a good husband and knew that mostly this was between Dana and Sam and he'd be called for advice if needed.

"Honey," Dana said, "it's a little chilly to stand outside."

"It's okay, Mom. I'm not a little kid."

Apparently he thought she was concerned for him, not for herself, which was every kid's mother-child relationship, wasn't it?

"I couldn't go back to school until I apologized. Until you know how sorry I am for what I did. And for the part about you finding out."

"Which is it, Sam? The fact you slept with Kitty or the fact I found out?" Her tone was biting; she wished it wasn't.

"Either. Both."

She might have said it was okay, but she wouldn't have really meant it, until she saw the big tears that had sprung up in his eyes. "I told Ben we had to turn around. I told him you and I had a fight. I'm sorry, Mom. I'm so sorry and ashamed."

Sorry and ashamed. She sighed. She knew those were tough words for anyone to say. Anyone, let alone her sensitive, too-caring son.

Sorry.

Ashamed.

And then Dana remembered when she'd heard those words before. They were in a note, written by her father a long, long time ago. Written on a piece of paper that had been sent from a jail cell, accompanied by her mother's obituary.

I'm so sorry.
And ashamed.

She sat down on the steps. "I'm sorry, too, Sam. I didn't mean to judge you. Sometimes parents . . . well, sometimes we overreact when we think our kid's welfare is at stake." That was what her father had done, hadn't he?

"But you were right, Mom. It was wrong, what I did with Kitty. It doesn't matter if it was her fault or mine. It was wrong. I knew that all along."

He sat next to her and she put her arm around him. And that's when she decided it really didn't matter if they ever learned who'd murdered Vincent. It really didn't matter if Bridget ever knew that Dana knew Aimée wasn't Randall's daughter, or if the entire town knew Caroline liked women.

It didn't really matter if Lauren resurfaced after the supposed quarrel with Bob.

What mattered was taking the time to try and understand one another. Having patience, learning tolerance. What mattered was forgiving and being forgiven.

"Honey," Dana said, stroking Sam's hair, "how would you like to help me with a little project?"

He groaned. "I'm off the case, Mom. I'm thinking of changing to corporate law instead of criminal stuff."

"What if it's something we can do on your 'indispensable Internet'? Something simple, like a missing person search?"

He sat up straight. "Missing person?" He might be like his father, but he had Dana's knack for gathering details, for wanting to craft the world's problems into a solvable puzzle.

"Yes," she said. "We need to start in Indiana. It's time we found your grandfather."

Thirty-seven

The house looked the same but smaller, closer to the sidewalk, dwarfed by the giant oak trees that now were way too big.

It was made of red brick and was almost cottage-size, with a single dormer above the roofline of the small front porch. The dormer held the window that had been in Dana's bedroom.

How many times she'd sat there watching for her father to walk up the street on his way home from work, his navy uniform still neat and clean, his gold badge shining in the late afternoon.

How many times she'd come home from school and found her laundry neatly stacked on her bed, smelling like bleach and strong detergent, sprinkled and ironed and folded by her mother.

How many times she'd sat at her desk, working on her homework, the aromas of her mother's cooking wafting up the stairs, though all Dana really wanted was for dinner to be over so she could go to the library with Becky or to Burgertown with Jane and Sue.

She sat in the passenger seat of the Chevrolet Impala rental car and studied the porch post where black metal numbers read 6–8–2–0. She remembered going with her father to the hardware store to buy them, then helping him screw them into the post. He'd always planned a Saturday project when she was young, something they would do together. It was years before Dana realized it had less to do with accomplishing a project and more to do with spending time with her, making memories, like the 6–8–2–0.

"Do you want to go in?" Steven asked. He sat behind the wheel, her patient, understanding husband, having skirted a business trip to Chicago to go with her to Indiana. "I'm sure if you rang the bell . . ."

But Dana shook her head. "I just wanted to see the house. I don't want to bother anyone." Turning back to the MapQuest printout on her lap, she said, "Okay, let's go. According to Sam, he lives on the other side of downtown. I think I can remember how to get there from here."

Like the house, the streets seemed smaller, the intersections narrower, the trip across town shorter. Before Dana was prepared, a sign in front of a two-story townhouse complex read *Meadowe Crest*. She pushed aside the MapQuest printout and got out of the car before she could change her mind.

* * *

He was old. His hair was white, his shoulders drooped, he stood a little shorter, his blue eyes seemed lighter. He was old, but it was he.

"Daddy," she said, because that was what she'd still called him when she—when *he*—had been sent away.

His eyes came to life. His mouth turned up into a grin. He opened the screen door and took her into his arms.

"Your mother was sick," he said to Dana while they sat, with Steven, in the small living room that had tweed-upholstered furniture and an old-fashioned ham radio set up in one corner. She'd forgotten he'd loved that, that he'd sit for hours and listen to the crackle waiting for voices to come from Russia or Europe or even Australia right into Indiana.

She hadn't forgotten the picture of her mother with a baby—*her!*—that now stood on an end table. He'd taken it at the Ohio State Fair in front of the exhibit of the world's biggest tomato.

She wondered what Bridget and Lauren and Caroline would think about that.

"You knew Mom was sick before . . . before you were arrested?" As they sat on the sofa, Steven lightly touched her leg, his hand a surge protector in case her emotions sparked. She was grateful that unlike Randall Haynes or Bob Halliday or Jack Meacham, Steven had always known about his wife's not-so-perfect past.

"Laetrile treatments were thought to be a miracle cure," George Kimball, once the head of the police union, said. "The treatments were illegal here, but not in Mexico. The trouble was, we had no money. The medical bills were already huge . . ."

She listened to the rest. How he'd embezzled all the money but then he'd been caught.

"When I went to jail, only five thousand dollars was left. It kept your mother going for a while." He laughed a sad laugh. "It wasn't as if I used the money to buy her diamonds, though I often wished I had. I mean, I lost my job, I lost you, and she died anyway."

Dana's throat was dry, tears leaked slowly from her eyes. "But you came back here. Why did you come back? Wasn't it . . . hard? To face everyone?"

He smiled a half smile. "I was away ten years. I came back in case you ever tried to find me. Even though I lost the house, I figured if you came to town, you'd ask around and someone would know where old George Kimball was."

They sat quietly together, after more than thirty years. Then Dana asked her father if he'd like to move to New York. "You have three terrific grandsons," she said, "who would love to know you. And we live in a nice town, if you ignore some of the stuff."

🍃 *Thirty-eight*

Bridget strutted into the oncology department Monday morning in teal satin pajamas trimmed with silver sequins that were great for staving off hot flashes. The Haynes family had spent Sunday afternoon at Victoria's Secret, where Aimée selected and Bridget modeled and Randall sat in the "gentleman's chair" and laughed at his two *jeunes filles*. Before heading home they stopped at the nutrition store and loaded up on immune-boosting wheatgrass and ginseng that Randall announced he would use to create a new cocktail for Bridget, a temporary (she hoped) substitute for wine.

Today she'd downed the drink, then jumped into the teal, which she now wore with dangling sequin earrings and silver satin mules. Randall said she never looked more ravishing.

She warned him he might regret those words if she threw up on the ensemble.

He marched up to the reception desk beside her, having canceled golf with Jack Meacham, the epitome of New Falls sacrifice.

"If anyone's going to poison my wife," he kidded the woman behind the desk, "I want to be here as a witness." But as he said it his voice quivered and his eyebrows knitted together and a touch of moisture filled his eyes.

Bridget smiled at her corny husband and his ill-fitting toupee and took him by the arm. It was nice now that her cancer was out in the open. It was nice that Luc was back in France, four thousand miles away by land and sea, a million miles and a lifetime away from her heart.

"No golf today?" Caroline asked her husband as she strolled past his bedroom and realized he was still under the covers and his draperies were still drawn though it was after ten.

He didn't answer right away, then said, "Caroline, come here."

"Are you ill?" Yesterday she'd gone with Chloe to the Cloisters for the day. She'd greatly needed to get away from New Falls and her husband and the bitter aftertaste of the gala.

"Come here," he said again.

Aside from announcing he was bringing someone or other home for dinner, or expecting her to keep their social calendar arranged with all the have-tos and the RSVPs RSVP-ed, Jack rarely asked Caroline for anything.

"Please," he said.

She moved into the room with tentative steps.

"I'm sorry about the gala," he said. "I'm sorry it wasn't everything you'd hoped."

"We raised four hundred and sixty thousand dollars. It wasn't a total waste." One of his hands was under his head, under his pillow. The other was still under the comforter, perhaps holding his penis.

"Please," he said, "sit down."

"I'd rather stand."

He didn't push the issue. Instead he asked, "Do you love her, Caroline?"

She waited for the longing to crush her chest. When it did not, she asked, "What is love, Jack? Was it what we had?" It certainly wasn't being cruel, as Elise had been cruel to Caroline at the gala, almost mocking it, mocking her, using the gala as a soapbox for Yolanda's shock-news.

"I don't know what love is, Caroline. I can't remember. We've spent so many years being the Meachams, I've forgotten who Jack and Caroline really are."

Her eyes adjusted to the light; she saw the questions in his. "Jack was a young man out of business school who wanted to take on the world," she said. "Caroline was her father's perfect hostess who wanted a husband."

"I'm not sure, but I think you've sold us short."

"No I haven't, Jack. The problems started when we took ourselves too seriously. The rest of the world did, too."

He seemed to think about that. Then he said, "I once loved having sex together."

She blanched. "You did?"

He rolled onto his side. "I always thought no matter what the next deal would net or what the market did or didn't do or what my golf score was, well, I always thought of you as the one thing I could count on."

"It wasn't always about you, Jack."

"You made me think it was."

"I did?"

"Well. Yes. You were the doting, dutiful wife. And when you weren't doting on me or on Chloe, you were doting on New Falls. Why would I have ever thought that wasn't what you wanted?"

She sat down on the bed because she had grown weak.

"I'm sorry if I didn't measure up to your expectations," he continued. "If you'd rather be with Elise, I'll go quietly. Or let you go quietly. Don't worry about money. I'll take care of everything."

He slid his arm from beneath the pillow. He started to reach for her, then was content to rest his hand on the straight pleat of her pants. How long had it been since he'd touched her like that? Since he'd touched her at all?

"I thought about asking you to stay," he continued. "But that sounded stupid. I couldn't come up with a way for the three of us to live here. Especially since it would be four now that Chloe is back home."

"I wouldn't have wanted that, Jack." Despite the lust, the craziness she'd felt for Elise, she'd never entertained the idea of having her live here, in the house that Jack built. Just as she'd never really imagined not being a New Falls wife.

"What do you want?" he asked.

And suddenly she knew. "I think I really only want what I've always wanted. I want you to love me. To touch me, really touch me. To make love to me and have the feeling linger. To stop being such a driven, self-centered man and think about me as a woman. Who likes to be held. Who sometimes needs tenderness."

He could have laughed at that, at Caroline Meacham wanting tenderness. He could have laughed, but he did not.

"I want us to try again. I want to forget about Elise. I want you to forget about her, too." She hadn't realized until then that was indeed what she wanted.

He looked at her a moment with bemused eyes. "You think it will be easy for this man to forget his wife has been with a woman?"

She smiled quietly. It was all she could do.

He smiled slowly back. Then he slid his other hand from beneath the comforter. She thought that he was going to pull her close, maybe make love to her. She thought she might like it. She was so busy thinking that she was surprised to hear such a thundering noise followed by a blast that ripped right through her head.

🍃 Thirty-nine

Dana couldn't wait to tell Bridget about her father. Steven had gone on to Chicago from Indianapolis, so she'd flown back to New York alone, adrenaline pumping from takeoff to touchdown, despite that she'd talked half the night, telling Steven stories of her childhood, of her mother, of Daddy.

They'd driven her car to the airport so she only had to jump in and head north to New Falls. By the time she got to Bridget's, it was after two o'clock in the afternoon.

"My, don't you look perky," Dana said as Bridget opened the door dressed in teal and sequins. She hadn't yet told Bridget about her visit from Luc, about the wildflowers, about the fact he was sorry. There would be time for that later; for now,

Dana wouldn't disrupt Bridget's newfound contentment.

"We had a family outing this morning at the chemo room," Bridget said. "It wasn't the same without you. Randall is *trés terrible* at pedicures."

Bridget made tea and bemoaned the fact she'd lost her taste for wine. "I couldn't even drink one tiny sip at the gala. Not that it mattered. Oh, what an awful night that was. All that business with Caroline and Yolanda and Elise."

They settled at the table.

"I wonder what Caroline is going to do," Dana said.

"Leave him, I expect. The way Lauren has left Bob."

"Has she really left him?"

"She has."

"Dear God."

"Oui, oui."

They sipped.

"Lauren called a little while ago," Bridget continued. "She said she couldn't get through to Caroline. And you didn't answer your cell. Where have you been anyway? You look tired."

"I'll tell you later. First tell me about Lauren." Once she started talking about her father, she knew she wouldn't want to stop, not even for news of Lauren.

"Well, she's on Nantucket! She really did it. Sold her Mikimotos and left that old geezer high and dry. She's staying in an apartment above a scrimshaw store. Can you imagine? Lauren? Living above a shop?"

Could they imagine any of them doing such a thing?

"I'm happy for her," Bridget went on. "She sounded really, really excited. She said in a while, she might look for a man. Someone down-to-earth."

"A far cry from Bob."

"Or Vincent. *Mon dieu*, every time when I think of those pink diamonds on Yolanda's neck, I wonder if Vincent bought them with my two hundred thousand."

"They *are* beautiful diamonds," Dana said. Then something nagged a bit. "Seriously, though. When did he buy them for her? Before or after he blackmailed you?"

Bridget frowned. "After, I think. Yes, of course. The first time we saw them was only two weeks ago, at Caroline's rite-of-spring luncheon."

The day that Vincent had been shot. Kitty had mentioned that the money for the diamonds must have come from Vincent's secret stash.

Suddenly the thing that had been nagging jerked Dana's thoughts.

"Oh my God," she shouted as she bounded off the couch. "Kitty did it, Bridget. Kitty killed Vincent after all!"

"What?"

"She did! She killed him! I knew something bothered me when my father said it. That he never bought my mother diamonds."

"Your father? What father?"

"Get up," she commanded. "We're going to visit Detective Johnson."

Bridget said Dana was insane but she stood up anyway.

Dana tugged her by the wrist. "Don't you see?" she jabbered as she led Bridget toward the door and Bridget grabbed her raincoat on the way out. "Kitty knew about Yolanda's new pink diamonds. But Vincent had just bought them for her. *The first time she'd worn them was to Caroline's luncheon.*"

Bridget nodded as she buckled the seat belt around her teal satin middle.

"It's true," Dana kept sputtering as she turned on the ignition and backed out of the drive. "Kitty mentioned the diamonds the day Sam and I went to see her. When we asked if Vincent was broke, she said how could he have been when he'd bought those pink diamonds?"

Bridget held on to the door as Dana shoved the gearshift into drive and they sped off down the street.

"The only way Kitty could have seen them would be if she was near Caroline's that day. But she wasn't invited! She must have been outside the party, watching. She must have used the opportunity to dump Vincent's gun into Caroline's water garden."

It all made sense to Dana. And Bridget could not disagree.

Detective Johnson said it would be highly irregular for Dana and Bridget to follow them to Kitty's apartment in Tarrytown. He did not comment that on top of the irregularity, Bridget was wearing pajamas.

"Please, Detective," Dana pleaded. "If I talk to her, she might admit it. It would save you lots of time, and the state a lot of money, if she just confesses."

She suspected it was the part about saving him time that made him acquiesce.

They bullied their way into her apartment, Detective Johnson, his three officer-sidekicks, Dana and Bridget, plus a Tarrytown cop they'd picked up on the way, which had something to do with "jurisdiction."

"We know you did it," Dana said. "You wouldn't have known

about Yolanda's pink diamonds unless you were watching Caroline's house the day of the luncheon."

Kitty clutched the robe more tightly to the breasts that Sam must have fondled. Dana pushed the thought from her mind.

Then Kitty shrugged. "I told Vincent to meet me at our old house. I said the buyers for the Oriental rugs would be there."

Detective Johnson read her her rights the same way he'd read them the day they'd found Vincent.

But Kitty's eyes had glazed over and she didn't seem to hear.

"I brought the gun Vincent bought me. He was so paranoid about muggers. Anyway, I meant to kill him. But when he said I looked good, I saw the chance to really make him pay." She rolled her eyes and smiled. "Vincent always was so easy when his penis was involved."

At first no one seemed to know what she meant. Then she stepped toward Detective Johnson, placed her hands flat on his chest.

"I did this," she said, moving her hands over his chest. Then her fingers darted inside the detective's jacket. He grasped her wrist. She laughed.

"So you don't carry a gun in the same place Vincent did. Well, as usual, his was there. I called him a bastard, then I shot him with his gun." She pointed her finger at Detective Johnson's left ear. "I guess the neighbors didn't hear that shot."

"Then what?" the detective asked.

"Then I left Vincent there. I went to Caroline's—that was very smart of you to figure that out, Dana. You always were smarter than the rest of us."

Dana chewed her lip.

Bridget slid one foot in and out of her silver sequin mules.

"I hid in those bushes by the water garden. Even from there, I could see Yolanda and the pink diamonds. Imagine that. They're so big I didn't need opera glasses."

"But you went back to the house," Johnson said.

"I tossed Vincent's gun into the water. Then yes, of course I went back. Maybe I needed to be sure the bastard was dead. Or maybe I needed to see him one more time. Whatever. When I got there, I took out my gun in case he was still breathing. When I bent down to check him, my gun went off and shot the rug, and the police were there in a flash."

That's when Kitty laughed. "The worst part is, it really was worth it," she said. "I've had more attention than when I was Vincent's wife. Besides, it was fun, wasn't it?"

The police officers handcuffed Kitty and led her from the place. Just before they filed down the stairs, Detective Johnson's cell phone rang.

"Johnson," he said. Then "Yes. I see. Good God. Okay, we'll be right there." For some reason he turned and looked at Dana and Bridget. He hesitated briefly, then motioned to his partner. "Let them take her in," he said, pointing to the other cops. "We've got something more urgent."

"Something more urgent? In New Falls?" Bridget laughed. "*Mon dieu*, not again."

The detective paused, closed his eyes, took a breath. Then he rushed past them and raced down the stairs.

"Hey!" Bridget shouted over the railing. "You forgot to thank us for our help!"

The detective waved his hand. "I'll come and talk to you

both later," he called back, which seemed rather foreboding, but then, life was like that sometimes.

Dana smiled and said, "Come on, you beauty queen. I'm going to take you to The Chocolate Flan for lunch. I have a lot to tell you, now that Vincent's killer has been caught and we can get back to normal, whatever that is."

❧ Epilogue

It was the perfect spot for a hair salon, right in the center of New Falls, right on Main Street where she could keep an eye on everyone and everything. It even had a perfect apartment on the second floor, where she would raise her baby—a girl! she had learned.

Three months had passed since Vincent died. Yolanda wondered if she would ever stop missing him.

The baby, of course, was his. Kitty seemed to really believe he'd had a vasectomy; Yolanda was pretty sure it wasn't the first or only time Vincent had lied to Kitty. He'd told her once how Kitty made him crazy with her nonstop nitpicking. In the end, even Paul Tobin didn't want to handle Kitty's case, which wasn't really a case, because she'd confessed. "Shot her big mouth off," Tobin had said, then disappeared, probably fearful that the others would come looking for him, would have him arrested for the way he had tried to cash in on Vincent's misdeeds.

"Would you like to make an offer?" the real estate agent who stood beside her asked.

"Yes," Yolanda said, "I'll pay the asking price. It's exactly what I want." She had decided to stay in town. It was what Vincent would have wanted for her, and for their daughter.

Money would be easier now that Marvin and Elise had given her half of the two-million-dollar insurance, now that Kitty no longer "qualified" as the beneficiary. They said they still had plenty to keep their grandmother well-cared for upstate.

Of course, even with a million, Yolanda didn't have a New Falls fortune left, now that she'd sold the house, paid the taxes, and returned the blackmail money:

Two hundred thousand dollars to Lauren Halliday, who was working in a flip-flop shop on Nantucket, dating a scallop fisherman, and planning to buy a cottage so Dory and Jeffrey and little Liam—and any of her stepchildren, if they so desired—could visit from time to time;

Two hundred thousand dollars to Bridget Haynes, whose hair had fallen out and now grown back, who said she'd use the money for something other than lunches and wine, that perhaps she'd do some good in the world, because, *mon dieu*, the world surely could use it;

And two hundred thousand to Caroline's daughter, Chloe, who needed every cent she could get now that her mother was dead and her father, like Kitty, was going to prison for the rest of his life. The Meacham family assets had been frozen, like Chloe, pending settlements from attorneys and business partners and who knew who else. So Chloe had hawked the diamond Lee Sato had given her and had reclused herself somewhere in South Hadley, Massachusetts, where she'd gone to college and apparently felt safe.

Dana Fulton didn't get any money because Vincent hadn't blackmailed her, though the town was buzzing now that her long-lost father had moved into their house. Rumor had it that Dana and Steven paid for Caroline Meacham's headstone and her funeral, though few people attended. If Dana or anyone else knew who brought the yellow tulips to the gravesite each week, no one was saying, no one was gossiping about that, at least not out loud.

Yolanda, of course, knew. Just as she knew that if she didn't make trouble, the women in town would eventually come to her shop, would share their stories, would, in time, forget all that had happened.

It was funny, Yolanda thought, as she looked around at her new beginning, but aside from the jewels and the houses and the cars and the clothes and the silly facelifts, well, the wives of New Falls weren't a whole lot different than those in the Bronx.

Mais oui, as Bridget would say.

A+

**AUTHOR
INSIGHTS,
EXTRAS, &
MORE...**

FROM

**ABBY
DRAKE**

AND

AVON A

"It's her second facelift!" my cousin Linda shrieked one night as we picked at salads and pretended the real reason we got together was to have dinner out, not to share the latest gossip of who-did-what-to-whom. She was speaking of a neighbor's friend, a librarian, of all people. I mean, who would think a librarian would have one facelift, not to mention two? "This time," Linda added, plucking a leaf of baby spinach before E. coli interrupted, "they extracted fat tissue from her butt to plump up her lips."

Good grief.

Dinner continued and our conversation moved on to other people, other situations, her job, my job, our mutual Aunt Lois who was in assisted living. I forgot about the facelift.

A few days later I was at a ladies' luncheon in a posh community that's a five-carat stone's throw from Manhattan.

Let me take this opportunity to say that, as a writer, I suppose I am always on a behind-the-scenes hunt for good material—plots, characters, that sort of thing. I do not, however, wave around a notebook, at least not overtly, though I usually have one within arm's reach. (I have, on occasion, resorted to jotting notes or great one-liners on the backs of envelopes, bank deposit slips, and receipts from Wendy's window, always remembering that Abraham Lincoln scribed the Gettysburg address on a brown paper bag or something, and that worked out pretty well for him.)

But back to my story.

So there I was at this sophisticated, very proper, elegant, ladies-only, holiday party in the commodious home of my friend Eileen, the most elegant lady of all, whom I have known since college. I was standing in the music room listening to the chitchat of women whose full-time jobs consist mainly of husbands and children, yet whose housekeepers and nannies and gardeners and cooks enable them to have way too much time on their perfectly lotioned hands. All that, of course, is said with a twinge of envy from this lady who has been in the punch-the-clock-workplace far too many hours a day for far too many years.

One of the guests was a delightfully perky woman who was chatting with another, discussing the fallout of her divorce. Thankfully they stood close enough that I could absorb each delicious word.

"The #@%!-er took everything," she squealed.

I assumed the #@%!-er was her ex-husband.

"He had a mistress for about a hundred years—the *same one*, for godssake. For some reason he thinks that makes it all right!"

I nibbled a scallop ceviche and pretended to be fascinated by the raspberry that bobbed in my champagne flute.

"I thought he was a spy," the perky woman said. "I thought he worked for the CIA and that's why he left the room whenever his phone rang. I mean, he couldn't very well talk in front of the kids and me, could he? Not with government secrets at stake?"

The last question brought an eye roll from her companion.

"At least it's finally over," she continued, her voice dropping a bit.

I leaned forward and tilted my good ear toward her.

"It's been four years. Today is the first time I've been out since I was shunned at the deli."

Huh?

I swallowed the rest of the scallop, then, as if propelled by a demon gossipmonger, I took a step toward them. "Nice party," I said, insinuating myself into their twosome.

"You're Eileen's friend from college, aren't you?" the perky woman asked.

I nodded.

"The writer," the other one said.

I nodded again.

Ms. Perky perked up. "Wow. Do I have a story for you."

I was hoping she'd say that.

Without spilling the details, I'll just say she confided that, one day at the deli where the locals all shop, a woman raised one polite eyebrow at her, then turned to a friend and haughtily said, "I knew her when she was married."

Apparently, in that town, a woman is only considered to be one of "the wives" and ceases to exist, socially or otherwise, once her husband has left.

It is Stepford in the twenty-first century.

The absurdity gnawed at my subconscious.

A few days later I heard from another old friend, this one an editor for a large publishing house. In her e-mail she bemoaned the fact the holidays were here and she did not have a man, a clean-shaved arm candy, to tote to all the parties. She wondered if she'd attract one if she had a facelift.

"You don't need a man," I responded. "Who wants one any-way?" I then spewed forth a laundry list of unsolicited advice, including the tale of the librarian's surgeries and a few snippets from the wives at Eileen's party, especially Ms. Perky's story.

The editor responded: "Your advice was hilarious. Please tell me it's going to end up in a book."

Hmm.

I didn't tell her that was not going to happen, that I was working on a lovely novel that had nothing to do with hilarity or women who have been wronged by rich, arrogant #@%!-ers.

That night I slept until two-fifteen A.M., when I was jolted awake by a sentence, as if the sandman had crept into my bedroom and clubbed me over the head with a subject and a verb and a little punctuation.

I squeezed my eyes closed, willing dreamland to return, willing the sentence to go away. Besides, if it was that great, I'd remember it in the morning, wouldn't I?

Of course not. I'd tried that many times and knew better.

Okay, so I turned on the light and jotted the words in the notebook I keep next to my bed. Then I turned off the light and closed my eyes again. Surely I could go back to sleep.

Any minute now.

If I just counted sheep.

Or tried yoga breathing.

Or . . . never mind.

I snapped on the light again, picked up my notebook, got out of bed, and stomped down the hall to my office.

I turned on my computer, sat down with a sigh, and slowly, with determination, I began to type:

It started because of a facelift . . .

Walt Steinmetz Photography

Abby Drake

A graduate of Skidmore College in Saratoga Springs, New York–two and a half hours due north of "New Falls"–**ABBY DRAKE** understands the social pecking order of Manhattan's bedroom towns. Like many of the wives she portrays, she does not play golf but can drive a cart; unlike many, she owns no Mikimotos and has not had a face-lift. Yet. She currently lives in Amherst, Massachusetts, where she feels life is simply less stressful.